Merry

Christmas

Mom !!

Enjoy Love

Janis

The Secret Life of

Damian Spinelli

The Secret Life of

Damian Spinelli

As told to

Diane Miller

By Carolyn Hennesy

New York

Library of Congress Cataloging-in-Publication Data has been applied for.

ISBN 978-1-4013-2413-1

Hyperion books are available for special promotions and premiums. For details contact the HarperCollins Special Markets Department in the New York office at 212-207-7528, fax 212-207-7222, or e-mail spsales@harpercollins.com.

Book design by Ralph Fowler / rlf design

FIRST EDITION

10 9 8 7 6 5 4 3

THIS LABEL APPLIES TO TEXT STOCK

We try to produce the most beautiful books possible, and we are also extremely concerned about the impact of our manufacturing process on the forests of the world and the environment as a whole. Accordingly, we've made sure that all of the paper we use has been certified as coming from forests that are managed, to ensure the protection of the people and wildlife dependent upon them.

For Donald

Contents

Publisher's Note

Roughly one year ago, the following manuscript appeared at our offices in a manila envelope bearing no return address. A note inside read simply "No one fires me and gets away with it. From the files of Ms. High-and-Mighty Diane Miller. Publish it . . . and blow the lid off Port Charles."

It was the mention of one of New York State's more infamous cities that got our attention. For years, veteran journalists and cub reporters alike have been searching for ways to infiltrate that warren of iniquity, psychological mayhem, debauchery, and ancestral (potentially incestuous) families residing on gated compounds and private islands.

Now, thanks to one disgruntled employee, we have a glimpse inside the high stone walls and elaborate defense mechanisms of New York's very own riddle, wrapped in a mystery, inside an enigma. These are the tales, dating, as close as we can guess, from 2009 to 2010, of one man's nearly superhuman crusade to save, protect, heal, and fight for what is right for the citizens of Port Charles . . . a town not his birthplace, but one he has taken to his heart.

These pages contain only a fraction of the stories found on Ms. Miller's stolen computer disk; judicious prudence determined what has comprised this volume. We have striven to protect the residents of Port Charles and are also dubious as to exactly what effect the entire collection of tales of derring-do might have on a populace sorely in need of a hero; we do not want either the citizens of Port Charles or Damian Spinelli to be swamped with groupies, stalkers, and fanatics (the city has enough problems).

It is doubtful we will ever see more clues, more insight into the man himself than what Mr. Spinelli and Ms. Miller have, unwittingly, provided us on that disk. To that end, we regard it as something approaching a national treasure; a man like Damian Spinelli comes along very rarely.

And so . . . we ask you to . . .

Enjoy.

The Secret Life of

Damian Spinelli

1

A Late Night Chat

Brusque Lady . . .

Please meet the Jackal at the bar in the Metro Court at 10:00 PM sharp. Although it is somewhat past ~~my~~ his bedtime, he must speak with you on a grave matter concerning many of your clientele. Do not fail ~~me~~ him.

Regards,

The Jackal

———————

I'd been sitting at the tiny table for about an hour, twirling the note around in my fingers and wishing, as the minutes ticked by, that the note was Spinelli's neck. The cocktail waitress was giving me the evil eye and I didn't blame her. The look said I had better tip big for taking up a prime seat or I'd never be welcome back at the Metro Court.

I like the Metro Court. Max and I both like it . . . a lot.

Ten minutes and two bowls of cashews later, I'd had enough. I was stashing my tape recorder, notepad, and Uni-ball fine tip into my purse when suddenly I got a tap, hard, on my shoulder.

"Ms. Miller."

The voice was soft but commanding. I turned to find my

panzer tank of a guy standing in a three-piece suit, complete with matching tie and pocket scarf. Classic.

"Hi Max." I coughed. There are times when the sight of this man still does the strangest things to me. "Why so formal, handsome?"

"I hope I didn't startle you. I just came by to give you a message from the Jackal."

"Oh, sweet-Jesus-on-a-popsicle-stick, are you in on these shenanigans too? What's going *on,* Max?"

"Mr. Spinelli . . . he apologizes for being late. Said he ran into some trouble on the waterfront, but he's on his way and asked if I would relay the message to you."

"Are you working for him too now?"

"Me? Work for Spinelli? Of course not, Diane."

"So why are you relaying a message from him?"

"Because I'm a nice guy."

He turned to go, his glutei maximi straining the seams of his Armani slacks.

"Have mercy!" I thought. "Yes . . . yes you are."

"Max?" I called after him.

He turned around.

"Buy some Häagen-Dazs and warm up the sheets. This shouldn't take too long."

"You got it, lamb chop."

I unpacked my purse, laying the recorder and notepad carefully back on the table, and ordered my third Southern Comfort Manhattan . . . very dry vermouth, up, with a twist. I spent the next few minutes clicking the cap of my Uni-ball and thinking about Max Giambetti's set of glutes and that getting to squeeze those cantaloupes made me a pretty lucky lady.

Suddenly my reflection in the martini glass dimmed slightly. Before I could look up, a slim figure in a cheap black suit slid into the chair across from me. More precisely, the upper half of a cheap black suit, as I noticed the cargo pants and a bizarre green shoulder sack slung across his sunken chest.

"Most profound apologies, Brusque One. The Jackal is deeply and most assuredly mortified at having kept one so prestigious as you waiting a jot past our appointed time."

Once I got past the jacket, which hung on him like a wet sheet, I took note of the pencil-thin tie loosely knotted around a tie-dyed crew-neck, and the fedora, which was also cheap but fit him to a tee. Sinatra goes to the skate park.

"Um . . . that's okay, Spinelli."

"Jackal, please. Thank you for coming at my request."

It was only when I spent any length of time with Spinelli alone that I remembered that he talked like an idiot . . . an idiot right out of Dashiell Hammett. And *Star Trek* . . . with maybe a little Shakespeare thrown in.

"Did you ever find it?" I asked.

"Humble apologies once again . . . I don't understand. Find what?"

"The Maltese falcon."

I laughed. Hard. He just smiled and tried to straighten his sad little tie. I got a queasy feeling in my stomach. There was no way Spinelli could afford to buy drinks in this saloon, and I'd just hurt his feelings with a bad joke. Nice, Diane. Nice way to start off.

"Sorry. You just . . . you look . . . great. You look great."

"I know, and thank you for agreeing to pen my memoirs. I think you'll find . . ."

"Whoa! Your *what*? Wait just a second, Spinelli . . ."

"Jackal. Or Grasshopper, if you prefer."

I took a sip of my drink and wondered if a "trip to the ladies' room" could actually get me out the door.

"Look . . . Jackal. I haven't agreed to pen anything. I didn't even know what this meeting was really about."

I tossed his note across the table.

"I find this under my office door . . . You say you have information of a serious nature about my clients. *That*'s why
I'm here, Spin . . . Jack . . . hop . . . Jackalhopper. Not to write
the story of your life . . . as if I even have time . . ."

"The tiniest of interruptions, She Who Stands For
Justice . . . This is not the story of my life. These are the stories of my life. And they all involve your clients or those close
to them; their actions and behaviors in times of crises and
triumph. These are tales of incredible cases . . . episodes . . .
actions yearning to be told. While I don't feel that anything
would be of an embarrassing nature to those you know . . .
I . . . I . . . I harbor the strongest hope that you will find what
I have to say worthy of notation. I'm staking much upon it, in
point of fact. I am to embark on a journey upon the morrow
from which I may return or I may meet my untimely fate. It is
on the chance that I will not return that you must listen to
what I have to say tonight." He ran his forefingers across the
brim of his fedora.

I was silent for a moment.

"My clients, you say?"

"And those connected to them in intimate and not-so-
intimate relationships."

Well . . . damned if the skinny kid didn't have a point.

"Yes, well, I don't necessarily want or need to know where
you're headed tomorrow morning, but if you have something
to say about Sonny . . . or Jason . . . or anyone else for that
matter, whether I represent them or not . . . it's . . . it's probably best that you *do* tell it to me. I can afford you attorney/
client privilege, thanks to Jason Morgan's wide-spreading
umbrella of protection and Sonny's generous retainer. But I
don't know about creating a memoir. I don't have time to turn
around, Mr. Grasshopper, let alone . . . Why are you . . . why
are you dressed like that?"

His face fell and nearly oozed across the table. I kept for-
getting; this guy bruised easily . . . like a banana.

"To what do you refer?"

"Ol' Blue Eyes meets Tony Hawk. The combination of gangsta and suave, if slightly . . . extra large . . . sophistication?"

"I am not clothed cap-a-pie in any one period . . . this is true and an astute observation on your part, solicitor. But I was attempting to fly under a certain radar tonight, hence the post-Depression togs, and I found that when I had completed the assignment and returned to my base camp . . . some of my clothes had been poached by hoodlums of the night."

"I'm sorry. The pants, the shirt . . . you look like a regular Joe. But the jacket and the hat say you've been watching *Sunset Boulevard*. A lot. It's just that it's so . . . so . . . of a certain period."

"The era in which I like to think I would have flourished to my fullest potential. The American late 1930s and '40s. Most of my exploits, which involve your clientele and hence are the reason you are here, as you will see, are, to no credit of my own, almost rotogravure reproductions of the feats of daring and action that dotted that landscape. It's almost as if the Jackal is channeling Sam Spade!"

I was getting a headache.

"Okay . . . but why me? Why don't you just write these yourself?"

"My prowess and forte is in the technical arena. Words fly out of my mouth, but when I attempt to put pen to paper, as it were, my fingers go numb and nary a line is written. Also . . ."

Suddenly, a slow sly smile wiggled its way across his chin, and damned if there wasn't a twinkle in his eye. I chalked that up to the Manhattan, but then the smile broke into a grin, and suddenly I found myself in Wonderland.

". . . I've read your work."

"My *what*? What work?"

"Your contributions to the *Law Review*. Your articles for *American Jurisprudence*. *Law Today*. *Attorney Style*. You write particularly well."

"Thank you."

Come to think of it, I had always liked the boy.

"Also," Spinelli went on, "in many of our brief inter-
actions, I have come to feel as if you also share in my deep
appreciation for the noir, yes? The darker side of things. I
occasionally hear it in your own patterns of speech. The less
than fragrant underbelly of society."

"I'm a lawyer. A working one, you understand, not just some
name on an office shingle. I've seen it all. I'm jaded for my
years, I've lost whatever idealism I once had and I watch *Sunset
Boulevard*. A lot. Patter like this is standard issue. Ask Max."

The cocktail waitress set down a bowl of potato chips and an
orange soda in front of the brother from another planet. And
she slammed down another Manhattan for me.

"Thanks, Madison," said Spinelli.

"'Madison.'" I laughed as she sloped away. "Have you noticed that everyone around here has a name you'd only hear on
a soap opera? I got off the elevator tonight and Carly brushes
by me. Jax was just paying the check and he calls out, 'Carly,
hold the lift!' And she just giggles and says, 'I'll race you up to
the penthouse, Jax!' The elevator doors close, *boom*, just like
that. And Jax dashes out of the stairwell, laughing like he's
going to the circus! And then I realize, I can't remember: Are
they divorced? Are they back together now . . . again? How
many times? The back and forth . . . well, of everyone, really.
The whole place is a roller coaster, but those two are ridin' at the
front."

"The Valkyrie and the White Knight."

Maybe it was the Manhattans . . . or maybe it was the fact
that, with that fedora so close I, too, was really mouthing it like
Jimmy Cagney . . . but I was starting to get the hang of this guy.

"Yeah."

"Carly . . . the Valkyrie and her White Knight, Jax . . .
are the subjects of my first tale. How the White Knight was
taken from his ladylove and she, being the unstoppable war-

rior maiden of myth, decided to find him. She engaged the Jackal in the quest only to fall madly in love . . . shouldn't you be writing any of this down?"

I looked at my Uni-ball and my notepad. I looked at my watch and thought about Max and the pint of Vanilla Swiss Almond he was already scooping into. Then I looked at the eager face of Mr. Spinelli aka Jackal aka Grasshopper aka certifiable nut. And yes, there were a thousand different things I should have been doing at that moment. But I uncapped the pen, just in case a thought struck me, positioned the notepad, and hit the "record" button on the tape recorder. I wasn't going anywhere.

"What the hell, Mr. Jackal . . . talk to me."

2

Damian Spinelli

and the Case of the Vamping Valkyrie

I had just walked back into the offices of Spinelli/McCall, P.I. The corned beef on date-nut bread with sweet pickles and extra mayo was sittin' heavier than usual in my tummy . . .

"Tummy?" I interrupted.

"You object?"

"Not if you're a fourth-grader."

"But I always refer to my gaping maw as my tummy," Spinelli said.

"How far could this guy's face fall?" I wondered.

"If you're gonna do this," I said, getting into the feel of the memoirs, "then do it right."

"I bow to your intellectual magnificence."

"You bet you do. 'Gullet.'"

"Oh, Ms. Miller! That's sheer . . ."

"Whatever."

"Uh . . ."

. . . sittin' heavier that usual in my gullet. I chalked up the ringin' in my ears to the six orange Nehis. Too much sugar for an already sweet guy. Then the ringin' became a five-chime train whistle on a diesel headed straight for my head.

" '*Cabeza*,' " I said.
"Right, '*cabeza*.' "

. . . I realized the phone was ringin'. I picked it up, but the call had already gone to voice mail. A good thing, too . . . because if I had actually heard her voice, I wouldn't have been able to say no. Ultimately, I didn't say no anyway, I just wouldn't have said it a lot sooner. I tossed my hat onto the hat rack, un-holstered my rod, put my feet up on the desk, and hit a button on my cell. "Listen to your messages," the nice lady said. "Yes, I will, Gladys," I thought. One new call. It had to be from a minute ago. I had only heard the first few frightened words when, from the sound of shatterin' glass, the outer office door blew off its hinges.

I grabbed my heater, levelin' it at my private office door. A silhouette loomed large in the yellow light from the hallway.

"Stone Cold? That you?" I called. "Timmy Two-Fingers? Mister Sir? Joey the Squirrel?"

Suddenly, the silhouette shook its hair. I mean a mane-full, and I realized this was no guy . . . no regular guy, anyway.

"You can come in, but just know that you won't be talkin' only to me; I got my best friend here." I patted my gun.

She opened the door and walked in. Blue eyes the color of billiard chalk and blonde hair so bouncy I wanted to jump all over it. She had legs that could cause a heart attack in a caribou, and they went all the way up under her mink mini-jacket. At least, I hoped they did.

"That's good," she said, wipin' away a tear. "Because I need a friend right now myself."

Carly Corinthos Jacks was standin' in my office. She lifted

one leg onto a chair and set it down like she was stampin' out a ciggie.

"I called a minute ago, but there was no answer, so I decided to take my chances and come on by. I told myself I'd wait all night if I had to. Got a light?" she purred.

I went all tapioca inside, but kept the outside cool. In the day-to-day world, this woman wouldn't speak to me in the supermarket, she wouldn't stand five feet from me in any direction . . . but now she wanted my help. They all wanted my help. Sooner or later. I had the upper hand.

"You don't smoke," I said.

"I never said it was for a cigarette."

"I'm fresh out."

She took her leg off the chair and sat down.

"May I sit?"

"No."

If she was going to play coy, she was dealin' with a master: I learned at my momma's knee.

"Jackal, I'll be straight with you, all right?"

My eyes wandered over her shapely calves.

"Your words will be the only straight thing about you, doll."

"My husband's been kidnapped and I know who took him. His brother Jerry."

"Why has Jerry become his brother's keeper?" I asked.

"The last unresolved item from their father's will has finally cleared probate. We thought that everything had been divided up years ago, but then we found out about the . . . diamonds!"

My heart started beatin' a little faster. Yeah, I was all guy, but I liked the sparklies. The mere mention of ice in a cocktail sent me all a-flutter . . .

"Lose this part," I recommended.

"But why? If I am going to expose to exploration and analysis the innermost workings of my soul, then it must be fully," Spinelli said, taking a tiny sip of his orange soda.

" 'Cause it makes you sound like you should be served on a plate with cheese."

"If I may offer a different opinion . . ."

"Never mind." I sighed, reaching for a potato chip. "No one ever listens to me until it's too late. Go on."

"Diamonds?" I inquired . . . casually.

"Five flawless diamonds, perfect in color, cut, and clarity. The smallest weighs in at seven and a half carats. The largest . . . is bigger than the Hope. John, Jasper and Jerry's father, left them specifically for Jasper . . . I mean Jax . . . God, I hate using his first name; it's like he's a five-year-old. I didn't even know about the diamonds. Jerry has been holding them up in probate for years, so Jax didn't even bother to tell me . . . an oversight which he and I will discuss at a later time. Jerry has taken Jax and is holding him prisoner—torturing him so that Jax will tell him where the diamonds are!"

"How do you know this, Mrs. Jacks? How do you know your husband hasn't gone out for a shot of tequila and a redhead?"

"First of all, my husband's Australian . . . He would never drink tequila. And second, I have *this.*"

She reached in between the lapels of her mink and withdrew a scrap of paper. As she was drawin' it out, a tiny pink ribbon-end came with it. I recognized the color: "Hinky Pinky" was only found on certain items of Victoria's Secret lingerie . . .

"Okay!" I said, slamming my pen on the table. "I'll say it again . . . you talk like this and people will think . . ."

"A brief interruption, learned solicitor," Spinelli countered. "I only know this because my own true love, the fair Maximista, wears almost nothing but items in Hinky Pinky."

"Oh, all right, then," I said, begrudgingly. "But you might want to mention that somewhere."

"As you wish."

"Okay," I said, suddenly craving a cheeseburger . . . and a Rob Roy.

". . . and I realized that Mrs. Jacks was wearin' precious little under her mink sweatshirt."

She handed over the note. In that childish scrawl common to many psychopaths, the note read:

> My brother's life for a few simple stones. I know you know where they are, darling Carly. If I don't have them by tomorrow evening, I'll finish Jax, and then I'll come for the kids.
>
> Understand, sweetheart?
>
> Don't go all white on me, lady . . . 10:00 PM. And come . . .
>
> . . . alone.

"It doesn't even say where I'm supposed to go!" Carly moaned.

"When did you get this?" I asked, wantin' to slap her . . . for no reason.

"About two hours ago."

"Do you have the diamonds?"

"Jax insisted that I sew them into the hem of my mink, because I so rarely take it off."

She flashed open the mini-trench, letting me catch just a peek of Hinky Pinky and five dark lumps at the bottom of the fur.

"And you haven't called the police?"

"No . . . I mean the note specifically didn't say that I shouldn't, I just thought it was best."

"Good girl."

"Does that mean you'll take the case?"

She looked up at me with those pool hall eyes, brimmin' with tears. Her mink fell off her shoulder the teensiest bit. She'd brought all the weapons with her; if the waterworks didn't do it, the striptease just might.

"I'm four hundred dollars a day, plus expenses."

"Well," she said, snifflin', "counting today and tomorrow, that's only eight hundred dollars. What a deal!"

"I'll have a lot of expenses. Startin' with a new car."

"But we don't even know where to look for Jax."

"We could hop in a cab and be there in five minutes. Or my new car, if I had one."

"Whaaaa? You mean you've already figured out where Jerry is holding him?"

"Simple, sweetheart. It's in the note. Why would Jerry tell you not to go all *white* on him, lady, huh? I mean who writes crapola like that? What does that even mean?"

"I . . . don't . . . know?"

"That's right. So I have to figure it's one of those stupid sentences that somebody says when they want somebody else to look a little deeper. So I did, and what did I find?"

"I . . . don't . . . know?"

"That's why you should always stay pretty, Valkyrie . . . Brains ain't your department. White and lady. Ring any bells?"

"You mean, our yacht? The White Lady?"

"You do all right when it's spelled out for you, kiddo. That's right, the White Lady."

"But she's not in Port Charles. She's docked up at our every-other-summer home in Bar Harbor."

"Then it looks like you and I are takin' a road trip . . . in my new car."

"No new car."

My autobahn dreams never materialized, but bright and a little too early the next morning, Carly Corinthos Jacks pulled up to the building, two cups of steamin' something in her Porsche's cup holder. We'd decided not to take my Toyota Echo . . . even though it was silver . . . all right, primer . . .

Jerry was expecting to see Carly's silver 2010 Porsche Cayman S Coupe.

"Venti chai lattes, breve, sugar-free vanilla, no water, no foam, extra hot."

I nearly spit the creamy concoction all over her tinted windows.

"You don't like it?"

"No . . . it's good. It just reminds me of Christmas. And I hate Christmas."

The late October woods were on fire, like my derriere after a bowl of Dennison's. The drive up to Bar Harbor was uneventful until Carly started to open up, and I don't mean the throttle. We were only a couple of hours outside of Port Charlie when she asks, real casual like, what goes into my idea of the perfect woman.

I start tellin' her: a pound of sass, gams like a couple of flagpoles, a pouty mouth, and brains enough to know when to keep it shut!

I look over just in time to see a big Karo syrup tear run down that high cheekbone.

"What's with the waterworks, doll?"

Her lip started to quiver. I get nervous when the lip starts to quiver.

"I try to be all that and more for Jax. But it just seems like we're fighting all the time. I know he's not happy . . . but I swear, Jackal, I try, I really do. If we get him back . . . I'm going to make him the happiest man in the world!"

"First of all, toots, it's not a question of if, but when we get him back. And second . . ."

I watched as she reached for her chai latte with the thing and the thing. I realized she'd been suckin' on it since we left the city. There was no way there could be anything left. Then I saw the move. Sly and quick . . . real cute. She pulled a hip flask from under her mink mini-trench, took off her cup lid, poured about six drops of . . . what was it? . . . whiskey . . .

into the cup, popped the lid back on, and slid the flask back on her thigh like she was passin' a note in grade school. The whole thing took about three seconds. I was impressed. Then I tightened my seat belt.

But Carly was drivin' like an ace. It was just her emotions that were getting all screwy.

". . . and second, I'm sure you'd make any man feel like a high-roller. You're a champ, Carly . . . You're Big League."

"Do you really think so?"

"Of course, I wouldn'ta said it if . . ."

She took her eyes off the road for the first time and trained those baby-blues right on me.

"Do you . . . really . . . think so?"

"Sure," I said, drownin' in those two cups of blue curaçao, not realizing she'd slammed the Porsche to the side of the road.

"I'm glad to hear it," she purred, grabbing the parking brake. Then she planted one on me that made me happy to be alive. And a man. And glad I'd never had a tonsillectomy, 'cause she was givin' one to me now. Suddenly, what little sense I had left returned, and I pushed her away, rough, but not too rough.

"Oh, Jackal, I've wanted to do that ever since you showed up in Port Charles. When Jax was kidnapped, I was glad . . . glad, do you hear? I knew I could get close to you for a fairly decent reason. I could get you alone and let you know how I really felt."

"Hang on, sister," I said, tryin' to keep this clawing kitten at arm's length, "this isn't you talkin', it's the eighty-proof in your latte. Calm down."

"I am calm," she said. "I've never been so calm in my life. Don't you see, Jackal? The way I've treated you all these years . . . it was just a ruse, an act, a put-on, so you wouldn't see my true feelings. But I'm tired of the games . . . tired of trying to make my incredibly rich husband happy. He only loves one thing. He won't tell me what it is. But it's not me. I can turn this car around and let Jerry have him and we can put the diamonds in a safety deposit box and my car in your garage."

I hesitated for only a moment. It was the bad guy in me, the thug, the torpedo.

"The car . . . can I drive it?"

"No."

That was the slap I needed.

"No dice, doll." Then I softened. "Look, I can't blame you for the way you feel, but you and I both know that it would never work. Your problems don't amount to a hill of beans. Mine, of course, are another story, but the point is you love Jax and he loves you. If you let him go down without tryin' to save him, you'll regret it."

"But what about us?"

"We'll always have two chai lattes and a summer drive to Bar Harbor."

"You're right."

"And that time you kicked my shoppin' cart into that pile of avocados in the supermarket."

"Of course."

"And that time you let the door slam on my hand when you were comin' out of the Metro Court."

"Yes . . . yes . . . stop now."

"Let's go get your husband."

She wiped away those pretty tears and six hours and one speeding ticket later we pulled into the Malvern Hotel. We were gonna use it as a base camp. Then I realized Carly had only rented one room. She'd been pretty sure I'd fall. She was one good-lookin' dame, but she was hard . . . too hard . . . and I was glad I'd let her down. I told I'd sit in the car while she went in and freshened up. Smart woman, she took the keys.

At ten on the button, we pulled up to the docks and saw the *White Lady* in her slip. A single light burned in the main cabin. I stayed in the car while Carly went onboard. Of course, we'd

taken the diamonds out of her mink, and now they were safely
stowed in the secret pocket of my pants. Suddenly, the light
went out, there was a crash, and then the sound of a cabin door
openin', and I heard Carly scream. I was out of the car and
creepin' up the gangplank in a flash. Making my way down
the side of the yacht, I tripped over a large sack of something
just outside the main cabin door.

Turned out to be Jax, trussed up like grandma's turkey on
Thanksgiving. He was out cold. I dragged his body down the
gangplank and propped him up against a tackle shed. Back
on the boat, I crawled on my belly till I reached the main
cabin, then cautiously opened the door.

I saw the flash of a gun. The first bullet ricocheted off a
bronze bell and broke a window on its way out. But Jerry had
given away his position and he couldn't move along the windows without being seen in the moonlight. I drew my heater.
Jerry was a lefty. He dressed to the left, politics were to the left
and his left eye was sharper than his right. He would be holdin'
Carly, in a very uncomfortable position for her, I was certain,
to his right.

"I've already frisked my sister-in-law, which she thoroughly
enjoyed, didn't you, darling? Unfortunately, I didn't find any
diamonds."

"Maybe she's hidin' 'em someplace special," I said.

I heard Carly protest; sounded like there was a hand over
her mouth.

"Hmmm . . . I didn't think to look there. But now that
you mention it . . ."

"Keep talkin', ya big maroon," I thought. "I almost have
you."

". . . I just might," Jerry went on. "Sweetheart, would you
mind just turning around . . ."

I followed the sound of his voice and aimed right just a hair;
I knew I only had one chance or Carly was gonna look pretty on
a coroner's slab. I squeezed off a shot. Carly screamed again and

then there were three thuds as Jerry crashed into the cabin furniture. Then . . . silence.

I high-tailed it to Carly in the darkness. Suddenly, Jerry's figure towered in the moonlight filterin' in from the windows. I shot again and this time Jerry spun around and crashed, face-first, through the glass. A split second later, we heard a splash in Bar Harbor.

I hustled Carly off the yacht, got Jax untied, and by midnight we were all enjoying the "lighter-fare" menu at the Malvern. I handed over the diamonds and said good-bye to Carly that night. As she helped Jax up to the room, she looked over her shoulder. I tipped my hat and picked up a Greyhound back to Port Charlie.

The ride home in her Porsche was one I didn't want to take. Not with Jax there. Not with so many memories of what could have been . . . if only I wasn't such a sweet guy.

3

Damian Spinelli

and the Case of the Quartered Main

Port Charles gets a different kinda rain.

It's not the steamy, bluesy Southern kinda they see in New Orleans or Memphis . . . the kind that makes you want to sit on your front porch with a bowl of cheese grits until you remember exactly why your wife left and ain't never coming back. It's not the endless, dull Seattle kind that makes you wanna take a heater to your melon after a couple of days.

Port Charles rain blows cold off the big pond. It's never seen land; it knows only itself . . . only water. And it's the kinda rain that puts to rest any doubts: Port Charles is a town that God forgot.

It was the day after Thanksgiving and I was sick of turkey. Talkin' it and eatin' it. I was in the office later than usual; I wasn't thrilled about takin' on the weather, and Maxie, who couldn't care less about a little deluge, was comin' by with some cheap Chinese . . .

"Oh, Ms. Miller," Spinelli said, his eyes wide. "Do you think that's a bit . . . ?"

"You're talking about take-out food?" I asked.
"Well, of course," he answered.
"People will get it," I said. **"Go on."**

. . . and I thought I might feed her some chicken lo mein while she was sittin' on my desk lookin' all sweet.

Then the phone rang.

Being after hours, I didn't wanna pick it up, but then I thought it might be Maxie at Yun Chow's. Maybe she was havin' a little trouble decidin' on the dumplings . . . so I caved.

"Spinelli!?"

It was Big Alice, the Quartermaines' maid.

"Speakin'."

"You gotta help! Mr. Edward . . . he's gone! I think he's out at sea . . ."

I'd never heard panic in the voice of Big Alice. Whiskey, yeah. Barroom brawl, you bet . . . But panic, never. I was concerned.

"Slow down, Big Alice, slow down," I said, leanin' back in my chair. "What do you mean he's at sea?"

"It will be easier if I explain everything in person."

"It always is, doll." I sighed. So much for the dumplings. "Okay, Big Alice, I'm on my way."

"Thank you . . . Oh, and I'm not so big anymore."

"Come again?" I said, caught off-guard.

"I'm not going by 'Big Alice' these days. I've slimmed down. Gone vegan, become heart smart, and I've done several marathons. It's just 'Alice' now."

She waited for me to give her an atta' girl, but it was hard to think of Alice as anything other than a gorgeous lady of wrestling . . . or a bobsledder . . . or a bobsled.

"Good for you, Alice. Guess I'll see for myself, won't I?"

"Hurry!" she said. Then the phone clicked off.

Just then, Maxie appeared in the doorway, arms full of take-

out and a couple of bottles of Freixenet (I don't say nothin',
'cause she likes it . . . but the stuff gives me the willies).

"I couldn't decide between pork dumplings and chicken
wontons . . . so I got both. Oh, and I slept with the counter
guy. I'm sorry . . ."

"I'll hear it later," I said. But I'd heard it fine; it was the
same old story. She'd slept with someone, she was sorry, and
I could hurt her all I wanted in return. Trouble is, I didn't
want to. Not right then, anyway.

"Keep the foo young hot," I said, bussin' her cheek. "I'll
be back as soon as I can."

"Are you going on another caper?" she asked, her baby-
blues gettin' all curious on me.

"Case!" I said. "It's a case! A caper is something in a Nancy
Drew novel, or a good chicken piccata. Get it straight, sweetheart. Be good . . . at least try."

I left her fondling the wontons and headed away from the
cheap streets and into the expensive part of town. Quartermaine country.

Even through the downpour, one could tell that the Quartermaine mansion would take up an entire mid-city Manhattan
block. And that was just the house. It took me a good fifteen minutes to navigate the winding drive in the wind and
rain.

Big Alice answered the door on the first knock. And yeah,
she'd slimmed down; she'd lost a whole person. Okay, she
wasn't gonna blow away on the next nor'easter, but she was, in
a word, fine.

"Lookin' good, bub . . . I mean, lady . . . Alice. You look
real good."

She grinned.

"Well, if someone messes with this family, I can still break
them over my knee like a Luke Spencer promise, but thank
you. Come in."

She was about to lead me into the Quartermaine den, but then she sidestepped into the butler's pantry.

"They're all in there," she said, noddin' toward the den. "They know Mr. Edward is gone and no one is lifting a finger to do anything. That's why I called you."

"Are you sure he didn't just step out for the evening?" I asked.

"Not a chance. First of all, it's the night after Thanksgiving, which means leftovers; day-old pizza—his favorite. Also, I checked his closet; his evening suits are there but his yachting clothes are gone."

"Why do you think he took the boat out?"

"Because of this."

She held up a piece of paper with a few items listed in a tidy column. There was a childish scrawl underneath. I reached out to take it from her when the sound of glass shatterin' in the den made her freeze.

"Alice!"

I followed her into the large . . . really large . . . silly large room. I had only been here once before when Maxie had delivered a fancy-schmancy dress to one of the Quartermaine dames and I went along for the ride. Bright daylight made the room easy on the eyes, but now, with the lights down low and all that expensive silk and satin, I thought I might have wandered into a mortuary.

And the stiffs were all there.

Monica Quartermaine: brilliant and beautiful. She was a sawbones once, and a pretty good one, but someone put the kibosh on that ever since she started hangin' out with Jack . . . Daniel's. Apparently she was a real firecracker in her day, but since the death of her husband, Alan, she was cold and sad, like a mackerel on ice.

Tracy Quartermaine Spencer: a tough broad, and also beautiful, but in a hard way. She was angular and edgy, like a Harley that would skid you off the road if you sat on her wrong.

Tonight she was lounging in orange silk pajamas with two chopsticks poking out of a hair bun stuck on the back of her head . . . lookin' like a bad dream you'd have after too much egg drop soup.

And Luke Spencer. Bad boy, rough and tumble. Made me look like a cream puff. His own man . . . and occasionally Tracy's. Sometimes Laura's, if she was conscious. Sometimes Skye's . . . but mostly Tracy's. So he was back in Port Charles. For how long? I wondered.

The shattered glass had been his, and now the mahogany slats at his feet were covered in whiskey.

"Hey, everybody!" Alice said, tryin' to act chipper. "Look who's here!"

"Alice, I seemed to have tumbled my tumbler," Luke said.

"No problem, Mr. Luke. I'll be right back with a rag and a dustpan."

She slipped from the room like she'd been used to cleanin' spilled hooch for a long time, leaving me standin' in the middle of the waxworks.

"Why are you here?" Tracy asked.

"Your pop's gone missin'."

"Isn't it delightful?" She grinned. I could see the molars filed down to fine points. "Will, will . . . where's that will?"

"Not that you'll be getting anything, you transparent, ungrateful witch. I happen to know it's all going to the grandchildren," Monica said, laying down a card on her solitaire game.

"Be quiet, you shopgirl-in-a-borrowed-dress," Tracy cawed. "Or you might just find all your pretty things in the reflecting pond. You're only still here, you know, because my father is too silly and sentimental to put you out on the street."

"It's MY house, tranny!" Monica shouted back. "Alan gave it to me! And when I go, Ned will inherit this whole mess and toss you out on your considerable derriere."

She put a hand to her forehead as she turned toward the window. She was shakin' . . . a little.

"If only I had the strength to do it myself."

"Maybe another shot of bourbon, Monica, darling," Tracy said, crossing to the bar. "Oh, that's right . . . you really shouldn't drink, should you? Oh, come on . . . what's one little nip between us girls?"

"Assassin!"

This crowd was rough.

"Would you mind very much shooting me in the head?" Luke asked me.

"I didn't bring my pal," I said.

"You'd never go anywhere without your pal, pal," he said. "You're a bad liar."

I was a great liar . . . he was just better.

"Did any of you see Mr. Quartermaine tonight?" I asked.

I'd been in the room for less than two minutes and already I thought I was gonna lose my lunch: cream cheese and bologna on wheat with green-goddess dressing.

"Nope," said Luke.

"Not me," said Tracy. "Not that I wouldn't have shoved him toward the door . . ."

"I saw him cross the foyer on his way out," said Monica, playin' a queen.

"It's a pretty dangerous night," I said, lookin' at her cards. "The two goes on the three, not the nine. Why didn't you try to stop him?"

"He's a grown man. Besides, I have a game to finish."

I was gettin' nowhere fast. I headed back toward the front door. Alice was hurryin' out of the kitchen.

"How long has he been gone?"

"I'd say two hours, tops," she answered. "I was in the kitchen making myself some tofu tacos and vegan chocolate-and-peanut-butter pies when I heard the front door close . . ."

"Don't paint me a picture, Rembrandt, just let me see that

note," I said. I didn't want to stay in the House of the Living Dead any longer than I had to.

Alice shoved it into my hand as she rushed into the den.

"That's Mr. Quartermaine's handwriting on the bottom!"

I looked at the piece of paper: It was her shopping list:

Tomatoes
Eggplant
Lily-Fresh laundry detergent
Rutabagas
Sea salt
Yakatori sauce
Casaba melons
Code! Lila to rendezvous at sea with Cassadine on yacht!
   Must stop them!

So the old man's cheese had finally slipped off his cracker, and the only one who'd really noticed . . . probably the only one who still cared . . . was the maid. He'd confused "rutabaga" with "rendezvous" and "casaba" with "Cassadine." Yakatori meant yacht . . . and Lily was his own long-lost Lila. And now the poor devil was wanderin' the high seas in a perfect storm, lookin' for a pair of lovers that weren't there.

I had to get to the harbor, but quick.

———————

The Port Charlie harbor isn't one of the biggest . . . anywhere; it's low on the list. That's the reason it's one of the busiest. Any fed who's tried to bring down Sonny Corinthos will tell you that and plenty more . . . but that's another story.

The Quartermaine yacht, the *Smilin' Lila*, was nowhere to be seen and the tie lines alongside her slip were lyin' on the dock; they weren't wound and knotted the way old man Q probably insisted every time he took her out. This told me he'd just thrown the ropes from the boat . . . which meant there was no one else onboard.

I went over my options. I coulda swiped another yacht . . . I'd "borrowed" enough cars (and how) over the years; I could hot-wire anything. But I needed speed and the eighty-footers all around me didn't have it. Then I spotted a cigarette boat, a real speedster, down a few slips. She was bein' tossed about in the storm like a Caesar salad; a few more bumps into her dock and her owner could use her for toothpicks. Hell, I was practically doing the guy a favor by takin' her out.

Ten minutes later, the harbor jetty was three hundred yards behind me and I was racin' into open water. The rain was comin' down hard, like the sea was being punished. I flipped on the ciggie's bilge pump and cursed myself for not buyin' that waterproof trench coat Maxie had showed me in Manhattan. Too pricey at the time; now I woulda given my right nut.

"Really, Mr. Grasshopper?" I asked him. I could tell my eyebrows had gone into my hairline. "Your right nut?"

"Does the Smart and Sassy Solicitor feel that is too much?" Spinelli asked.

"Not if you'd do it."

My only problem was: Which way was the old man steerin'? It was a toss-up, so I went with my gut . . . which is never wrong, only sometimes I don't listen . . . like when Maxie says I should have that extra scoop of butter brickle ice cream and I know cow-juice doesn't sit so well . . .

"Spinelli . . ."
"Profound apologies."

I turned the ciggie south and opened her up. I should al-ways listen to my gut. It wasn't long before a white spot ap-peared off to my right, but the rain was doin' funny things to

my perspective, and before I knew it, I was bearin' down hard
on the yacht. I pulled her up just in the nick of time: three
more feet and *Smilin' Lila* woulda been smokin' the ciggie.

The boat was dark—not even her runnin' lights were twin-
kling. Made me think I was pretty damn lucky to have spotted
her in the first place. I saw the rope ladder bouncin' off her
side. I cut the motor on the ciggie, grabbed a tie line, and
climbed aboard. There was no time to tie the speedster off at
the back of the yacht, so I did a perfect monkey knot around the
railing. Then I took a quick look around.

Eddie Quartermaine liked his toys big and expensive and
the *Smilin' Lila* was no exception. She wasn't a racin' yacht; this
gal was pure pleasure . . . but she came from a different era,
just like Eddie. This baby was more schooner than cruiser.
She had to be ninety feet if she was an inch. She had three
masts and huge sails . . . I could tell because they were still
up and gettin' shredded. The *Lila* was pitchin' from side to
side, back and forth, like she was the head on a jack-in-the-
box. I had to hang on tight—one slip and I was shark food. I
made for the wheel at the back . . . no Mr. Q. Then I saw a
square shape farther toward the bow. Smart Eddie: He'd also
built an interior wheelhouse.

Over the sound of the storm, I heard yellin' as I approached.
The door was locked. I didn't want to smash it, but I had no
choice . . . The lighthouse at Farrin's Point was pretty damn
close, which meant the rocks were closer. The *Smilin' Lila* was
gonna end up like the ciggie would have: toothpicks. Only
there wouldn't be an Edward to stick 'em between his chom-
pers.

A coupla tries and I was in. The cabin was dark, but the in-
strument panel was glowin' like a dozen stars. Edward Quartermaine was standin' at the helm, straight as a rod. Even
soakin' wet, with his back to me, I could tell this man was a
smooth operator. White pants, navy blazer, cap cocked at a
jaunty angle. Smooth. Classy. His hands were at his sides and

he was starin' out the front window like he was lookin' at a ghost . . . or lookin' *for* one. He was mumblin' to himself; then all of a sudden he screamed, "Lila, you won't get away with this!"

"Quartermaine!" I yelled. "We gotta get you off this boat!"

He turned around and I saw the look in his eye. This was no billionaire, no capitalist tycoon, no captain of industry. This was only a broken man whose heart was in pieces all over the floor, like a crazy jigsaw puzzle. I don't know of many loves like his and Lila's . . . maybe Hollywood comes close with some of their flickers . . . all I know is that it was still there for this man, and the storm of the decade wasn't gonna keep him from his gal.

"Quartermaine! Lila's not here. We gotta get off the boat. The rocks! She's gonna break up on the rocks!"

Then his look went from crazy love to plain crazy.

"Cassadine! Where is she!? You took her . . . probably by force, you conniving Greek! Where is she!?"

"I'm not Cassadine! He's not . . ."

"I'll sail all the way to your stinking island, you dog! I'll go around the world for Lila! She doesn't love you!"

I knew when to play along.

"You're right, Quartermaine! What was I thinkin', eh? She loves you! Only you!"

But he was on a roll.

"I'll never stop, you hear me! Never! You'll never get rid of me. I'll be the shadow in the corner . . ."

There was a jolt and a splinterin' sound as the *Smilin' Lila* hit the rocks. I watched as the mainmast broke in two, then in two again.

". . . I'll be the face in the crowd. I'll be the voice telling you not to order the *ceviche*. You'll never take me. You think you're smart, wise guy. Isn't that right, soldier? But you'll never take Rocco. There's only one Johnny Rocco and Rocco's smarter than all of you! Gay Dawn's a lush!"

Any other time, I coulda played out *Key Largo* from start to finish, every line, every look . . . even Bacall . . . especially Bacall. But just then the yacht pitched to starboard and smashed sideways into the rocks. The wheelhouse windows blew inward and Quartermaine took a header into the wall.

I dragged him onto the deck, as unconscious of the world around him as a D.C. senator. The *Smilin' Lila* was goin' down, and I had to get Eddie back to the ciggie, but fast.

I got him to the railing and went to find the tie line.

Gone.

The speedster was lost, and so were we.

Then I spotted the dinghy floatin' in the water on the starboard side. She was all wood, but well cared for: She was our only chance. I dragged Eddie across the yacht, the sea comin' in at my feet, and loaded him into the dinghy. Jeez, I thought to myself, the man even crumpled with style.

Then I remembered seein' somethin' in the wheelhouse . . . somethin' I might need later. Quartermaine was startin' to come 'round by this time, and I told him to hold on and not to move . . . that we were gonna go get his ladylove. Then I hightailed it back to the middle of the yacht.

It was tough findin' what I was lookin' for, with the sea water lappin' at my delicate unmentionables . . .

"I'm not writing that," I said, putting my Uni-ball on the table.

"As you wish . . ."

. . . with the sea water up to my waist. I got turned around pretty fast. But then I saw it, just above the radio. I made a grab and headed back to the dinghy.

"You planning on telling me what 'it' was?" I asked.

"Perhaps," Spinelli said. "Perhaps it will appear in another tale."

"Perhaps I am missing out on spoonfuls of Häagen-Dazs topped with Max sprinkles and I should be heading home!"

"Indulgence, I beg of you, Lady of the Law," Spinelli pleaded. "All will be revealed . . . or most of it, I assure you."

"Keep going."

Quartermaine was still there, lookin' like Little Lord Fauntleroy . . . or some other equally scared kid.

I loosened the ropes and took up the oars. Seconds later, a wave took out what was left of the *Smilin' Lila*, sendin' shrapnel flying. A plank missed me by inches, but the top section of the quartered main landed in the dinghy, nearly capsizing it.

I rowed for hours, wrackin' my brain trying to remember if there was a small strip of beach anywhere close to the lighthouse. Nothin' . . . but rocks . . . which is probably why they built the lighthouse there. Quartermaine was out cold again . . . so cold that I checked his breathing once or twice.

Finally, close to dawn, the rain stopped, and the sun came up but beautiful. It was such a beautiful morning, I thought if I stuck my finger out, a little bird might land on it. And there was the Port Charlie harbor in the distance. I rowed hard, but an hour later, I realized we hadn't budged. The Atlantic currents were keepin' the dinghy trapped at sea.

Quartermaine woke up around eight, by my calculation, with no recollection of the night before. He was a little peeved at first, until I set him straight. Told him I wasn't no hero, just a gumshoe doing a job, but that if it wasn't for me and the dinghy, he'd be playin' nine-handed poker with an octopus in the Marianas Trench right about then. That softened him up, like butter.

Two hours later, the sun was doin' a little softenin' of its own, and I was gettin' worried for both our noggins. Big Alice knew I was out here . . . She, at least, had some concern for her employer. If she hadn't lost her smarts when she lost that weight, she'd send help. I had to believe that.

Quartermaine and I spent a few hours discussin' the weather, fishin', the best way to unhook a brassiere, and the markets; he talked stock, I talked black.

Then, around three, Eddie's eyes got all glassy, and I saw the sweat roll down outta that silver hair. We hadn't eaten all day, and I thought he might have been lookin' at me like I was a big roast chicken.

"I went out too far. I'm sorry."

"Yeah, but your family will send . . ."

"Nothing has defeated me . . . I went out too far. But pain does not matter to a man!"

It mattered to me . . . and the fact that Eddie was losin' it.

"It was the sharks. They took my fish."

The Old Man and the Sea. Just perfect.

"Okay, Santiago," I said, goin' along. "But you still have to get this boat ashore. Gotta show the villagers what those sharks took from you . . ."

"It was a big fish . . . Christ, I did not know he was so big. I could not let him know of his own glory."

Quartermaine was wringin' his hands, tears streamin' down his face. But even as the sun did its worst to his sunburnt face, I could tell they were tears of joy. That's when I saw movement off to the right.

A Coast Guard cutter was makin' fast toward the dinghy . . . and none too soon.

Eddie was still talkin' Hemingway when they brought him aboard, gently, like he was a dame. I watched as they took him into the infirmary.

"He'll be fine," the captain said. "A little sunstroke, that's all. Could have been dicey at his age, but he's in terrific shape. You did fine out there, son. You should be proud of yourself."

"Just my job, skipper," I said. "Just my job."

But even as they closed the infirmary doors, Eddie's last words were still ringin' in my ears. It was Port Charles in a single sentence:

". . . everything kills everything else in some way."

4

Damian Spinelli

and the Case of the
Un-Tracy-able Underworld

Lulu Spencer is a cute kid.

Really cute.

She fell hard for me when I first arrived in Port Charlie, and I had thought about givin' her a go for a bit (about the time it takes a shot of whiskey to find my ulcer). But Lulu's a peppermint ice cream cone and I'm a four-minute egg. She's a wand of cotton candy and I'm the rind on a three-week-old wedge of room temperature Parmesan. She's a . . .

"Spinelli!" I said.

"Whaa . . . ?" he gasped. "Oh. Forgive me, Brusque Lady. Was my epicurean compare-and-contrast becoming too much?"

"I just don't have the time to see where it eventually ends up," I answered. "'She's a spoonful of Nutella and I'm the crusty end of a date nut loaf.'"

"Oh, that's good!"

"Keep it moving."

. . . We're different, the kid and I. Didn't stop her from lovin' me, but I had to let her down. I made it easy on her . . . because she's cute.

Really cute.

"I got it . . . She's cute. Now I'm gonna let *you* down, if you understand my meaning, and it won't be easy. Move it along!"

When her call came in that night, I thought about ignorin' it; I wasn't in the mood for a Lulu Spencer sob fest, her verbal crawl across the floor. Because, if I'm tellin' it square, she was comin' real close to wearing me down. But it was late, maybe eleven or so; she usually calls to beg me to take her back before I've had my morning coffee . . . Something was up. I picked up the phone.

"Spinelli?"

"Doll-face . . . you changin' to the night shift? It's not five in the AM. You're gonna get me all confused."

"I know, I'm sorry, but I need you!"

"Look, doll . . ."

"It's not for me this time. I swear. I know I can't have you. I'm trying to make peace with that. I think the therapy is help-ing. It's my father. I think something has happened to him."

"Somethin', huh? Like what, doll? Like he's not keepin' three sets of books like he used to? He's off the hooch? He's not a rat anymore?"

I'd lost five hundred clams at Luke's joint, the Haunted Star, the night before; my pal Luke had been winkin' so hard when he told me to play red-22, I thought he was havin' a stroke. If Senor Spencer was floatin' in the harbor now, it was no skin off my back.

"He told me he was leaving town," Lulu said. "That was three days ago . . . but I don't think he's gone anywhere."

Her voice was all Shirley Temple . . . the drink . . . with a couple of extra cherries.

"Why not?" I asked.

"Because he didn't say good-bye to me in his usual way."

"What's that?"

"A ten-thousand-dollar check and a package of Pez," she said.

"Your old man gives you ten thousand dollars every time he cuts out of town?" I coughed.

"Uh-huh."

I needed to take a better look at Kid Spencer.

"Why Pez?"

"It used to be Valium, but Dad realized that's a gateway drug. He doesn't mind if I get hooked on Pez."

Using the twisted logic of Luke Spencer, this made perfect sense.

"I went to the Quartermaine mansion to talk to Tracy about it," Lulu went on, "but she just laughed in my face. Said she had no idea where he could be. I didn't want to tell her why I think he's not really gone. She'd probably say any money he gives me is really hers . . ."

Lulu knew her Quartermaines.

". . . But as I was leaving, I noticed something weird."

"What was that, doll?"

"There was a black enamel chopstick lying about halfway up the stairs and Alice was scrubbing the floors in the foyer . . . There were shoe prints in a red dust."

Suddenly the case got interesting.

"I want to hire you, Jackal," Lulu said. "I can't pay you much right now; I don't have my ten thousand . . . but when I get it, I promise, I'll make it worth your while."

"I'll keep a tab . . . and I'm gonna add the five hundred samolians your daddy took off me the other night. Go get some sleep. I'm on it."

"Can I still call you tomorrow morning?" she asked.

"Give it a coupla days, doll," I said. "I don't know where I'll be."

If I asked Tracy Quartermaine about her better half, I knew she wouldn't talk to me; she might throw a plate and scream a few things, but it wouldn't be anything I could use. But Alice might know something, havin' cleaned up the red dust, and that chopstick made me think of the night I saw Tracy Q all done up in those crazy orange pajamas.

I headed out to the Qs', but as I steered my car up the drive, I realized I might be spotted from the window of the den. That's where they always were . . . all of them. In fact, I didn't think they used any other room in the house.

I ditched my car about halfway down the drive behind a tree and hoofed it the rest of the way. I stuck to the shadows and the bushes, which was a smart move 'cause Tracy came poundin' out the front door just as I stepped onto the brick porch. I threw myself behind a *Cornus stolonifera* . . .

"Stop!" I said. "What's with the Latin?"
"It's a tree," Spinelli said.
"Then call it by a tree name . . . no Latin. Jesus!"

. . . a red osier dogwood . . .

"Criminey . . . that's just as bad. Tough guys don't usually know these things, Mr. Grasshopper."
"My fields of study extend far and wide, Ms. Miller. If I am able to discern a dogwood from an elderberry, I think that should be taken into consider . . ."
At that moment, Spinelli jumped in his seat, then from a pants pocket he fished out his cell phone, which was on vibrate . . . high. He looked at the number, then mumbled a few words, of which I only caught ". . . if I do not recognize

your number, then you do not exist . . . villain!" He put the
phone away and looked at me once more.

". . . as I was saying, Lady of the Law, I don't feel that I must
come under censorship and scrutiny simply because my arbori-
cultural acumen spans . . ."

"Sorry, Spinelli," I said. "Yes . . . yes. You're right. It's
your story. I'm just trying to keep you from getting beat up by
the other kids on the playground. Please, go on."

. . . uh . . . a tree. Tracy had on a different outfit this
time: tight-fittin' dark blue Chinese dress, two jade brace-
lets, and five-inch silver stiletto heels. She got behind
the wheel of her mint-condition 1967 green Jaguar and hit
the gas.

If I didn't hurry, she'd be out of sight fast. I was leanin'
heavy on the pedal of my Toyota Echo when I saw the Jag's
taillights turn left onto the main road back into town. I had a
good quarter of a mile to make up, and if I lost her, I'd never
find her . . . and I'd never learn why she was lookin' like a
Hong Kong travel brochure.

Turns out my luck was runnin' hot that night: the Jag had
a missing taillight. Bad Tracy.

Good Tracy.

She flew through several stop signs and a couple of red
lights on her way into downtown. I couldn't figure what she
was doin'. She blew by the ELQ offices, blew by other buildings with Quartermaine interests, and shot out of the high-
rise section like she was a cannonball.

Suddenly, I realized where she was going:

Chinatown.

On either coast, every port city, big or small, has a Chinatown. Usually, they're tourist attractions; sometimes they're
the place to get the best dim sum, if you know where to go . . .
or a nice mah-jongg set. But mostly they're reminders of

another time in this great country when some folks didn't treat other folks with an ounce of respect.

Port Charlie was no exception.

About a hundred years ago, we got a whole passel of Chinese who'd had it with New York City's special type of discrimination and headed north, only to find that upstate manners were just as bad.

They'd banded together, making their solitary way, and had established some fine, legit businesses. But outsiders were not welcome. You could eat some roast pork and buy a fake Ming vase, but it wasn't wise to be on the streets of Chinatown after dark unless you wanted to see the inside of a rice-cooker firsthand.

Most of the shops were dark; a few ugly fluorescents pocked the darkness of a second floor or a backroom.

The Jag was like a homing pigeon; Tracy wasn't takin' one wrong turn. Maybe she was lookin' for a rug. Maybe it was a nice paper lantern. Maybe she was in the mood for late night mu shu. Whatever it was didn't matter; Tracy Quartermaine had been here before.

I hung back as far as I could until she started windin' through a few back alleys. I thought for a moment she'd made me, but there was no speedin' up or doublin' back. She took a final left and then she slowed in front of an herb shop. She slipped into a curbside parking space like she was slippin' into a booth at Jake's: real easy. I drove across the intersection nice and slow, then found a spot of my own. I cut the engine and headed back, stickin' my peepers around the corner.

It looked like Tracy was standin' in front of a door, but I couldn't tell for sure. Then I saw her knock. She waited, then knocked again. Someone must have answered, 'cause Tracy began yammerin' in Chinese . . . fluent Mandarin. The dame had traveled. So had I . . . just not that far; I was pickin' up every fourth or fifth word, but it wasn't enough.

Then . . . Tracy was gone.

I crept around the corner, huggin' tight to the walls. I hit the herb shop. Right next to it was a travel agency with posters of Shanghai, the Yangtze River, and, of course, Hong Kong. But both of these places were darker than my morning coffee and closed up tight.

Then a street lamp popped across the street, and I saw a little flash in the empty space where one shop ended and the other began. Lookin' real close, I just made out a thin black door in the side of a black wall. It was painted to look like black brick . . . even the handle. But a little black paint had been rubbed off and the metal underneath had caught the flash.

There was no way I could knock . . . I didn't know exactly what Tracy had said, and if word got to her that someone was snoopin' around, she'd probably take off out the back. I looked up high . . . nothin'.

No . . . wait . . .

There was some kind of lettering . . . a sign maybe . . . up high. It was a dark bronze, but it wasn't black, and even though my Chinese was as sketchy as a Picasso notebook, I stared at it long enough to finally make it out.

THE PALACE OF THE FIVE TIGERS.

A tiny bell went off in my head . . . Where had I seen that before?

I paced off steps back to the corner, then crept around to the alley that ran in back of the block. I backtracked down the alley the same number of paces. No door. For twenty feet on either side of where a back door should have been . . . nothin'.

Then I flashed on the lettering again. I'd seen it, I knew I had. The same sign. But where? The question was bangin' around my noggin and I knew if I didn't figure it out, I'd never get another night's sleep. It would haunt me till I cracked up but good, started doing crazy things, and some judge would lock me up . . .

Judge?

Judge!

That was it!

I ran to the car. As I was hittin' the gas, I looked up . . .
and there it was. Exactly what I needed to see: the Port Charlie Courthouse.

I gunned the car outta Chinatown and headed back toward
downtown. Then I started thinkin'.

A long time ago, the Chinese had their spot on the little
hill where the courthouse now stood. They were hard-working
folks, bent on makin' a better life for their families. But
the upright natives didn't quite take to the idea. They didn't
force the Chinese out, but they didn't want to even see them
on the street. Story goes, it was that way all over the country.
Oh sure, America, you bet. "Give me your tired, your poor,
your huddled masses . . ."

"You're sermonizing," I said.

**"A thousand apologies," Spinelli said. "It's just that I get so
angry thinking about it."**

**"You're also preaching to the choir, Mr. Grasshopper," I
replied. "It was a raw deal. But it's history . . . shameful . . .
but history. Go on."**

The entire Chinese population was forced to vamoose when
the wiseacre city planners decided that the view of the harbor
from that particular hill was as pretty as a Ziegfeld girl and
just right for the hall of justice. But the construction crews
had a big surprise waitin' for them. They kept findin' tunnels
and secret rooms as far down as a hundred feet. That's how
everyone had been gettin' around from home to work and back
again without riskin' bein' seen. And these tunnels went everywhere. Some led right underneath the fancy homes of Port
Charles's finest, including the mayor's mansion; some led
down toward the harbor . . . perfect for smugglin' . . . and
one even led off underneath the train depot.

And then there were a few that led east . . . just east. Maybe a mile, if you were shootin' straight. Of course, no one found out just how far they went until a few construction patsies went explorin' and came back missin' an eye, or an ear, or a head, and tellin' tales of arrows shootin' outta walls, floors that just dropped out from under 'em, and walls that closed in and would crush a guy down to the size of a Ritz cracker box.

Turns out that these particular tunnels led out underneath a few shacks in the middle of a field that, in the past, nobody had paid much attention to. That's because nobody knew what they were hidin' . . . Port Charles's own little vacation spots.

Secret opium dens.

And now these leisure lounges were right underneath . . . the new Chinatown. Instead of leaving a cash business to be discovered by someone else, Port Charlie's most enterprisin' citizens moved right on top of it.

I'd heard rumors of what it was like, back in the day. The tunnels were crawlin' with coppers (including the chief), snot-nosed lawyers, senators up from D.C. with wads of payola, local brass, and crooked judges, all of 'em knowin' the traps and all lookin' for a little time in dreamland. And sometimes, from what I heard tell, if the bright lights and rubber hoses weren't workin' and a perp just wouldn't talk, the cops would take the guy through the tunnels into the Palace of the Five Tigers and get him real . . . happy.

Story goes that a whole lot of canaries sang after a few hours of just breathin' in deep.

As I was drivin', I realized I was one lucky son of a bootlegger. It was only because of my mandatory presence a couple of years ago during the trial of my right-hand man, Jason Morgan, for the murder of Lorenzo Alcazar, that I had been in the courthouse so much. One morning, when the DA du jour, Ric Lansing, was makin' his opening wisecracks, I needed to see a man about a horse. I was walkin' the hallway from the courtroom to the waterloo when I suddenly noticed a door with a padlock on the handle. And that was it . . . no sign, nothin'. Until I looked a little closer. Up over the arch, there were faint outlines of Chinese letters etched into the marble. Someone had pried them off and had even tried to cover these up with black paint. But I could just make out the words . . . on a door right in the middle of the PC courthouse corridor!

THE PALACE OF THE FIVE TIGERS.

I guess subtlety wasn't high on the to-do list, back in the day. It couldn't have been more obvious if they'd painted an arrow.

I didn't think much of it at the time. But now . . . it was my way in.

I screeched to a halt at the bottom of the courthouse steps and hopped out. There was no one around . . . The streets were as empty as Monica Quartermaine's martini glass.

Getting into the courthouse was like takin' candy from a baby . . . especially a Spencer-Webber baby . . . those kids practically throw their jujubes at you. Cameron's been known to lob an ice cream cone at perfect strangers . . .

"You're digressing," I said.

"Apologies," Spinelli said. "But I have the Rocky Road stains to prove it. That little boy, that pint-sized picture of perfection, ruined my best Megadeth vintage tee."

"Keep going."

I used my skeleton key and whammo, I was in. I headed down the corridor, past the night watchman who was glued to SoapNet on a portable black and white, catchin' up on his serials. He had his headphones on . . . I coulda been the 4:19 outta Rochester and he still wouldn'ta made me.

I found the door and tried the lock. It was old . . . I didn't think my key would work and I was right. I tried a standard

pick . . . no dice. I ran my hand through my hair; I was in a
spot, all right. I then felt one of Maxie's hairpins at the back
of my neck . . .

Spinelli stopped and stared at me for a moment.
"I'm not even going to ask," I said.

I had nothin' to lose. I tried the hairpin in the lock and she
sprung open like a Texas debutante on a New York weekend.
The door creaked inward. Right off, I was covered in dust and
cobwebs. And it was dark . . . really dark. I got about five feet
and realized I was never gonna make it. I thought about turnin'
around and tryin' to find a way in from Chinatown; then I
remembered something I had on my utility belt.

"Stop it *now*!" I yelled. "Utility belt?!"
"May all the gods on Olympus strike me dead if I lie,
Brusque Lady," Spinelli said. He opened his coat to reveal a
bungee cord around his waist replete with various pouches,
one handcuff case, and one Hello Kitty cosmetic bag.
"I give up."

I still had the item I took from the *Smilin' Lila*, when I saved
Eddie Quartermaine's bacon: a flare gun.

I closed the door behind me and took it out of my jacket.
One flare in the chamber and three taped to the side of the
gun. I fired straight ahead. The first flare hit the wall of the
tunnel about eighty feet away and lit her up like a Christmas
tree. I figured I had about two minutes until the flame went
out, so I sprinted the first few yards . . . and good thing I
did. Three yards in and I heard a crumblin' sound behind
me. The floor was fallin' away as soon as my feet hit it. Obviously, there was a button or lever I had missed on my way in, but
no time to think about it now. I ran like the devil himself was

chasing me. I ran past the flare and was headin' deeper in darkness when the sound stopped. I slowed down and looked behind me. The floor was solid right up until the flare. I tip-toed back, like a friggin' ballerina, and pried the flare outta the wall. I was gonna milk the light as long as I could.

I carried the flare deeper into the tunnel. The flame was goin' longer than I expected, but eventually it started to sputter. I held it out in front of me as long as my arm would go . . . and then, suddenly, somethin' cut out the light.

I froze like a twelve-pack of veal chops in my grandma's cold chest. Then I took one step forward and felt something whiz by my forehead. I didn't wanna use up another flare right away, so I pulled out my silver lighter . . . the one inscribed "We'll always have Pearis. Love, Maxie."

"You're joking," I said.

"My non-bride is indeed beautiful, sexy, and smart," Spinelli replied. "Spelling is not her forte. Fortunately, there is spell check for most things."

"Uh-huh."

The tiny flame gave me damn near bupkis by way of light, maybe a foot in any direction. But I could see holes on either side of me and as I moved forward, I saw an arrow shoot across my face and bounce off the opposite wall. I hit the floor and whaddya know . . . there were no holes close to the ground. I crawled on my belly . . . the way I had when the Gerrys had us pinned down in the Argonne woods . . .

"Oh, please."

But that's another story.

There were no more arrows because there was nothing to trigger them, except once when my ass got a little too high and an arrow gave my dungarees some unwanted air-conditioning.

That's also how I got a little ass shrapnel in the Argonne woods . . .

"Stop it!"

But that's another story.

I got past the arrows, and the rat pit, and the bags of scorpions, and the lye waterfall, and the chopping blades, and the crushin' walls. I used all the flares, and the butane in my lighter was almost gone when I heard muffled voices just ahead. I thought I might have been hallucinatin' . . . or it was another trap: the room of a thousand waggin' tongues. Then I heard . . .

"You'll never get away from me, you blackhearted dog! I have you and I'm going to keep you."

"You can't hold me here forever, Spanky."

"Oh no? Just watch me! I hope you like pork chow mein, scoundrel, because that's all you'll be getting from now on!"

"Can I at least have a little toot from one of those pipes?"

"Oh, Luke," Tracy's voice dropped to a disgusted whisper. I could barely make it out. "There hasn't been any opium here for years. That's why no one comes here anymore . . ."

I reached out in front of me and felt a door. I took a chance and pushed. It swung easily on its hinges, and I stopped it at about four inches—just enough to let me take a gander into the room.

". . . That's why I drugged you and brought you here."

"I had a Pop-Tart for dinner. How did you drug a Pop-Tart?!" Luke said.

"I have my ways!"

Tracy was standin' in the middle of a bad Chinese dream. Maybe it had been a hot spot once, and nothing actually looked out of place, but now the rugs were faded and the wooden chairs had damn near been eaten where they stood, their red lacquer flaking into a fine dust on the floor. Long metal/

wood opium pipes were rusting beside low sofas, opium resi-
due thick around the bowls. The paper lanterns were covered
in cobwebs and the cushions had all seen better days. It was
like time had stopped marching and, one day, everybody had
just walked away. Luke Spencer was lying on a long couch . . .
probably the most comfortable in the room . . . with his hands
tied to a metal ring in the wall behind him. On either side, at
a distance, a beautiful girl fanned him with woven bamboo.
Tracy began to pace the floor in front of Luke.

"And don't think of bribing either Mei Lee or Trixie,"
Tracy said, looking at the two gorgeous fortune cookies. "I've
paid them too much money; Mei Lee is sick of practicing law
and Trixie says being a venture capitalist was turning her
prematurely gray. I've warned them both of your tricks."

Then she sat down on the couch next to Luke.

"I can send them away with a flick of my wrist," she
purred . . . like a lion before it eats a wildebeest. "And you and
I can have this love nest all to ourselves. No more wondering
where you are. What country you're in. And with whom. When
you're coming home. If you're coming home. What rashes,
insects, and parasites you'll bring with you. You are now and
completely mine! And you know what the really beautiful
part is?"

"Enlighten me, wife," Luke said, grinning.

"I'm still free as a bird!" she yelled, startling Trixie, who
had fallen asleep. "I can see anyone, do anyone . . . thing . . .
any*thing*. I can go on trips to Rome or Milan, and you'll still be
here when I come back. Now you'll know what I've been suffering all of these years! The waiting . . . the wondering. The
booze-filled minutes of torture until you came home again!"

"You said you never minded, Spanks."

"Well, I lied!"

"Tell you what," Luke said, looking up at her. "You untie
these ropes and we'll take off . . . just you and me . . . on a
pleasure cruise around the world. And we'll make it last as

long as you want. We'll rent a yacht, just say the word . . . or
we can buy an island. Or a mountain. Whatever your tiny
black stone of a heart desires. And it will be just the two of us.
Italy, France, Spain . . ."

"On MY money, you freeloader!"

"You can't take it with you, Tracy," Luke said. I couldn't be
sure from where I was, but I think I actually saw the man bat
his eyelids. "And we'd have one helluva time!"

"Until you ditch me for some scoop of gelato outside the
Uffizi? No thank you. I'll keep you here . . . in my own private Peking. You know, egg rolls aren't just for breakfast anymore."

"What does that even mean?"

"Hell if I know. And now, I must be going. I have a date."

"You do?" Luke asked.

"No. But you were scared there for a moment."

"Oh, wife," he said, lowerin' his eyes. "You know me too
well."

The boy could play coy, I'd give him that.

"Damn straight!" Tracy spat out the words like they were
weak gin. "Oh, and even if you could get past Trixie and Mei
Lee, you would never get past Mr. Fists-of-Iron at the door.
He has orders to snap your neck like a pea pod. Fair warning."

"Thanks."

Tracy sauntered back through the abandoned rooms like
she was on her way to a Southern ladies' social.

"Hey, Spanky?" Luke called.

"Yes, Bluebeard?"

"I like your style."

"Flattery will get you a bowl of lychee nuts . . . and that's
about all."

She started up a flight of stairs. I heard a door open and
slam shut somewhere overhead. Then silence.

I swung the tunnel door outward and walked into the room.
I would free Luke and the two of us could probably handle

Mr. Fists-of-Iron . . . or, if Spencer was too weak from his stay in Tracy's pleasure palace, I was certain my hapkido black belt would be just the ticket. And Trixie and Mei Lee weren't gonna get wise and give me any trouble.

How wrong I was.

I didn't even see Mei Lee drop her fan, but one moment I'm walkin' toward Luke Spencer, his eyes buggin' out at the sight of me, and the next I'm on my keister, Trixie has me folded like a wonton, and Mei Lee's doin' a little chop-sockey number on my thinkin' parts.

These girls were trained, but good. Fortunately, my kung fu was just a little sharper . . .

"A minute ago you said hapkido," I mused. **"Now it's kung fu. Which is it?"**

"The Jackal is proficient, nay, expert in several of the most dangerous martial arts. So much so that I have blended them into a single subtle form and coined my own name for the skill. Jukidokafu."

"Gesundheit."

I got out of Trixie's knot and folded back up on her like a Venus flytrap. Two taps, right between her shoulder and the base of her neck, and she was out like a Cubs batter in any game . . . pretty much ever. Mei Lee took a little more effort. She'd worked out her own little Asian smorgasbord of death kicks, and suddenly I found myself in the middle of flyin' feet and hands that packed a wallop. I couldn't go twelve rounds with this broad on my best day. I saw one opening, kicked her feet out, and sent her flyin'. She landed right between Luke's calves and, being a quick thinker, he clamped down hard, holdin' her. I knew I only had a second before she broke free . . . and probably broke his legs. I towered over her as she went to make her move. I moved first.

One touch . . . right at her throat.

Her eyes got all glassy and her arms went limp. She struggled in Luke's grasp, then she stopped long enough to gimme a look that said she knew what was comin'.

"Sorry, ginger-root. It was you or me. Just doin' my job."

Mei Lee nodded, gasping for air. She held her hand out . . . all she really needed was somebody to hold onto.

"I'm scared," she wheezed.

"Don't be," I said. "I'll bet you got folks waiting for you and a big golden pagoda to live in on the other side."

"But I was a venture capitalist . . ." she said, her eyes growing dim.

"Oh . . . well, in that case, karma's gonna be a bitch," I said. "Sorry."

Luke and I watched the lights go out, then we rolled her off to the side.

"You killed her?" Luke asked.

"Not a chance," I said. "That was the Touch-of-Revelation. She'll be out for a couple of hours. Learned it when I was at the Tashi Lhunpo Monastery in Tibet. You go so far under, you actually get to see what's waitin' for you when you go for good. Kinda helpful. She may wake up and turn her life around. Or not. Now, let's get you outta here before Mr. Fists-of-Iron comes down for a walkthrough," I said, reaching up to untie the monkey knots holdin' Luke to the wall. Then I stopped short.

"Actually, before I untie you . . . let's talk about the five hundred pieces-of-eight you took off of me the other night at the Haunted Star."

"It's called gambling, my friend," Luke said, reclining against the wall, acting nothin' like a man who was trussed up like a roasting chicken.

"You practically pointed to the number I shoulda played. It's like you wanted me to set my chips right on top of red-22."

"And you bought my line. That's why the house usually wins."

"Well then," I said casually. "Maybe I'll just walk outta here and tell Lulu I couldn't find you."

"Go ahead," Luke said, a slug of a smile inchin' across his face. "I'll be right behind you."

Then he slipped his ropes and wiggled his fingers like a crazy elf.

"You've been free?!" I practically yelled, then I remembered we still weren't alone. I dropped it some. "You've been able to scramola? For how long?"

"Pretty much since she tied me up. Only, of course, because Tracy insisted on doing it herself. Said she wanted the ropes to be on the other hand for once."

I just learned a little somethin' about Luke Spencer.

"You called my bluff you son-of-a-horse-trader," I said. I had to give the man credit.

"Hey," he said. "You took a big fat chance coming down here . . . How did you get in, by the way?"

"Old tunnel; leads from the courthouse."

"Fantastic," Luke said. "At any rate, you risked a lot for me . . . so come by the Star next week and you'll get your money back. Unless you want to try and double it on red-22?"

"No thanks," I said. "But why next week?"

"I'm gonna stay here a few more days."

"No foolin'?"

"I owe it to the wife," he said, and by God if he didn't get a little misty. "She puts up with a lot from me. This is making her happier than I've seen her in years. I can play along for a while."

"How you gonna eat?" I asked.

"Mr. Fists-of-Iron and I worked out a deal. He gets me pizza, ribs, tacos . . . anything but Chinese, and next week I'm gonna get him some 'paperwork' so he can see his family in Hong Kong on the government's nickel. In fact, I'm gonna go with him."

"So, you're gonna leave again?" I asked. I already knew the answer. Yeah, there's such a thing as a stupid question.

"Hey, man . . . a rolling stone, y'know?"

"I know."

I turned to leave. I was gonna head up the stairway and cab it back to the courthouse; didn't want to face that tunnel again.

"Don't worry about Mr. FOI," Luke said. He must have seen that little falter in my step. "We talk about Tracy. He's got his own lady-troubles back home . . . but we love our wives. He's very understanding. He's cool."

I looked at Luke Spencer . . . wild man, rebel . . . legend . . . roped to a wall in a passé opium den, eatin' juke-joint ribs and greasy slices of 'za just to keep his wife from losin' what was left of her mind.

"So are you, my friend," I said.

"The same at'cha."

"See you next week for the five hundred."

"If I'm not there, Ethan will get it for you," he said, closin' his eyes. "Don't worry; I'll let Lulu know I'm fine . . . and I'll send you a postcard from Hong Kong."

I walked up the stairs and exchanged a nod with Mr. Fists-of-Iron.

"Hey Fists!" Luke called from below. "Tonight, let's eat Greek."

5

Damian Spinelli

and the Case of the Jumping Jax

The Port Charles oil refinery is small; that's because the Empire State has no oil. The crude boom of the 1920s and '30s was high-cotton for Texas and Cali-Flake-ia, but the upper East Coast started feeling left out. No big hats and Cadillacs with steer horns for Philly and Buffalo. A few states decided to put in an oil refinery anyway, because they knew it was only a matter of time until God pointed the way to a deep well. After all, God had pretty much blessed this part of the country with everything else, He certainly wouldn't leave the upper states out of the party for long. Port Charlie was the lucky draw. Small harbor meant small refinery: God would show the way all right, but don't block anybody's view.

Needless to say, the two big, round tanks have sat empty since they were built; a couple of years back, the refinery was turned into artist's lofts for the fancy-nancy set. Somebody put a chowder joint on the dock and used the crane as an elevator to the second floor. Cute gimmick. Sonny Corinthos moved in to the neighborhood, decided he didn't like chowder, and the place went under . . . no questions asked.

But the local punks still used to take their girls and climb all over the tanks . . . and each other. Regular jungle-gym, those tanks. Then, story goes, in the late '50s, during one spring break, somebody decided the game was gonna be "how many kids can you cram onto the little platform on the top?"

Turns out it was twelve.

Unlucky thirteen took a header and there was a fence around the works the next morning. Didn't really stop the juveniles, but the flatfeet had to patrol a little more often. Then, spooning on the tanks became old-fashioned . . . like root-beer floats and the electric chair. Kids found dance clubs . . . discos and the like . . . other ways to occupy their time and their hands. Nobody cruised the tanks.

So it was a little surprising when I got a call from Mac Scorpio tellin' me to meet him at the refinery, pronto.

Sun was settin' early that time of year, so Mac-the-Knife had the place lit up like a church at Christmas. And I hate Christmas. With all that wattage, a nice crowd had gathered to rubberneck at the shenanigans.

"What's up, Mac?" I asked, flashing my PI badge to a nosy beat cop. I don't like pulling rank, but I will when I have to. This palooka didn't know me; now he does.

"We've got a potential bird," Mac said, never taking his eyes off the tiny platform at the top.

"Come again?"

"A bird, a swan, an Acapulco diver."

"Stop talking like a Reuben and cut the ham!" I said. "Give it to me plain, Mac."

"We've got a jumper."

"That's better," I said. "What do we know?"

"Only a little. Several of the guys have tried talking him down," Mac said, motioning to a bullhorn lying in the dirt. "Nothing. Not a peep. I thought about trying it myself . . . but . . . ever since . . ."

He stopped short.

"Don't go over it again, Mac."

I knew why Scorpio didn't want to try his hand at talking the guy off the tank. It was common knowledge, but we'd all just put it deep in the backyard, so to speak. I hadn't heard anybody bring it up for years.

Years ago, Mac had built himself quite a reputation as a slick negotiator with a 100 percent success rate. Robbers out of banks, hostages freed at filling station holdups, jumpers off ledges . . . he even talked an old man into giving himself up during a standoff at the old Aces-High Casino and Lounge when the joint had taken the last cent of the man's pension check. Mac told him the casino would give him a refund and the health insurance company would reinstate his wife's policy so she could continue her chemo. And damn if Mac didn't make it stick.

Then, one night . . . his luck ran out.

A woman, standing on the edge of the roof of the old Bijou flicker house. Didn't seem crazy at all, Mac said later, just desperate. Husband had been killed in the service. Parents gone. Two kids, no job . . . and the landlord was throwing her out of her cold-water walk-up. Even worse, turns out Mac had dated her a while back . . . really liked her, too. Now he was trying to save her life.

He was on top of the movie house for a good four hours . . . thought he was gettin' through. Then the dame just turned a couple of sad eyes on Mac Scorpio and walked off the edge.

No one saw Mac for a few weeks after that, except the takeout delivery guys and a couple of bartenders. Then one day he walks into the Port Charles Police Department and sits down at his desk. Nobody cracks wise . . . nobody says nothin'. And that's the way it's been. Except I happen to know, because I gotta friend at the First National Bank of Port Charles, that Mac Scorpio has been taking care of that woman's kids for the past fifteen years. A real St. Nick . . . or St. something . . . He's tops in my book.

"You're our last hope, Jackal," Mac said.

"Nobody comes around here no more," I said, pulling my collar higher. "How'd you get wise?"

"Michael Corinthos was giving some girl a tour of Daddy's waterfront holdings," Mac answered. "Kids decided to see the view from the top of the tank like in the old days. This guy ran 'em off. Poor girl nearly fell off the metal stairs. As Michael was leaving, he heard the guy saying something about how Michael should come back in an hour . . . it would all be over by then. How he'd be just a memory . . . but a good-looking one. Of course, Michael got scared and called us . . . because he knows the jumper."

"Knows him?"

"Yep," Mac said. "Couldn't mistake the accent. It's his ex—step daddy . . . or are he and Carly still married? I'm never sure with those two."

"You mean it's . . . ?" I said looking up.

"Yeah . . . it's Jax."

———————

My first step on the stairs told me I was in trouble. My Buster Browns were gonna cause quite a hubbub as they hit the metal. Jax would know someone was on their way up . . . no telling what that would do to the man. A man can do desperate things when he's backed into a corner, especially if it's a corner on a five-by-five platform two hundred feet high.

I took off my *zapatos* and started the hike.

Five minutes later, I was leaning hard against the tank, like a bear scratching an itch. Only a few more steps and I'd be on the top. I ducked down as long as I could, then I craned my head for a peek.

Jax was standing with his back to me, staring at the harbor. Poor fool didn't even know I was there.

"I knew they'd send you, Jackal."

Okay, so I was wrong.

"Don't know what you're talkin' 'bout," I said. "Came up for the view."

"Top of the world, Jackal. Top of the world."

"Close enough," I said, putting on my shoes. "Yeah, real pretty. Now what say we head down, grab a coupla steaks, coupla redheads, and soak the whole mess in a coupla gimlets?"

"Not this time, Spinelli," Jax said, finally turning to look at me. "Game's over."

"Whaddya talking about?" I said. "I don't see no game up here. You want a game? I know a back-alley craps game that'll give you six-to-one. Or we could cab it to Saratoga and play with the ponies . . ."

"Stop it, Jackal. It's no good . . . not anymore. I'm ending it all now."

"Cut the coleslaw and give me the straight beef."

Jax looked at me real hard.

"What?" I said.

"What do you mean 'what'?" he asked, as if I should know.

"Whaaat?" I was startin' to get steamed. "Toss out the egg salad, Chester, it's old news. What gives!?"

He still just stared, but harder. I was gonna push him over the side myself.

"Don't you see it!?" he finally yelled.

"What?" I yelled right back. "What am I looking for? What's got you all nutso?"

"Right here!"

And Jax moved his hand so fast, I thought he was gonna deck himself right in his noggin. Suddenly, like some kind of spooky mechanical toy, he's pointing at his head, just above his right ear. I bent in for a look. Nice ear . . . like a pink kidney bean.

"You get your ears pierced?"

"NO! Right here!"

"I'm not seein' nothin' except skin and hair," I said.

And then, outta the blue, he gets all teary-eyed.

"What color is the hair?" he said.

"Brown? Sandy blond, maybe? Clairol #57 if I'm guessin' right? Am I right?"

"Look closer, damn you!"

"Hey, stop with the lip. Ain't no call to be talkin' . . . wait. Wait a minute. What's that?"

The sun was dropping into the sea and the last little glint caught a single hair. A single, pure white hair.

"THAT?" I said, nearly falling over my feet as I pushed my fedora back on my head. "You're pullin' my leg, but good. That's what's got you loco? A gray hair?"

"It's white! It's skipped gray entirely. And it's only the beginning, Spinelli. More are on their way. It's finally happening. I'm getting old. And I know why . . ."

"What do you mean, 'why'?" I said, getting a little concerned now. "Happens to everyone, Jax."

"You don't understand. It was never supposed to happen to me. Everybody was gonna get pruny around me, but I was gonna outlast them all. This face was gonna stay young and gorgeous forever!"

"You just crossed the line, Barrymore," I said gently. "Now you got me worried for real."

"It was the deal, Spinelli. The deal my father made with . . . I don't know . . . I just know the terms. My father John had a hand of five playing cards that never left his person. They were always on him somewhere. Aces and eights. As long as my father had the cards . . . his lucky hand . . . Wild Bill's hand . . . he was fine. Healthy, strong as an ox, and a handsome devil. But Sam . . ."

"Sam?" I cut in. "McCall . . . my partner?"

"Long before you showed up in Port Charles," Jax went on, "Sam stole one of the cards. I can't even remember why anymore. She got her hands on an eight . . . a lousy eight . . .

and my father went downhill. In no time, he was in the hospital. I didn't think it was anything but superstition at the time; I didn't believe, you hear me? I just knew it mattered to my father! I managed to get the card away from Sam . . . I rushed to the hospital, but . . . but . . ."

I'm not comfortable with grown men crying . . . unless it's me . . . but his story had me riveted, so I got past wantin' to smack him.

"I showed my father the card . . . held it right under his nose, you understand!? But it was too late. With his last gasp, he looked me in the eye and said he was passing the secret of the hand to me. Told me where to find the other cards and that I should always keep them close. They'd keep me young and handsome."

"Aw, come on. This is voodoo talk, Jax! This is chicken bones and . . . and . . . stickin' pins in little dolls! You can't tell me you believed . . ."

"And sexy. And virile."

"Yeah, yeah . . . I got it! But this is candles and sand circles and . . ." I said, getting the urge to shove him off the tank again.

"A lust machine."

"All right . . . I savvy! Don't need to hear this part."

"Incredibly well endowed. Able to go for hours . . ."

"Aces and eights, you say?"

"Spinelli . . . how old do you think I am?"

Now, if this had been a dame I was talking to, I knew how to wise up, and fast. Maxie had pulled this on me once. Cost me two hundred bucks in silk, lace, and bonbons. And the tears! Cripes, I didn't know a person could make that much salt water. These days, if Maxie even started getting that look in her eye like she was gonna ask me how old she looked or if she looked fat or some other female nonsense, I gave one right on her kisser, pulled out a Franklin and told her to go buy herself something pretty. But this was Jax . . . askin' a skirt question.

"I don't know, Jax," I said. "Maybe thirty-five, thirty-eight at the outside?"

A smile started movin' across his face real slow, like a snot-nose kid crossing the gym floor to ask a girl to dance.

"I'm sixty-seven and a half."

It was like someone stopped my heart for a second. I hadn't realized the boy was this far gone.

"Yeah," I said, "and I'm the Pope."

"Your Eminence," Jax said, bowing slightly.

"Cut the corn!" I yelled, as the moon started to rise over the city.

"I'm not kidding, Jackal," Jax said, his voice real low. "My father was one hundred and seven when he died. And he'd still be alive if he'd had his lucky hand. When he lost the card, he went fast . . . and it was painful. I don't want to go like that!"

He moved toward the edge of the platform.

"I want to go in the blink of an eye, and leave a good-looking corpse."

"You take that next step and they won't find enough of you to leave a good-looking anything. What they do find, they'll have to stitch together, and that won't be pretty."

"Just let me get it over with."

"Why don't we go down and talk this whole thing over with . . ."

I stopped short. Real short. Maybe it was the night air or the altitude playing tricks with my head, maybe it was this guy's belief that his fate lay in one hand of cards . . . or maybe I just hadn't seen it before, but there was a second white hair growin' close to the first. I shook it off.

"They got doctors, see? Real good ones . . . at Shady-brook . . ."

"I didn't expect you to believe me. Look, maybe it's better this way. I won't outlive any wives and won't look younger than the bridegroom when I walk Josslyn down the aisle. I appreciate you trying to help . . . Now step aside, Spinelli."

Right in front of my peepers, I coulda sworn I saw a third hair go white.

"Okay . . . okay . . . let's just think about this," I said, trying to buy some time before Jax bought a one-way ticket. "Where'd you lose the eight?"

"It doesn't matter. I've retraced my steps. It's gone."

He took two steps closer to the edge; one more and he'd be a pavement burger.

"Hey look!" I said, pointing off to my left. "Carly's naked in a 'copter!"

"Where!?"

I caught his chin right on the square. What surprised me is that it shattered, like it was made of glass . . . or the bones were old. Jax looked back at me, his pretty face kinda outta whack now.

"That hurt," he tried to say, just before he passed out. He started to fall backward and woulda taken the plunge if I hadn't caught him by his tie. He slumped forward on top of me and I was glad I'd spent all those years lifting sacks of beans on that coffee plantation in Costa Rica.

But it was all too easy: the punch and the pass-out. This was one of the most . . . all right, there's no other word for it . . . "manly" men in the mid-Atlantic state area. Jax was a straight arrow; an Eagle Scout who grew up into Cary Grant. He was the clean-cut altar boy with a little Clark Kent on the side. This guy even gave Sonny Corinthos a run for his money in the lady-killer department and he could almost out-muscle Stone Cold Morgan. I shoulda never been able to take him like that. But I could think about it tomorrow, after I'd gotten him into a nice, cozy ambulance.

"C'mon, Mumbles. Let's get you down."

———————

The next morning, after a cup of Colombian and a chat with the docs at General Hospital to check on Jax's condition (his vitals were weak, but stable, and he was sleeping like a baby, or like me after a sleeping pill with a beer chaser), I headed over to his penthouse at the Metro Court. My skeleton key let me in, and I went over the place like it was Rockefeller's last will and testament. Nothing. Not one beauty product out of place.

I drove over to Carly's house, the one she got when she and Jax divorced. I was gonna tell her about Jax's condition and see if she could explain some of her ex's crazy talk.

I knocked twice, then after a few minutes I let myself in. Didn't look like anyone was home; then I heard Carly's laugh comin' from the direction of the pool. I poked my head out from behind one of the floor-to-ceiling curtains and saw the former Mrs. Jax, wearin' a doll-sized swimsuit, makin' very merry with two cabana boys, one of whom didn't look much older than her son, Michael.

"Nice," I thought. "Nice broad. Keep her *ocupada*, boys, and thanks."

I turned around. I had the perfect opportunity to shake down the joint, if only the laugh twins would buy me the time. I backtracked through the yellow and black living room and was heading to another part of the house . . .

. . . when I saw it.

Carly's purse sitting on one of the long, white couches. I might have gone right by it, but a flash of red outta the corner of my eye brought me up short. I walked over . . .

. . . and there it was. Sticking right up out of a side pocket. The eight of diamonds.

It was tattered and dog-eared. The print on the back wasn't from any brand of cards I'd ever seen, and I'd seen some. And the size was all wrong. It was smaller than a normal card . . . kinda like it was from a different time and place.

Why Carly had taken it in the first place was anyone's guess. She was a walking roulette wheel and the ball always landed on "crazy." She'd gotten everything she'd wanted in the split, but her emotions had been blended like a margarita. She hated Jax . . . but she still loved him, deep down, where it counts. She was suffering plenty just wakin' up in the morning. My guess is that Jax had let her in on his crazy little secret during the whole "I can tell you anything" phase of their relationship, and then after the divorce she had gotten her mitts on the eight just to make him tumble over the edge. If she was gonna be miserable, so was he.

Suddenly, I heard Carly on the patio just outside.

"No, Emilio, I don't want you to freshen my Tom Collins. You do it wrong every time, dammit! Besides, I want to change into something fun and festive!"

Fun and festive? All that was left was her birthday suit, and while it would have made for a pretty picture, that was my cue to scram.

I grabbed the card and was burning unleaded in less than thirty seconds. I knew where I had to go. Even if it was only superstition, a silly idea running around like a hamster inside Jax's brain, maybe the idea of the card could help. The mind is a powerful thing; bendable at certain times, immovable at others. I thought about Maxie. When she got it into her head that she wanted hot Krispy Kremes, I knew I was goin' for a drive to the nearest shop. Unfortunately, it was in North Carolina, but there was nothing else I could do. Her mind was like the walls of Sing Sing . . . no way around.

I walked right past the nurse's desk . . . Epiphany Johnson was yelling at a new resident; something about his charts being messy. I liked Epiphany, she was a real pro; no bull crap, fierce, but underneath . . . hell, I'd seen her toss full-grown men outta the hospital after visiting hours, then turn around and give a sucker to a frightened little kid. Or had she thrown out the kid and given the sucker to the . . . ?

Either way, Nurse Johnson was tops.

I left her telling the intern not to let the ER doors hit him in the ass, and went to Jax's room.

At least a dozen tubes and wires were stickin' outta him in

every direction. He looked thinner than he had on the tank the previous night . . . and the hair at his temples was completely gray. Maybe . . . I couldn't tell, not really. The room was dark, the blackout curtains were drawn, and the nightlight was on.

I didn't want to wake him, poor bastard; he looked almost peaceful. Then he rolled a bit to one side and his hand flopped off the edge of the bed. He was clutching four cards; I could only see their backs, but they matched the eight of diamonds I had in my pocket.

And he was holding on to them like they were a rosary.

I gently slipped the eight into his fist with the rest.

Now, maybe I was dreamin' this next part. Maybe I got a little spooked myself. Maybe I had a piece of wax in one ear the size of a Brazil nut and it decided to fall out just at that moment. Or maybe what Billy the Bard says is true and "there's more stuff in heaven and earth than we really know about, Harry," and I just wanted to believe in something, anything, the way Jax believed in those cards, but . . . I'd swear on my mother's grave, if I knew where it was . . . His heartbeat got a little louder. And the green line on the monitor started movin' a little faster. A light went on over his bed that I knew was gonna send Epiphany Johnson on the run. I hid behind the door and, sure as bathtub gin'll get you six months in the slammer, Epiphany Johnson and Dr. Patrick Drake were in his room in a flash. I slipped away like a ghost and walked out past the intern, cleaning up his charts and emptying a box of Kleenex.

On my way out of the General Hospital parking structure, I put in a call to my favorite gal.

"Hi, honey!" Maxie said. Her voice was real high and sweet on the other end of the line.

"I woke up and you weren't here. I got sad."

"That's why I'm calling, doll-face," I said. "Put on something nice; I'm pulling up in ten minutes. We're going to North Carolina."

"Krispy Kremes!"

"A whole dozen just for you, baby."

"What's the occasion, Jackal?"

"Does there have to be an occasion? It's nothin'. It's you and me, is all. It's a drive on a nice day. We're young, and good-lookin', and we ain't dead yet . . . so we're gonna live a little. Today, Wilmington . . . tomorrow, who knows, kiddo, I may fly you to Paris."

"Oh, Spinelli!"

"Yeah, well don't put on your beret just yet. Just slip into your dungarees and be waitin'. Oh, and . . . doll?"

"Yes?"

"I love you."

6

Damian Spinelli
and Great Alan's Ghost

She let me in the bathroom window.

"I feel like I'm breakin' in," I said, easing my unmentionables out of the begonias and over the sill. "It's been a while
since I've used a window in a crapper, pardon my French, and
usually I'm hightailin' it out. Jealous husbands ain't my favorite dessert, if you know what I mean, doll."

"It's Doc . . . I mean, you may call me Doctor," Monica
Quartermaine said coolly, but I could tell she was nervous . . .
underneath. "I couldn't let you in the front door because
Tracy has the whole place alarmed like Fort Knox. She changes
the code every night and keeps it a big secret, the evil she-
man. This window is the only open spot in the house. And I'm
not interested in your back window exploits, Mr. Spinelli . . .
For heaven's sake, I could be your mother."

Suddenly my guts went all loosey-goosey. I was gonna have
trouble holding down my Spam and cream cheese on sprouted
wheat with a cup of tapioca on the side.

"Are you?"

"Am I what?" she said.

"My mother?"

"Oh, for pity's . . ."

"Oh . . . oh, Ma!"

"Stop it!" Monica said. Then she hushed herself and looked up toward the second floor. "No, I am not your mother."

"Sorry, doll . . . Doc," I said. "I just got a little excited there for a second. Not many people know that one of the reasons I came to Port Charles was because I got a bead on my mother, see? Trail got cold after I arrived, but I ain't givin' up hope, y'know."

"Well, I am certainly not her."

"It's jake," I said, feelin' the Spam settle back down . . . along with my hopes. "So what's with the squeezy phone call to my office? Why the jitters?"

Monica looked around the bathroom. She stared at the expensive hand towels, the gold toilet handle, and that funny contraption that washes your prat n' parts. It was a nice place to take a powder.

"Doc? You gonna talk or do I call Madame Rosinka, the psychic on Sixth and Pine, and have her tell me, huh?"

"It . . . it's . . . well, now that I am actually about to say it, it's just going to sound silly," Monica said, rubbing her hands together.

"Nothing's silly if it pays the rent. Come on . . . you musta called for some reason."

She took a deep breath.

"I'm being haunted."

That's when I remembered that Doc Quartermaine enjoyed her hooch. I tried to smile real big.

"Can I leave by the front door, or do you want me to smash a few more begonias? Oh, that's right . . . the alarms."

"I'm not joking!" she practically yelled. "I know how it sounds . . ."

"Yeah?"

". . . but it's the truth."

"Yeah? Haunted, huh? A 'haint'? Well, is he here right now? Maybe his name's Jack . . . or Jim . . . or Johnny . . ."

"What?" she said.

". . . or Jose . . . or Absolut . . . or Belvedere . . ."

"I have not been drinking!" she screamed. Then she put her hand over her mouth.

"I have not been drinking," she whispered, her eyes gettin' all wet and her mouth twitching. Suddenly, I knew she was on the level. I could tell an honest twitch from a drunk twitch. I'd learned that in Saigon.

"Come on, Mr. Grasshopper," I said. **"I will bet you a case of orange soda that you have never been in Saigon."**

"My contradiction means no disrespect, Surly Solicitor," Spinelli said. **"But where do you think I obtained the moniker 'Grasshopper'?"** It was closing in on 2:00 AM, and I knew Max had finished the Häagen-Dazs, gone out for another pint, and polished off most of that as well. In fact, if he were true to form, he'd taken the second pint to bed to watch the late, late show on the Hallmark channel and fallen asleep, mid-scoop, and now there was Vanilla Swiss Almond dribbled all over my Egyptian cotton sheets. It was the couch for me no matter what time I got home.

"Forgive my doubts . . . Grasshopper."

Just then, Spinelli jumped in his seat and I knew his cell phone had gone off again. He fished it out and glared at the number before clicking the button to ignore it.

"Nefarious One! Desist!"

"Who is it?"

"I do not know."

"Then how do you know they're nefarious?" I asked him.

"Forgive my outburst," Spinelli said. **"But I have personal and in many cases intimate knowledge of all who possess this most secret of phone numbers. But, on occasion, I will be the recipient of prank phone calls from fellow yet lesser cyber**

lords. This is a number I don't recognize . . . it's not even a country I recognize."

"No wonder they're calling at such an ungodly hour. And it is. Ungodly. So let's push onward, shall we?"

"Okay, Doc, okay . . . you haven't been tipplin' tonight. But you can't expect me to believe that . . ."

"It's my husband."

"Your husband? The late Alan Quartermaine, one of GH's finest pill-pushers and general Port Charles gad-about?"

"Y . . . yes."

"How do you know?"

"Come upstairs. You can see for yourself."

I followed her out of the powder room, down the hallway, and past the maid's room where Alice was snorin' and mumblin' something about Johnny Zacchara and Pudding Pops. We headed up the grand staircase, but not before Monica put her finger to her lips about five times, warnin' me to keep mum.

We turned left and started walkin' down the longest damn hallway I had even seen—including the one in that big palace belongin' to that Frog king, Louis . . . the guy that lost a few pounds, head-wise. Yeah, I knew the Q house was big, but this was a Hitchcock hallway: one that just kept stretchin' away, the more you walked down it. It wasn't hard to see how Doc Quartermaine kept her girlish figure; I was gonna drop a few pounds myself whenever we got wherever we were going. Finally, she stopped at a set of double doors about twenty-five yards in, put a key in the lock, and turned to me.

"I called you because I think you're a man who doesn't scare easily."

"Only one thing scares me, Doc . . . and your see-through hubby ain't it."

"Good."

She turned the handle and we walked into a bedroom the

size of an airplane hangar. Strange thing was, it was cold. Really cold.

"You can't afford heat?" I asked, as she flipped on the lights. "Or you just like it like Oslo?"

"Look," she said pointing to a little box on the wall. The thermostat read seventy-five degrees.

"Right," I said, feelin' the hairs at the back of my neck stand at attention. "So, what's the story?"

"He's in the bathroom."

"Say again?"

"In my medicine cabinet."

"Doc . . ."

"That's where he spends most of his time, I think . . . but then he leaves me . . . messages. Over here . . ."

She motioned for me to follow her across the room. Two minutes later, I realized I shoulda brought a snack. Two minutes after that, we were approachin' what I took to be her bed. It was one of those silly affairs, high off the floor with piles of pillows . . . the lady needed a stepladder to get some sleep. Monica stopped right by her nightstand. She was shakin', hard; but it wasn't DTs. It was pure fear. I could tell the difference. I learned that in Rangoon.

"Oh, please . . ."

She turned on the lamp and looked away quickly.

"Tell me what it says," she whispered. "I don't want to look."

I took a gander at the nightstand. There was a pile of medical-type magazines, a jug of water, an open pound bag of peanut M&M's, and a pocket-sized Bible.

"What are you gettin' at?" I asked her, real nice. I thought maybe if I talked real nice and all, she might gimme a few M&M's for the trip back across the room. "I don't see nothin'."

"Behind the water pitcher."

I took a look.

One word.

Spelled out nice and neat with, maybe, a hundred little bright orange pills: MONICA.

"Somebody's been pill-paintin'," I said.

"What does it say?"

"It's just your name."

"God," she gasped. "Sometimes he spells out other things."

"That's it?" I said. "This is what you called me about? You, playing jigsaw puzzle with your meds?"

"I didn't do it!" she said. "I came into my room tonight and there it was. I just saw them lying there . . . but I couldn't bring myself to read it. That was three hours ago. That's when I called you."

"Uh-huh."

I was startin' to lose my cool. I didn't like losing my cool.

"All right," I barked at her. "How about someone else in the house, huh? Somebody trying to drive you around the bend in a 1967 green Jag with a bright orange interior? Like Tracy, maybe? You ever think of that?!"

"My door is locked whether I'm in my room or not," Monica said; she was turning on the waterworks, but good. "And I'm the only one with a key. One night, about six months ago, I caught Tracy standing over my bed with a frying pan, screaming something about kippers and a glue-gun. I called the locksmith's the next day. Tracy hasn't been in this room since."

"Okay, Doc," I snapped. I was tired and this was lookin' more and more like Monica Quartermaine was buckin' for a room in Shadybrook. "First of all, your sis-in-law couldn't stand over your bed, 'cause she'd have to be seventeen feet tall. And second, I'm headin' home. I don't know what kinda crazy game you're playin' . . ."

Suddenly, the Doc's eyes went all buggy in her head. Her mouth began opening and closing like a carp, and she pointed at the table.

I followed her finger . . . and felt my Spam comin' back up.

The little orange pills had been rearranged into two new words.

JOIN ME.

I started to back away from the table.

"How'd you do that?" I said, tryin' like hell to keep my voice calm.

"Spinelli . . ."

"Never mind," I said, realizing that if I lost my tapioca, two crazies in one room wouldn't do anybody any good. "Just start at the beginnin'."

She kept it brief. It had been happening for about four weeks . . . not every night . . . once, maybe twice a week to start; messages spelled out with pills. But not just any pills . . . sleepin' pills. The kind that could bring down a horse. Sometimes, like tonight, they were on her nightstand. But most of the time she found them on the sink or clingin' to the mirror. She'd read the message and the pills would drop into the basin. Once she found them floatin' in mid-air over the bathtub. But for the last three days, she'd found them everywhere: I LOVE YOU. PLEASE! COME TO ME. BE WITH ME.

"Why don't you call the goons on TV?" I asked. "Those palookas that go to the lighthouses and the old hotels and prisons. Sure, they never really see anything and the show's a steamin' pile, but they're in the business. Why me, Doc?"

"I know what you did for Edward," she said. Her shoulders slumped forward; she looked like she was curlin' into a bocce ball. "You saved his life in that terrible storm. Alice made sure we all knew about it and hasn't let us forget. That took a kind of courage I can't even imagine. I couldn't tell anyone here . . . Tracy's just waiting for an opportunity to put me in Shadybrook, and Edward wouldn't be able to stop her if I started talking about messages from beyond. You're the only one I thought of. Plus, the big bald guy on that show frightens me a little."

"Okay," I said, startin' to feel like a prize chump. The dame

was countin' on me. I didn't really know her history; she'd
already had her little deal with John Barleycorn going when
I'd first arrived in town. I'd only heard talk of her brilliance,
her skill with a scalpel, how many lives she'd saved. I knew it
took some tough times to turn an ace like that into . . . the
scared female standin' in the middle of her ballroom-sized
bedroom. I wasn't gonna let her down. Not if I could help it.

"I'm no witch doctor, see," I said, heading toward the
bathroom. "But I'll give it a go."

Monica Quartermaine's bathroom was as big as the penthouse I sublet to Jason Morgan.

"Now I happen to *know* that's just not true. Jason allows you
to stay in a room in . . ."

"A thousand pardons, Brusque Barrister," Spinelli interrupted, "but Stone Cold and I are not small about such things.
We don't keep books, as it were. And that is not the penultimate
and final point of this case."

"Is the Metro Court kitchen still open?"

"I'm sorry . . . ?"

"I am starving to my death," I said. "I would commit several
criminal acts for a Monte Cristo and a side salad."

"I am afraid the kitchen is closed," Spinelli replied. "But
I do know a spot, right around the corner, it just so happens,
that serves all night. Many's the time I have returned from a
stakeout and ordered a short stack of buttermilk hotcakes."

"We're leaving. You're buying."

"As you wish."

We settled into a booth at the Night Owl, a cozy joint that I'd
have to remember for those times Max and I got the post-nookie
munchies. No Monte Cristo on the diner's menu, so I ordered
my steak and eggs rare and poached respectively, and Spinelli

ordered a short stack . . . and asked if the fry-cook could make them into little pancake men, "like the last time."

I turned the tape recorder back on.

Her bathroom was just as big as the penthouse and looked twice as pricey. You coulda parked a Buick between the bath-tub and that funny contraption that washes your *arschloch*. Monica waited at the door as I started walkin'. And if I thought her bedroom was cold, her bathroom was a deep-freeze. A minute later, I was comin' up on the medicine cabinet sunk into the tiled wall, just over the sink. It was open, but every-thing looked like it was in its place. Then I checked the wash-stand. Sure as shootin', there were about eighty pills in a neat orange message, just to the left of the hot water knob.

I'M WAITING.

My skin was really startin' to go all clammy. I pushed the little pills around with my finger . . . they moved easy enough. It was a brand I was familiar with; hell, I used them myself when it was late and I wanted to stop thinking about Maxie's assorted shenanigans, so three or four somehow moved into my pocket. Now, the message read:

I'M WA TING

Yeah, the Doc coulda put it there, spelled it all out before I arrived. But there was no reason; it didn't make sense unless she was too afraid to flat-out demand a room in Shadybrook and this was the only scheme she could imagine. But that's not what I was gettin' from Doc Q. The lady believed . . . and even if I didn't, I was gonna find an ans . . .

That's when I closed the mirror on the cabinet.

"Hello, Spinelli."

My hands flew up so fast I nearly brained myself. If I hadn't been trained by ancient masters, I might have peed a little. Instead, I just backed up about ten paces. Fast.

Alan Quartermaine was starin' outta the mirror, right at me.

"What?!" Monica yelled from the doorway when she saw

me doing a box-step into the towel bar. I looked around for the gimmick . . . the projector, the tape recorder . . . whatever the trick was. Nothin'.

"Let's just say I believe you, Doc," I said, lookin' at the ghost in the glass.

"Why!?" Monica called. "What do you see?"

"Let's leave her out of this for a moment, shall we?" Alan said.

Suddenly the bathroom door swung shut. Mister Doc Quartermaine and I were all alone.

"I'm glad you're here, Spinelli. There's been a lot of talk around the house about you ever since you pulled Edward off of death's door. I was a little disappointed by that; he would have been nice company. At least I think so; he may be going somewhere else. At any rate, you're a good man, and I hope you'll help Monica. I was actually going to spell out a message that she call you, but the old gal beat me to it. Great minds, they say . . . Monica and I always did think alike. Well, most of the time."

"Look, Casper," I said, "I ain't tryin' to be rude, but what the hell are you doing leaving crazy messages with little night-night pills?"

"I want her to join me?"

"You want your wife to join you," I repeated . . . 'cause I couldn't think of anything else to say . . . "on the other side?"

"That's right," he said with a big smile.

"But why?"

"Because I'm lonely."

That's when my jaw hit the imported I-talian floor tiles. I'd heard that Alan Quartermaine, who was a fine chopper in the operating room, was also a spoiled rich kid who was a spoiled rich man until he popped off. He was used to getting what he wanted, but this took the cake.

"You gotta be jokin'!"

"Why?"

"Ain't nobody, livin' or deceased, ever been that selfish. Your wife is still livin' and breathin' over here on the bright side and you want her to off herself 'cause you don't have a play-mate?"

"Well, it's a little more serious than that, I can assure you. First of all, I didn't actually get into Heaven . . . it's sort of Heaven-Lite. It's not bad, it's just kind of a limbo. There's a veggie plate and cookies in the afternoons. And table tennis. But the women here are really down a few pegs. Oh, there are some that are all right, I suppose, but when you've had a woman like Monica, everyone here just pales . . . no pun intended. And I don't want to be unfaithful . . ."

I choked a little.

"From what I hear tell, Prince Charming, that's all you ever were."

"What's going on in there?" Monica yelled from the other side of the door.

"We're having a chat, throttle it back a little."

"I wish I could have handled her like that back in the day," Spooky Q said. "It was only in coming here that I learned a few things . . ."

"Yeah, well how to die and let live wasn't one of them, ya bastard."

"At any rate, that's one of the reasons I haven't appeared to Monica. This place is always rather dark and I didn't want her to get frightened off. I know she's been having, shall we say, troubles . . ."

I pushed my hat back on my head. They say . . . and who exactly is this "they" that everybody keeps talkin' about? I had an idea once that it was the Van Patten family, but that still didn't seem right. Anyways, they say that when you die, your whole life flashes and you see the error of your ways and all the choices you coulda made that would have let you do things a little better. I was bettin' Spooky Quartermaine had a black silk eye-mask over his peepers when the big moment hit. He hadn't learned diddley.

"So you thought you'd just frighten her to death? Hang on a second," I said. "She's gotta hear this for herself."

"Where are you going?" Alan said, getting nervous.

"Where do you think?"

"I won't let her see me!"

"You stay right there, shady!"

I walked over to the bathroom door and yanked on it. Spooky Q didn't want to open it at first, then I yelled that I would just tell her everything from inside the loo anyway. And that if he kept me there long enough to starve me, or if he managed to kill me in some way, I would be headin' to Heaven, but I'd arrange to make a stop at Heaven-Lite and settle his hash, but good.

"Doc," I said to Monica . . . she was standin' a little ways back from the door. "You need to see this."

I marched her back to the mirror.

"What?" she said. "I don't see anything."

"I told you," Alan said.

She obviously didn't hear anything either.

"I ain't surprised, you coward," I shouted at the mirror.

"Is he there? Can you see him? Oh, Alan."

"Yeah, well before you go all Niagara on me, you should hear the deal."

I told her everything. What her doornail hubby wanted and why. She kept her upper lip stiff, I'll say that for her. For about two minutes. Then she turned to the mirror and let Alan have it.

"Alan Quartermaine, I am a vital, vibrant, warm . . . fairly warm-blooded woman, who still has many years left in her . . . and if the Botox keeps working, no one will ever know that I'm not still in my forties! How dare you, you self-centered brute! I may be a little worse for wear these past few months, I may have crawled into bed with a bottle on my nightstand, but that was only in response to losing you, you pig . . . and now I see that you're behaving just as reprehensibly on the other side as you did here. If you think I am going to touch another drink, another ounce of whiskey, brandy, gin, or vodka in mourning over you, you disgusting lout, you have another think coming. In fact, I'm hereby off the sauce . . . Spinelli, you're a witness!"

"Got it."

"Thank you. And get out of my bathroom mirror, you pervert! My answer to you is a no . . . a big, fat NO! In fact, I am going to start doing so many good deeds, God will have no choice but to put me with your mother in Heaven . . . and you and I will never see each other again. You can just rot in Heaven-Lite."

She was all outta juice by the time she was done. She kinda fell onto my shoulder.

"Nicely done, Sawbones," I said, puttin' my arm around her. "Nicely done."

I looked back at the mirror. Alan had his arms folded across his chest. He looked like a little kid who just found out that Santa Claus is a big fat lie. Finally, he puffed his chest out like a rooster, then let all the air out again.

"Well," he said. "Then just ask her if I can date."

7

Damian Spinelli

and Yes, Sometimes It Really IS Brain Surgery

They say . . . the Van Patten family, that is . . . that everything happens for a reason. Everything from gettin' a parkin' ticket that you know you didn't deserve to marryin' the wrong dame two, maybe three times over. Sometimes we get to know what that reason is, like when I see Billy "Bag o' Donuts" Ludelski from sixty paces away walkin' into Domingo's Grocery for a cup of lemon ice and suddenly, bingo-bango, I remember I had a set-up date with his sister once about seven months ago and I sorta never showed . . . and this is God's way of tellin' me that I don't really need to walk by Domingo's on my way to get a bratwurst on raisin bread and that He let me see Jimmy to keep me alive.

And sometimes, you don't get to know the reason. At least not right away. If ever.

Like when the stoplight goes haywire at Eighth and Central and a busload of kids on their way back to school from a field trip . . . to a dairy farm, no less . . . slams into a car with one guy on his way into town to see his granddaughter . . . for the first time.

There ain't no reason for that . . . not that I can see.

I was at General Hospital donatin' my monthly pint, when suddenly there's a ruckus at the nurses' station.

I grabbed my cup of OJ and a coupla oatmeal cookies with the striped frostin' on top and started for the door.

"Now, Mr. Spinelli," said the nurse, with a wink . . . she was a looker all right, the kind that could make you forget you already had a looker back home. "I know Nurse Johnson has told you before . . . only one cookie per pint."

"What can I say, doll . . . I'm delicate. Besides, Michelle, you do things to me, know what I mean? I need my strength."

She hurried past me, also on her way to check out the fuss.

"See you next month?"

"If I ain't dead."

When I got through the door, Michelle had disappeared in a sea of GH uniforms and I knew this was no ordinary emergency. I headed for the nurses' station, where head nurse Epiphany Johnson was barkin' orders from on top of a chair.

"I need all available personnel on deck stat! Anyone with ER experience, get down there in the next sixty seconds. I need as many OR prep teams prepping every available room. And I need everyone else to scrub up and get ready or stay out of the way. Don't make me kick anyone's ass!"

My curiosity was eatin' away at me, but I knew she'd chew me up like spittin' tobacco if I made a peep.

I didn't have to wait long.

"What are we dealing with, Epiphany?" asked Dr. Patrick Drake, walkin' up. He was one of the best blood-letters in the business, just like his old man, and equally good at breakin' hearts as puttin' 'em back together again.

"There's been an accident," Nurse Johnson answered. "A passel of kids, the bus driver, and a single adult male. They're all on their way in. And it's bad. Bus flipped over twice . . . We've got multiple fractures, EMTs say there's a lot of internal bleeding and two severe cranials. No fatalities . . . yet."

"Don't talk that way, Epiphany . . . this is General Hospital," he said, straightening his white coat. "I'll handle both the cranials . . ."

"Doctor Drake," Epiphany interrupted, "I know you're the best neurosurgeon on the East Coast . . . maybe in the country . . . but one victim has a massive brain injury with a possible subarachnoid hemorrhage and the other is . . . is the youngest Corinthos boy. The EMTs say there's extreme pressure and swelling on the right side. Are you sure you want to tackle both at once?"

Drake put his head in his hands for a second.

"Dammit! Call McKinsey at Rhode Island Mercy and O'Leary at Long Island Good Samaritan."

"It may take them a while to get here."

"Just do it, Nurse!" he shouted. "I'll call my wife. Robin will handle the cuts and broken bones. She can take our baby to the police department; her uncle Mac promised to sit with Emma if we were ever in a pickle. She can be here in twenty minutes."

What I didn't see was Nurse Johnson lookin' at me sideways; otherwise I woulda scuttled out, but fast.

"We need more than just one extra set of hands for this one, Doctor. I think I might have an idea . . . but if I were you, I'd start praying."

"Will do."

Suddenly, the television in the waiting room next to the nurses' station blinked with an interruption of late-breaking news. The mouthpiece with the microphone was already on the scene of the accident, gettin' it all on film. The chaos, the bus on its side . . . and the used-to-be nifty blueberry-colored Fiat rag-top . . . upside down and flamin' like a Baked Alaska.

"No! Dear Lord . . . no!" Drake said, putting one hand on his forehead; the other he used to steady himself against the counter.

"Doctor?" Epiphany said. "Are you all right?"

"I'd know that car anywhere. Oh . . . no. And he said . . . he said he was coming back to Port Charles . . . to see Emma . . . for the first time."

"Doctor?"

Drake pounded one fist into another.

"That's . . . that's my father's car."

"Oh, Doctor . . ." Epiphany began.

"I'm fine, Nurse!" he said, straightening his coat again, and squarin' up his shoulders. "I'm fine. Let me know when his ambulance arrives."

He walked toward the stairwell and didn't look back. Epiphany clutched her hands together for a moment, shook her head, and started giving specific instructions to a coupla interns that looked like they were gonna hit the pavement.

I had all the information I needed; time for me to amscray or find my derriere on the business end of Epiphany's white shoe.

The nurses' station was now almost clear. I was nearly on the elevator, and I swear Epiphany had her back turned away from me, but suddenly, outta nowhere . . .

"Where do you think you're going, Mr. Spinelli?"

It was like I gotta shock; like when Maxie uses one o' them special toys on me she likes so much, the ones that need batteries. I turned back and Nurse Johnson was standin' in the middle of the corridor, given' me the evil-eye. I had to give it to her: she moved fast for an ample dame.

"Don't think for one second you are walking out of this hospital. Not today, sir."

"I don't know what you're talkin' about," I lied.

And it was a big lie. I knew exactly what she was talkin'

about. But there was no way . . . not after what happened.
Not after . . .

"You know damn well, and that's all we're gonna say about
it. Now get scrubbed."

"Epiphany," I said, feelin' my stomach do a few somersaults on its way to the floor, "I can't."

"You can and you're gonna . . . if I have to sit on you, you're
gonna."

"These doctors . . . they know what they're doin'. I don't
know my way around anything anymore."

"You gonna turn your back? Huh? You would walk away
when this hospital and those kids need all the help they can
get? I don't give a damn what those newspapers said. You got
the goods, and now you're gonna deliver. Come with me."

Normally, I don't let myself get tossed around, except by
Maxie, but Nurse Johnson was stronger than she looked. And
besides, if I didn't go with her, I had the feelin' she'd personally be drawin' my monthly pint from then on.

We were alone on the elevator. Epiphany wasn't even
lookin' at me, that's how much she meant business.

"How did you find out?" I asked, watchin' the floor indi-
cator lights blink on and off.

"I'm extremely well informed . . . Jackal. I read as much
as possible; not just the newspapers, but medical journals as
well. Hell, I read twice as much as any of the big-shot doctors
around here. How do you think I get away with talkin' to
them the way I do? They know that I know more than all of
them put together. You think I didn't recognize you when
you first got to town, huh? Graduated top of his class at Johns
Hopkins, and he doesn't think I'll recognize him; one of the
top neurosurgeons in the U.S. of A."

"*Was*, Piffy. *Was*."

"If you didn't need to be alert for the next few hours,
I'd smack you upside so hard. It's not 'Piffy' . . . it's Nurse
Johnson."

"You know so much about me? Then . . . you must have read about . . . what happened."

"I did indeed," she huffed. "And I think those papers gave you a raw deal. I went over all the facts and the testimony. Way I see it, there was no way you could have saved all those lumber-jacks in that camp . . . especially that boy . . ."

Suddenly, Piffy's voice faded away and I was right back there: the Northern Pacific Logging Camp, Flume, and Saw-mill. I'd only been out of medical school for a few months. I'd been workin', literally, under a microscope for years and I'd got a tooth-on to get my hands around some big things for a while before I started my residency. Big . . . like trees . . . even if I was, kinda, killin' 'em. One day, a rogue log came down the chute too fast and the flume broke close to camp. Seventeen loggers were either killed outright or pinned un-der the wreckage, water pouring down on the poor sons o' bitches, some of 'em shot through with splintered boards and such. I was tending the vertical boiler in the sawmill, but when the cry went up I raced to the scene. I worked my keister off that day . . . the camp doctor was drunk as usual and no-body else had any kind of medical know-how. Three men were already gone, but the others . . . the others all had a chance. I handled the worst first and had worked my way through everyone in a few hours. I thought I had set the last broken bone and sutured the last internal bleeder, when all at once, they brought in . . . Kenny.

Kenny . . . the slow kid. The camp favorite. Fascinated with trees all his life. Just wanted to be a logger, but nobody would let him near a chainsaw. He'd stare at the forest for hours until somebody needed something—then Kenny was the go-to guy.

They'd missed him at first under all the wood of the flume, but somebody saw the toe of his work boot and started dig-ging. But they got him too late. There was already a swelling of the brain. I tried . . . I tried. Damn it, I tried!

Turns out Kenny's parents had a load of dough. That's how Kenny got to stay at the camp . . . his folks basically paid the management to keep him there. They had a lawyer on me so fast it's like they were doin' a rhumba and I was standin' still . . . said I shoulda treated him first. And they saw to it that I never picked up a scalpel again . . . again . . . again . . .

"Anyway," Epiphany was sayin' when I snapped out of it, "I don't think anybody's been harder on you than you've been on yourself. You saved fourteen men that day, Spinelli. You musta had a . . . a faith in yourself back then. And I have that faith in you now."

The elevator doors opened.

"It's not Spinelli," I said, staring at the big mess in the ER.

"What?"

She'd done a good job on me, all right, and I felt like I could handle anything; just like one of those fightin' guys back in old Rome, the ones that wore the little skirts and tangled with the tigers.

"It's Doctor Spinelli . . . Nurse."

Epiphany got a grin on her face the size of the crazy cat in that kids' book.

"Very good . . . Doctor."

She took me to the ER nurses' station and filled them all in. Not the whole history, mind you . . . just the savin' lives part. Next thing I know, I'm in full scrubs.

"Spinelli!" called Dr. Drake, as I walked into the operating room. "Who do you think you are, Jackie Kennedy?! Get out of here. It's restricted, for hospital personnel only."

"Just a minute, Doctor Drake . . ." Epiphany started to say.

I was gettin' uneasy with how much explainin' she was havin' to do . . . about me.

"I'll take it from here."

I held my hands up for the OR nurse.

"Gloves, and step on it!"

Then I turned to Drake, as the latex slid over my grabbers. I flashed on Maxie . . . just for a second.

"Johns Hopkins, graduated . . . well, let's just say I graduated pretty high up . . ."

"Top," said Epiphany.

"Thanks, Nurse. Now look, Drake, I know I haven't been slicin' and dicin' for a few years, but I was damn good with the cutlery and these two cases that are comin' in . . . they won't be askin' any questions, see? I'm here and I'm good . . . I'm better than good. But I guess you'll have to put a scalpel in my hand to really find out, won'tcha? So are you gonna wait until McKinsey or O'Leary decides to show up? Huh? Are you gonna stand there with a bright light and a rubber hose to see if I know leukodystrophy from a lumbar drain or are you and I gonna go save some lives?"

Just then, the two head injury cases were wheeled in. One was little Morgan Corinthos . . . and if it was one thing that family didn't need, it was another kid with a bum thinker. The other . . .

"Oh, sweet Lord," said Drake, looking down at the gurney, then looking up to the ceiling. "It's my dad."

He stepped back. His hands started shakin' slightly.

"Which one?" he started mumbling. Before, during, and after, it was the only time I ever saw Drake lose his cool . . . and his cool was pretty damn sizable. It wasn't a choice I would have wanted to make either. Sonny Corinthos ever found out that Drake had chosen his pop over Sonny's kid, there wouldn't be enough of the doc to pick up with a blotter.

"Stand back, Drake," I said, kinda shovin' him aside. "I'll handle your old man. You work on the midget."

"But . . ."

"But nothin'. The decision's been made," I said. "Let me see those x-rays! Uh-huh. Now, gimme the MRI . . . I didn't just order a Tom Collins, nurse, I don't have all day . . . hit the gas! Okay, now we're gettin' somewhere. Scalpel! I'm gonna have to cut through the leptomeninges. Then I have to relieve the pressure . . . that's it. Now, where's that bleeder . . . ?"

About three hours later, McKinsey shows up, pickin' some prime rib outta his teeth.

"How can I help?" he asks, like he's Jesus comin' to touch the poor or somethin'.

I looked at Drake and he looked at me.

"Thanks for coming, Scott," he says, without even turnin' his head. "But we're doing just fine in here. Be a pal, would you, and go see if Robin needs anything? Thanks."

McKinsey's puss fell like it was goin' over Niagara in a barrel.

"Sure . . . sure. Whatever you need. Who's the new guy?"

"Scott . . . Robin? Please?"

McKinsey shut his trap and walked outta the OR. Just then, I tied off the last knot of catgut. Two of the nurses gave me a little applause. Real girly like, real sweet.

"That's some of the finest micro-work I have ever seen, Doctor Spinelli," said one.

"If your father doesn't make a full recovery, Doctor Drake," said the other, "well, I'll just eat my thigh-high nylons."

Then she gave me a wink.

I walked over to Drake as he was clampin' off an artery.

"How's things?"

"Because you were here, Spinelli," Drake said, resetting a section of Morgan's skull like it was a perfect piece of a jigsaw puzzle, "I had time to redirect part of his carotid artery to an avascular section of his cerebellum. His father has the same condition . . . not enough blood to one part of brain. I think it's why Sonny behaves the way he does . . . lack of blood . . . and the fact that Sonny's brain is slightly smaller than normal. Morgan could have ended up just like his father, but now, because of you, this little boy has enough blood flowing inside his cranium to let him lead a normal, productive life. As opposed to his father . . . who's a thug. Thank you."

"My pleasure, Drake."

"I'm done," he said, throwing his hands up as one nurse removed his gloves and another mopped his brow. I took a gander down at Morgan and at Drake's sutures: perfect, each one of them. There wasn't even gonna be a scar. Yeah, I was good, all right . . . but this guy was somethin' else. And they call that somethin' . . . the best.

"I have to go check on Robin, but after that, can I buy you a cup of coffee?" Drake asked.

"No thanks," I said. "I should be gettin' home. Been gone so long, Maxie will think I'm steppin' out on her . . . which would really be a switch. And I gotta go tell a certain someone . . . that she was right. Another time."

"Name it," Drake said, putting on his white coat. "Thanks . . . Doctor."

"It's just Spinelli, Drake. Just Spinelli."

I left the OR and couldn't find Epiphany Johnson anywhere—until I looked straight across the corridor. People were runnin' in between, rushin' gurneys at the speed of light, racin' back and forth with charts, and organ coolers, and pints of blood. But Epiphany was just standin' there like an eye in the center of a doozy of a storm.

"I saw Doctor Drake coming out and he said you weren't far behind," she said. "I hear his daddy's gonna be fine and the Corinthos boy, too."

"It was touch and go there for a while. But it looks like this will just be a bad memory for both of them in a couple of months. How are you holdin' up?"

"I've been on my feet for the last three hours and it looks like I ain't getting off them anytime soon."

"I can stay if you need me," I said. If it was for the kids, two more hours wouldn't make much difference now, and Maxie would understand. At least, I thought so.

"We've got it under control. Everyone made it just fine and

it's mostly mopping up at this point . . . and you'd just be in the way," she said, tryin' to look real serious.

"Yeah, well, we wouldn't want that, now would we?"

"Okay, then . . . we'll be seeing you next month."

"You bet," I said, waddin' up my OR mask in my hand. "And . . . thanks. For thinkin' of me . . . the way you did."

"I may be a lot of things, Spinelli," she said. "But wrong about people ain't one of them."

"I'll see you later."

I turned to walk out of the ER.

"Spinelli?" Epiphany said.

I turned back around.

"For the road."

With a big grin, she handed me a brown paper bag and headed back into the storm.

I walked through the doors thinkin' that maybe them Van Pattens is right: Maybe there is a reason for everything. I ain't so high on myself that I think a broken stoplight and a dozen banged up rug rats was the reason for me gettin' to . . . to . . . well, revisit a little something about myself, something I'd shoved under a fedora and a heater for the past few years: People matter, and you don't get to walk away. Ever.

But that's the way it worked out.

Coincidence? Hell if I know.

When I got out into the late afternoon sunshine, I opened the bag.

When Piffy was good, she was good.

It was a whole package of those oatmeal cookies . . . the ones with the striped frostin' on top.

8

Damian Spinelli

. . . Back in the USSR

The former Union of Soviet Socialist Republics has some fine points. They say parts of it are beautiful, like no place you've ever seen on earth. You can get a good bowl of borscht . . . not like the Russian Tea Room in Manhattan, but still. And you can see one of their former big-wigs in his coffin right in the middle of Moscow . . . and he's been there for years, no mold, nothin'. That's kind of a bonus. And let's not forget about all that art . . . all the stuff the Sovs decided to take with them when they marched outta Paris during the war—the big one. Even if nobody gets to see it, Russia still has it all stuffed away in that big building in St. Petersburg, and possession is nine-tenths . . . and whatnot.

But it ain't no place to raise kids. It's cold. Even in the summer, the place is an icebox. And most of the people suffer from a slight depression at the fragility and bleakness of their lives . . . which still ain't worth a nickel with the higher-ups. Not ideal for rug rats.

Maybe that's why a lot of 'em get snatched up and shipped over here. Takin' a kid out of a bad Baltic situation has become chi-chi and simple as Simon for good American folk with the dough to spend greasin' a few palms at an orphanage or two. And the kids turn out okay, for the most part. Apple pie moms and pops get instant families, kids stay warm (unless you take 'em to Maine or Michigan), and the we-ain't-Commies-anymore economy rolls along. Everybody wins.

Which is why I was kinda surprised to hear Olivia Falconeri's voice on the other end of my squawk-box. I knew she and Johnny "My-Daddy's-A-Real-Bastard-But-Look-Who-I'm-Keepin'-Company-With-So-Show-Me-Some-Respect" Zacchara had taken a red-eye to St. Pete's just a coupla days before to pick up a few little ones. Just before they left, I had run into Olivia at the Port Charlie farmers' market; Maxie was pickin' out cukes and I was wanderin' around, holdin' the bag.

Outta nowhere, Olivia told me that she and Johnny are gonna adopt a pack of Muscovite minis and she's over the moon about it. Then Johnny comes up . . . now he and I don't ever get chummy over beers, but I'm always civil . . . and he's lookin' kinda scared and happy at the same time. Olivia goes to buy a churro, which left Johnny and me standin' in the middle of the produce, starin' at each other like we were the only two guys who didn't get the joke.

"So . . ." I said, real friendly, "I hear you're gonna bring home a few more citizens for the good ol' U.S. of A."

"Yeah," he said, startin' to look kinda queasy-like. "When Dante . . ." (Dante Falconeri is Olivia's son by Sonny Corinthos; he's a cop and a good-lookin' guy, but seriously, she musta had him when she was three.)

"I know this already, Spinelli," I said.

"I only wish to clarify for posterity, Caustic Counselor," he said, "should these tales ever come to be in a time capsule, or before the, dare I hope, Pulitzer review board."

"These are only notes, Jackal."

"Certainly . . . I'm aware. But I have this meek and mild fantasy about being, one day, published. Of course this would not be the tome . . . not with the information contained herein."

"I made it clear these notes aren't going anywhere but onto my computer. Now, I believe John Zacchara was saying that when Dante . . ."

". . . came to Port Charles, Olivia was really thrilled at being a mom again, even if her son is a jerk. Her maternal instincts went into overdrive."

"Somebody reset her alarm clock, huh?"

"Pretty much," Johnny said. "Of course, there was nothing we could do about it, y'know, biologically. But I still want to make her happy, and we can afford it, and this particular orphanage made us a decent deal, so we're headed out day after tomorrow."

"Why Russia?" I asked.

"They contacted us," Johnny said. "I was looking into places here, but you wouldn't believe the red tape, the hoops they wanted us to jump through. And nearly every place wanted us to get married; can you believe it?"

"No kiddin'?" I said, slappin' my own face. "That's right outta the, y'know, last century . . . insistin' the parents have morals and all."

Johnny looked at me for a half-second, but I cut in before it could really hit home.

"So the Russians don't mind, and you're gonna have some kids without the sticky, fun part!"

"Yeah," he said. "We're coming home with seven."

"Seven?! You don't say!"

"They sent us pictures of seven kids. We couldn't decide, so we're taking them all."

"Lemme get this straight," I said, feeling my tuna with ketchup on an English muffin go south on me. "You were lookin' here, in the States. Hadn't put out any feelers in Russia. And just like that, the not-so-Reds ring you up? Doesn't that sound kinda, I don't know, suspicious?"

"I don't think so . . . It's all very technical, Spinelli," Johnny said, casin' a nearby crate of parsnips, tryin' like hell to look like he knew what he was talkin' about. "Probably has something to do with the Internet."

"Oh, well, sure," I said as Olivia walked up with two churros and shoved one into Johnny's pie-hole. "Yeah, that Internet . . . it's all over the place. Well, I gotta run. Good luck!"

Maxie was at Mr. Yu's veggie stand, waitin' by the leafy greens.

"Hi, honey," she says, handin' me a bag of kale. "You were gone so long I got lonely."

"Tell me you didn't sleep with Mr. Yu?"

"Of course not, silly," she said, slappin' me on my arm. "I just let him feel me up a little. He gave me a nice big head of romaine!"

That night, I couldn't tell which made me lose more sleep, Maxie playin' patty-knockers with Mr. Yu, or the funny coincidence about the Russian orphanage. I decided Johnny was probably right; it was an Internet thing . . . and all orphanages are probably on some big list, right? If prospective parents get turned down by one, there's gotta be a hundred others just dyin' to get their hard-luck kids into a good Yankee home.

Which is why I was sorta caught off-guard by Olivia's voice on the other end of the line. It was real low and real nervous.

"Spinelli & McCall, private eyes . . . If you can pay for it, the eyes have it. Spinelli speakin'."

"Spinelli? Oh, thank God! I only have a few seconds. It's Olivia and . . ."

"Olivia . . . how's the baby heist goin'?" I said.

"Spinelli, shut up and listen!"

"Whoa, I'm sensing a tone here," I said.

"Spinelli, they've got Johnny!"

I took a deep breath. I should know by now: When a dame is frantic on the other end of the phone, they don't want chit-chat, they want you to listen. Actually, that's pretty much all the time.

"Slow down, doll," I said. "Gimme the facts."

"A car picked us up at the airport. We weren't expecting it, but it had the name of the orphanage right on the car door. So we get in and nobody says anything at first. So Johnny starts talking to them . . . two bruisers, Spinelli, not orphanage men at all . . . Anyway, Johnny starts talking to these guys about the kids and when do we get to see them? Then one guy, right out of nowhere, smacks Johnny across the face. I don't know what's happening, but I lean over to see if he's okay, and the other bruiser holds me back. Then they both pull out their guns and the one who hit Johnny says, 'That was from your father. And there's more where that came from if you don't shut up.' They brought us to a . . . I think it's some kind of club. It's gotta be a club . . . there's been really loud music for the last two nights, but it's quiet during the day. They separated Johnny and me . . ."

"Okay, Olivia . . . just be quiet a sec. How are you callin' me?"

"I managed to hide my cell phone . . . someplace . . . someplace they didn't think to look. Well . . . maybe they wanted to, but they haven't yet. And they've been keeping me in a basement or a . . . a cellar for two days. But the only bathroom is on the ground level. So I've been real good, real cooperative ever since I got here, and today they let me come up here unescorted."

"Room gotta window?"

"Yeah . . . hang on."

I waited a minute, then she came back on the line.

"Okay," Olivia said. "I got it open and I can see a little bit."

"What street are you on?"

"The Nevskiy Prospekt."

"What kind of music does this club play at night?"

"What does that have to do with . . ."

"Dammit, woman, answer me!"

"ABBA!" she whispered, then her voice cracked "Just ABBA. Help me!"

My voice woulda cracked too if I had to listen to "Waterloo" for two nights straight.

"Oh, God, I think someone's coming!"

"Olivia, look across the street . . . What do you see?"

"I . . . I see . . . huh? . . . You gotta be kidding me . . ."

"Clowns, right?"

"How'd you know, Spinelli?"

"It's the State Circus. All right, it's an annex; the school. The headquarters are on the Fontanka River. And never mind how I know. They've got you holed up in the Club Prokofiev. It's run by the mob . . . I just never knew till now that it was the Zacchara mob. Hang tight, sweetheart, I'm on my way."

I clicked off, but not before I heard the bathroom door openin' on the other end and Olivia screamin' "It's occupied!"

"Stop it!" I said, flinging my pen down for the tenth time. "Stop it. You have never been on the Nevskiy Prospekt or in St. Petersburg, for that matter!"

"Your doubt of my veracity causes me no end of sadness, Brusque Barrister," Spinelli said, doing a terrific basset hound impression. "But I can attest, most assuredly, that I was a prize student of the comical arts. Perhaps you'll recall the Port Charles carnival of some months ago and how my 'clune' skills dazzled and delighted all who saw them?"

"I was away in Philadelphia on another case," I said. "I wasn't able to attend."

"Well, let me assure you, I was indeed a hit. And you, Lady of the Law, must know by now that Port Charles has not been

the first stop on my life's sojourn. I have, to use the common parlance, been around."

I honestly didn't know why I even bothered to say anything.

The flight was right outta a Roger Corman flick. Didn't get to sleep that night. All the way, the paperback was on my knee . . .

"Do not plagiarize Paul McCartney!"

"But it's the truth!" Spinelli cried. "I was reading *Love's Reckless Rash* and I didn't pick it up once!"

"I may have to strike you at some point."

I kept thinkin' about what Olivia had said. Somewhere over Helsinki, things became pretty clear. Anthony "Ant'ny" Zacchara, a mobster whose only rival for "big" . . . ego, mouth, reach, operation, you name it . . . was Sonny Corinthos, was due to get out of prison any day. And business had become, shall we say, difficult in the States. So Ant'ny was movin' the whole shebang to Blini-land . . . and he was gonna take his one and only son with him. He'd tricked Johnny into comin' to St. Pete's, and now it was gonna take a helluva lot to get Johnny back out.

Olivia?

She was expendable, like the nameless, red-shirted crew members of the USS *Enterprise* that beamed down in every episode to an unknown planet with Kirk, Spock, and McCoy. You knew they weren't beamin' back up. And if I knew Pops Zacchara, Olivia didn't have much time.

I had put in a call to Madame Blovotsky, my old clowning teacher at the State School . . . and a guy in drag if ever there was one. She was surprised to hear that I was comin' back into town . . . asked if I would do a master class for some of her new students. I told her I would be honored, but it would have to be some other time. I filled her in but little and asked if I could land at the school and just stay for a day or two.

The cab turned onto the Nevskiy Prospekt and I told the driver to stop a good two hundred yards from the State School doors. I went around to the back entrance and ran into a pack of kids on a ciggie break. I wasn't prepared for the reaction, especially since I had asked Madame Blovotsky to keep mum about my comin' at all. I didn't want to attract any attention.

"If you please, sir," said one kid on stilts. "You are the great Spinelski, yes?"

"Uh, no, mac, you got the wrong . . ."

"Oh, but you are!" said a cute little bird perched on a high-wire strung across the back alley. "We see the Spinelski portrait in the Hall of Master Clowns every day! Teacher takes us there for inspiration!"

"Yeah, well . . . you pegged me, all right!" I said with a little laugh, brushin' past another kid with a red bubble nose and a stuffed toy poodle who was starin' at me like I was the Second Coming. "Uh . . . you kids study hard now. Do your mamas proud and keep makin' with the funny!"

I hustled through the doors and down the hallway to Blovotsky's office. Her secretary let me right in. She was suckin' on her hookah with a bottle of vodka only inches away. Took me back: me practicin' pratfalls with her coachin' from the sidelines, glass of vodka in one hand, "Dancing Queen" pounding through the sewer pipes.

Old times . . . good times.

"Spinelski, darling!" Madame said, trying to get outta her chair. She'd put on about twenty extra pounds since my last tumbling run.

"Madame," I said with a little bow, bussin' both her cheeks. "I don't have much time, least of all not for gab. I need your help. Tell me, are the ventilation systems on both sides of the Prospekt still connected in that funny all-together, the-State-will-decide-when-you-need-to-be-warm kinda way?"

"*Da*," she said. "The new government promised us everything new when they took over. We would have our own heat and air. But that was thirty years ago and we still smell the piroshki frying from the café next door."

"And when Club Prokofiev turns on its coolers 'round one AM 'cause everyone is sweatin' to 'Super Trooper,' you guys still freeze over here?" I asked.

"I have had to cancel midnight practice, it gets so cold. In summertime, like now, is not so bad. But winter . . . it makes me cry," she said.

"That's all I needed to know. All right, I need a room where I can change. And I need your word there won't be any flappin' gums about why I'm here."

"I still don't know why you're here," she said. "Besides, Spinelski, I am an old woman . . . who would I tell?"

"C'mon, don't kid a kidder," I said. "We both know you were workin' both sides of the KGB back in the day. You had your own apartment, a car, and a swell, cushy job turnin' out funnymen for the State Circus. And I remember you always had meat during the week and more vodka than a person could drink in a lifetime. Nobody had things like that years ago unless they were kissin' up . . . or down, as it were. It's all jake, Madame. It's just that if the wrong person finds out I'm here, word could travel fast, and two of my friends just might find themselves heads-down in the Volga, see? Just gimme your word on this . . . for old times' sake?"

She looked at me from under those Brezhnev eyebrows and smiled like she'd just discovered the beauty of Capitalism.

"You'll do a master class before you leave?"

I sighed. She had me over a barrel . . . or rather, in it.

"Yeah. Yeah, all right. I give the kids a few pointers."

"Including . . ." She was zeroing in, and I saw it comin' a mile away. ". . . the Chicken Toss?"

"Aw, jeez," I said. "C'mon, not my signature act! Leave a little somthin' for history."

"I'm sorry, but the Chicken Toss was too great a trick for just one man to take the secret with him to his grave. Teach my students the Chicken Toss and I won't call President Putin and tell him that there is an American spy hiding in my school."

"Aw, what the hell," I said after a moment. "I'm not clownin' much these days, anyways. Okay, I'll show 'em."

"Then I have never seen you. I don't know you're here and even if I did, I would think you were, possibly, the new janitor."

"Thanks, Madame. Now pass me the vodka and show me where I can change."

———————

That time of year, in that part of the world, the sun was settin' late. Late late. So late as to be early. I wanted to get the show on the road right away, but Madame made me see otherwise: It would be a few hours until dark, and that's when Club Pro-kofiev would be in full swing, music blastin' out into the street. I needed to get my game face on, but with all that time, Madame finally got what she wanted: a nice long chat. I told her what I could about Olivia and Johnny, 'bout them comin' over to adopt a few kids. And I told her about Ant'ny and his dirty trick. She was onto the mob, understood that there was new blood comin' into the neighborhood. Had seen some unfamiliar muscle across the street. She knew the name Zac-chara and she was glad I was gonna try to take the Mob Prince back Stateside. I told her about the gumshoe racket and she told me about a few Cirque clowns she'd trained for Vegas . . . her greatest achievements after me . . . all the while givin' me guff for quittin' my true calling at the top of my career. The more vodka, the more guff. I took it with a smile.

"You still are having the dreams, Spinelski?"

I got real quiet.

"Come . . . tell me," she said.

"Only a few times a week now," I said.

"It is the same thing?"

"Always," I answered her. "I'm in my grandma's kitchen. She's handin' me a plate of cookies . . . snickerdoodles. She goes to grab the milk pitcher . . . the one with the clown face on it . . . but it falls out of her hand and comes flying toward me. That horrible face . . . it's like it's gonna . . . swallow me whole."

"I still say it is good you have this dream," Madame said. "This is what drives you to Russia, to this school, in the first place. You look this fear straight in the face! You still do. And you do not forget!"

Five hours later, after Madame and I had thrown back a few shots, and as the last of the light dimmed outside the frosted-glass windows of the school, the backbeat of "Knowing Me, Knowing You" started rattlin' the pipes. I tipped my hand to Madame and slipped below the sub-flooring and down into the ventilation ducts. My black Lycra bodysuit . . .

"Hang on," I said, holding up my hands. "I just visualized that . . . and I need a minute. I'm having a little trouble refocusing . . ."

"My darling Maximista reacts the same way when I don said article of clothing for her . . ."

"Yeah . . . not the same reaction, I can almost guarantee," I replied, forcing myself to think of Max, then a plate of nachos, and then a glass of Scotch. Then all three together. "Okay, I'm good. Go on."

. . . provided just the right amount of slip 'n' slide, so even though the ducts were narrow and slow going, my package stayed fit for delivery, if you know what I mean.

"And now I need a drink," I said. "Does this diner have a bar? And if you're curious, I have never been so serious about anything in my life."

"I believe that alcoholic libations are not to be purchased in this establishment," Spinelli said.

"Then it's a good thing I brought my own," I said, producing my hip flask from my . . . hip . . . and opening the top. "Ah . . . here we go. It was a heavy court day, not a lot of opportunity for a nip. Should still be pretty full. Just a moment . . . and . . . right as rain. Continue."

I was right under the middle of the Nevskiy Prospekt; all the traffic above was shakin' me like a paint mixer, when "Fernando" started playin' and I heard whoops and shouts from the other end. It was a good night at the club.

I hit the end and saw legs above me. I was gonna come up into one corner of the dance floor. I only needed about ten seconds to loose the ventilation grate, slip up, and roll into the shadows. I got the grate off all right, hoisted myself into a basic Martha Graham ball position, and started to roll. I was almost to the wall, the bodysuit makin' me damn near invisible under the black light and disco ball, when suddenly a stiletto heel comes down right in the center of my left hand . . . and I knew what Jesus went through, poor guy. Without thinkin', I screamed. Fortunately, it was during the four-part harmony of "Lay All Your Love on Me," so no one was the wiser.

I clung to the black wall and took a quick look around. I saw two dames comin' out of a little room, laughin' and puttin' their lipsticks back into their bags. That musta been the bathroom that Olivia had talked about. Right next to it was another door . . . with a big torpedo standin' guard. I skirted the dance floor as I took out my short billy club from my utility belt . . .

"I thought you said the duct was narrow," I said. "How did you manage a utility belt?"

"I have miniature versions of all necessary tools."
"Oh . . . well . . . sure. Where's my flask?"

The guy didn't know what hit him, literally. I slumped the lug against the wall so's he looked like he was sleepin', see? Then I tried the door handle. Not locked. I eased my way down some stairs and into a hallway that looked more like a blown-out bomb shelter. One overhead bulb and three doors: one to my right, one down a ways to my left, and one at the end.

Suddenly, I heard chatter from the room on my right. Door's open so I snuck a peek: three mooks playing cards in their undershirts. I figured Olivia's in one of the other rooms, but it'll take a bit more to get those doors open, so outta my belt I took a hairpin and a safety pin. The safety pin I tossed across the first room and it made a little "bang" as it hit the floor; nothing real loud and suspicious, but enough of a sound to make the mooks take a look. That's when I slipped past. I grabbed hold of my billy just in case one of them decided to take a walk, but the next minute I heard them yappin' away and throwin' down cards.

The hairpin worked on the second door and Olivia was lyin' on a cot at one end of the room. I motioned for her to be quiet before she could scream, and whipped off my black head mask. Her shoulders sagged a little bit, then she started with the tears but, smart broad, she kept quiet. She got off the cot and threw her arms around me, real tight. Johnny was a lucky man.

"Where is he?" I mouthed to her.

"Who? Oh! Johnny! I think he's somewhere that way," she mouthed back, pointin' in the direction of the end of the hall. "I've heard the most terrible things, Spinelli."

"Stay here," I mouthed. "I'll be back."

The hallway was still deserted and in two seconds I was

usin' the hairpin on the door at the far end. Turns out, I didn't need it.

Door was already unlocked.

The room was big and ugly. Looked like it might have been used for some painful hijinks during the cold war . . . or maybe a bit more recently. Rings on the walls, big pile of . . . ashes . . . coulda been . . . on the floor and a single wooden chair underneath a burned-out bulb. Suddenly, I was aware that there's light comin' from somewhere else in the room. I turned around and whammo! I'm in Shangri-La.

Johnny Z was havin' a bit of a lie-down himself, as the Limeys say, only he was on a wood-and-marble number that looked like it came right out of a czar's bedroom. Lots of feather pillows. Candles. They had him dressed in some sorta red silk smoking jacket, there was a hookah on the nightstand, and . . . I'll be damned . . . a broad lyin' across his legs wearin' nothing but lipstick and a toe ring. Daddy was takin' good care of his little boy.

I woke up Johnny and, real polite . . . even though I was slightly ticked off at the broad bein' there 'cause I happen to like Olivia . . . I told him that it was time to go. Johnny got this crazy look in his eye . . . like he was gonna protest too much, or somethin'. Like maybe he'd decided that he liked borscht and cabbage and nudies with toe rings. Like maybe he was thinkin' about stayin'. So I introduce him to Billy . . . club . . . and he got real . . . unconscious.

I flipped him onto my shoulder . . . glad I spent those months totin' two, sometimes three rail ties at once for the Bangor & Aroostook RR . . . and got him back to Olivia's room. She smothered him with kisses and I felt as if I was gonna bring up what was left of the in-flight meal. The guy didn't deserve the dame. But maybe, just maybe, he was so hopped up on hookah smoke and whatever else his pop's flunkies had pumped into him that . . . maybe . . . he didn't know what he was doin' . . . or had done. I decided to give him the benefit of the doubt until I was sure . . . then I'd brain him again, if he needed it . . . just for grins.

Then I got an idea.

"Olivia," I said, twirlin' the club. "Call them. Tell them you're sick or somethin'. See if you can get one of them in here."

Olivia nodded.

"Igor!" she called. "Igor, I'm not feeling very well. Can I have a glass of water please?"

"You know their names?" I asked.

"I've spent almost four days here, by my count. I passed the time. I made nice."

"How nice?" Johnny slurred.

"Shaddup, you," I whispered, shovin' him onto the cot. "Olivia, with me, back behind the door."

The door opened slowly, not because Igor suspected that anybody else was in the room, but because the maroon was carryin' not one but two shot glasses.

"Water is no good for upset, pretty lady," he said stepping into the room. "I bring you vodka."

Then he took a look at Johnny, sittin' on the cot with a dopey, doped-up grin on his face. Igor opened his mouth to yell but Billy stifled him, and how. I nodded to Olivia and suddenly, the whole operation became a Keystone Kops flicker . . . or an Arbuckle short, when Fatty was funny, before that cheesy starlet incident.

"Ivan?" Olivia called, real sweet. "Can I see you for a moment?"

There was laughter from down the hall, and someone cleared his throat and pushed back a chair. Five seconds later:

Ka-POW-ski!

"Nikolai?" Olivia purrs, like she's the motor of a '57 Chevy. "Let's make it a party! All three of us, how's that sound?"

BLAMMO!

I piled up the torpedos in the corner of the room and whacked them each once more where I knew it wouldn't kill 'em, just keep 'em dreamin' for a while. Olivia and I dragged Johnny out into the hallway and I grabbed a chair from the other room and wedged it against the door.

We got Johnny up the stairs. Then I opened the door to the disco real slow. We got the chorus of "Does Your Mother Know?" right in the eardrums, but it was still black as a bookie's plus column. I slipped out first, then Olivia . . . who, fortunately, was wearing dark blue . . . and I dragged out Johnny and propped him between us like he'd had too much Stoli, and headed for the door. Just then, I saw a couple of suits, non-disco types, comin' in from the street. We wheeled Johnny away from the door and out onto the dance floor. The suits stayed by the door, but I knew it was only a matter of time before they discovered Johnny Z had taken a powder. Our one chance was the ventilation duct. We danced over to it and I nodded my head. Olivia went all white and started to back away, but I grabbed her, gentle-like, by the arm and leaned in real close.

"It's now or never, kid. This is the only way. I'll take the point. We'll put the sleepin' prince in between us. I'll pull and you push. You gotta trust me on this, see? There's only one main duct. You won't get lost, I promise. I'll slip in first, then you lower Johnny and climb down after."

"I'm scared, Spinelli," she said, her lower lip jigglin' like it shoulda been in a go-go cage. "I hate small, confined spaces. It's why I left Bensonhurst. Don't make me . . . for God's sake, don't . . . !"

I hated smackin' dames, but she gave me no choice. I saw it in her eye; two seconds later and she woulda been screamin' loud enough to wake up Ivan, Igor, and Nikolai.

"I'm sorry, doll," I said, as she clammed up and looked at me with the widest eyes I'd ever seen. "It was for your own good. Now, you keep your eyes closed if you have to, but you're gonna get down in there and you're gonna crawl and crawl fast.

Okay, gimme some cover. Start dancin' and don't stop until Johnny's spats have cleared the floor. Now, move!"

Olivia just stared at me, then she started movin' like the game gal she was. Bensonhurst turned out a champ with this one.

Ten feet into the duct, Johnny was behind me, and I called out for Olivia.

"Right here," she said. There were nerves in her voice, but she was doin' her damnedest to hide 'em. "My eyes are closed, but I'm here."

"Good girl."

We shoved Johnny through the air duct like we was makin' bratwurst. I heard Olivia start to weep a little when we were under the Prospekt and the vent was doin' a rhumba.

"Keep moving, sister! Ain't nothin' comin' down or cavin' in. These ducts might be old, but you can't beat Red engineering."

An hour later, after pushin' and pullin' and squeezin', I stuck my head back into the practice room at the annex for the State Circus school. Madame Blovotsky was there to help us all outta the duct. And she had a surprise waitin'.

After layin' Johnny out on a tumbling mat and givin' Olivia a bear hug, Madame gets this enormous grin on her face . . . which kinda gave me the willies.

"I have present for you," she says to Olivia.

Then she walks over to the far side of the room, behind the trapeze rig, opens a door, and seven kids come runnin' out and knock Olivia flat on her patootski, shoutin' "Mama! Mama!" If Olivia had handpicked these midgets herself, she couldn't have done a better job. Each one was prettier than the last, and Olivia looked like she was a kid in a candy store, each fist full of jelly-beans and a sucker in her pucker.

"How did you know?" she asked Madame.

"I might have told her why you were here," I said.

"But how did you know we'd get out of there!?" she said.

"Because he is Spinelski," Madame said, real plain . . . like yogurt. "I make a phone call to local orphanage. I ask them for a nice selection. You are happy, yes?"

"Oh, yes," Olivia said, rufflin' one little boy's hair. "YES!"

That woke Johnny up. I sat him in a chair and told him the whole story while Madame went to get vodka and milk and Olivia learned all the kids' names. I was just gettin' to the part about slippin' down into the duct from the dance floor . . .

. . . when it hit me.

"Kee-rist! Olivia!"

"What?!"

"Did you replace the cover on the vent?"

"Huh?"

"When we got outta the club . . . did you make sure the vent cover was back in place?"

Her eyes went big again.

"N . . . no. Oh . . . God!"

I thought fast. How fast? NASA coulda used me to run a shuttle mission, that's how fast.

"They'll be comin' . . . anytime now."

Madame was right with me.

"We must hide the children . . . and Johnny and Olivia!" she said.

"No," I said. "We ain't gonna hide anybody. Kids? Can any of you tumble? Y'know, somersaults or cartwheels, that kinda thing?"

The older ones, maybe six to eight years old, answered me by doing perfect back-flips . . . in place. The younger ones did no-handed cartwheels . . . in place.

"You needed to ask?" Madame said. "They are Russian."

"Get 'em costumes. All of 'em. And find something for us. Olivia, you and Johnny are about to join the circus."

Ten minutes later, we were all in perfectly matched tights, leotards, red noses, and yellow wigs. The kids were doing

tumbling runs, and I had Johnny and Olivia up on the trapeze with me, which gave me a good vantage point and a de-
fensible position. Learned that in Korea. Johnny was still
kinda out of it, so I put him on the catcher's bar and told him
to just keep swingin' . . . upside down. He seemed to enjoy it
and worked himself into a damn good arc. Olivia was the real
surprise though. I told her to just fall into the net, over and
over again, 'cause I knew she'd never be able to do a trick,
see? But I'll be damned if the dame didn't keep tryin' to fly. I
was executin' layouts and doubles, then fallin' flat out into
the net, and then, I'll be a son-of-a-billygoat, Olivia would
try to match me. And she was good . . . real good. So good, I
almost didn't notice Igor's head stickin' up outta the floor
duct. But I had Madame on goon watch and she clobbered
him with a full bottle of vodka, then took a swig as he sank
back into the duct. Nikolai and Ivan were comin' in the
practice room door just as Madame covered the hole in the
floor with her skirt.

"What is meaning of this?" she yelled in a voice I hadn't
heard since she caught me not payin' attention in class once . . .
and only once. "We are in the middle of practice! You want to
distract my fliers?! Get out!"

"We are looking for two people, a woman and a man . . .
and someone else, perhaps. Did they come in here?" asked
Ivan.

"I tell you to get out! There is no one here who is not supposed to be here. We are State Circus school, hoodlum. Please,
you will go look for your hoodlum friends someplace else,
da?!"

Ivan and Nikolai shot a look at the kids, then they looked
up at the rig. I saw Nikolai shrug his shoulders and the two
of 'em turned to go. Right then, wouldn't you know it, Johnny
fell off the catch-bar and took a header into the net.

"Johnny!" Olivia screamed.

Ivan and Nikki were back in a flash.

"Up the ladder to the girl," Ivan said to Nikolai. "I will get the one in the net."

"Stay here," I said to Olivia as I dropped down like the other shoe. I rolled to the edge of the net just as Ivan was hoistin' himself up.

"Madame?" I yelled. "I could use that bottle of vodka right about now!"

With a perfect juggler's toss, she sailed it across the room and smack into my hand. Ivan looked up just in time to see some fine Russian hooch come crashin' down on his u-krainium. One down, one to go.

"Care to perform your rope trick, Madame?" I said.

"With pleasure," she said, grabbing a long length and tying Ivan up like a birthday present.

I hightailed it up the ladder to the catch-bar platform, hooked the bar, and brought it in. Nikolai was just about to reach Olivia on the platform at the other end of the rig.

"Okay, doll," I said, standin' on the catch-bar and startin' to swing. "Let's see that form!"

The timing had to be perfect, or we'd need a really big oven for all our cooked goose.

"And . . . swing!"

Olivia took off.

"And . . . drop!"

She let go of the fly-bar and hit the net . . . only inches away from Johnny. And that's when I flew off the catch-bar and caught the fly-bar on its way back to the platform. Nikolai was now standin' where Olivia had been, his gun in one hand and a goofy look on his face. I stuck my legs out like ramrods and launched cosmonaut Nikki out into space, while at the same time executin' a perfect landing back onto the platform. Nikki crashed into the wall and slid down onto the floor.

"He's still alive," Madame said, puttin' her hand on his neck.

"Then I smell a rope trick encore," I said, midair. I bounced in the net a moment, then helped Olivia and Johnny onto the floor. The kids were jumpin' and hollerin' all around us. The sun was startin' to light up the frosted-glass windows. It was a good way to start the day.

We dragged Igor from the vent and tied him up with Ivan and Nikolai. Then, right in the middle of a gorgeous St. Pete morning, Johnny (who was by now almost fully recovered from being hopped up by his dad's flunkies and then beaned by Billy) and I lugged the three muscle-"bound" mooks across the Nevskiy Prospekt and dumped them on the club door stoop. Then we rang the bell and ran.

"They let me get away," Johnny said with a grin, when we were back inside the school. "My father isn't gonna like that."

"Might go all Bolshoi on them," I said. "Do a couple of dance moves on their heads."

"At least," Johnny replied, laughin'.

"Now, if you'll *pardonnez-moi*," I said, "I have to teach a few kids how to toss a chicken."

The master class went better than I was expectin' and I realized I was leavin' my signature trick in good hands. And only one kid let the egg break on his head. We all had a good laugh and I realized that I had to make room, like a gentleman, for the new generation.

Suddenly, Madame came flouncin' up, all red-faced. I thought it was just the morning vodka, but it turned out she had news.

"I still have sources, as you must know, Spinelski. The news of Mr. Zacchara's disappearance from the club has spread like the wildfire. His father is having the roads, airports, rivers, and train stations all watched for any sign. I'm afraid you cannot leave the country."

"Oh, we're gonna vamoose, all right," I said, as everybody else ran up. "Pop is watchin' the usual routes, huh? Then we'll walk."

"Walk!" shouted Johnny, Olivia, the kids, and Madame all at once. Startled me so bad, I thought I was gonna crap myself.

"Madame, get the school bus ready. Everybody else, back in the red noses!"

Twenty minutes later, a big orange-and-purple bus full of clowns was headin' up the Prospekt . . . with no one thinkin' anything of it.

"Where are we going?" Madame asked as she drove.

"Finland," I said. "I have friends just across the border in Vaalimaa."

"I cannot cross. Even with artist's papers. They have become so strict."

"Don't worry your pretty, stubbled face, sweetheart. Just drop us down a ways from the checkpoint."

As soon as we got out of St. Pete's, we changed back into street clothes. Madame let us off at a deserted spot on the Finnish border and gave everyone a bear hug.

"I will miss you, Spinelski," she said in my ear.

"I'll see you again, Madame," I said, not wantin' to get all sentimental. "You gotta come Stateside for a visit."

"You will introduce me to movie stars?"

"You bet."

"Many?"

"Many as we can find."

"Johnny Depp?"

"Don't push it. Bye, Madame. Thanks."

We walked into Finland, no problem. Seven rug rats, their new mom and pop, and me . . . the Pied Piper. Few hours later, Vaalimaa was in sight. Wouldn't be long now before we were all on Main Street U.S.A., eatin' Mom's old-fashioned

apple pie. Outta nowhere, Olivia started singin' . . . said she
was thinkin' of a scene from one of those big-time Tinsel Town
CinemaScope musicals. We got about two choruses in and I
decided the sappy lyrics needed a little change.

Dough . . . the thing she likes to spend,
Ray, who owes me twenty Gs.
Me, the guy I like the best,
Far, fala with extra cheese.
So, I got no more to say,
La, it comes right after so,
Tee, off time's at noon today,
That should bring me lots of dough . . . oh, oh, oh . . .

9

Damian Spinelli

and the Case of the Treacherous Teacher

I was walkin' Maxie back through the park one night . . .

"Gaahhhh!" Spinelli suddenly cried. His cell phone was vibrating in his cargo pants again, only this time I could tell that it had somehow shifted position on his . . . person.

"Why don't you just answer it?" I said. "Don't you think it might be important?"

"There is nothing that can sway me from my date with destiny upon the morrow, hence these accounts must be related. That is of utmost, dare I say, paramount importance. Whomever this prankster is, whatever their odious and diabolical game, I shall have none of it," he said, hitting the "ignore" button. "Now, where was I . . . ?"

"Just a minute," I said, putting my hand to my head in a way that reminded me of Norma Desmond in *Sunset Boulevard.* "I think I have been very good for this last bit; haven't interrupted at all. I have just been a regular little stenographer and now I need a minute. Actually, about five."

"Is the Brusque Lady of Justice ill? May I get you a curative,

restorative, or tonic of some sort?" Spinelli asked, looking genuinely concerned.

"No," I replied. "I just have to process. I had no idea, Jackal-
hopper, that you were capable of astonishing me to such a
degree. So, we're going to sit quietly for five minutes and you're
not going to say anything. All right? No . . . don't even answer
that. Just . . . sit."

"May I . . . ?"

"I will take this pen and commit bodily harm. To you. Your
person. Sit."

He was good for, maybe, thirty seconds and I took a chance
on closing my eyes. Then, across the table littered with plates,
I heard him . . . *heard* him . . . open his mouth.

"If . . ."

"Stab you. Might have to stab you."

I tried to think of the next time I would be able to soak in a
tub full of my Himalayan bath salts . . . with or without Max. I
tried to think of the upcoming Lorente trunk show in Manhattan and how Kate said she would arrange tickets for Alexis and
me to attend. I tried to imagine the only decent martini in all
of Port Charles, the one made by my silent but wise three-days-
a-week houseboy, Kwan. I tried to recall Ella singing "A-Tisket,
A-Tasket." I tried to focus on my pet snake, Freckles.

Instead, all I could think of was Spinelli, in red tights, flying through the air with the greatest of ease; I realized I might
never have a decent night's sleep again.

"Okay," I said finally, opening my eyes. "You can con . . ."

Spinelli had, silently, pulled his fedora down over his eyes
and had his hands resting on the table, palms up. He was
delicately mouthing some sort of . . . chant . . . over and over
again.

"What are you doing?"

"I am invoking inner peace and harmony for you using a
traditional Shintoist prayer," he replied.

For some reason, I could think of nothing cute or cutting

to say. I found myself genuinely touched. There were stranger things that happened in the world besides what this scrawny, possibly deranged, but assuredly brilliant boy was telling me. Maybe it was all actually . . .

"Okay," I said. "I'm back. Where were we?"

Spring in Port Charles came early that year and Maxie said she wanted to stretch her gams. We'd just had about a pound of New York, rare for me, and a baked 'tater, fully loaded, each. We looked like those crazy snakes in Africa that swallow eggs whole, shell and all. We get back to her place and I go in for the big kisseroo . . . when my phone started vibratin'. For a second, I thought it was Maxie, makin' my heart race just a little faster, but she pulled away like she'd just been bit . . . which sometimes she likes, but not right then.

"What's up, doll?" I said. "Get back here . . . you're sendin' me!"

"Spinelli, it's your phone . . . either answer it or turn it off!"

I chucked it across the room.

Stupid move. It started vibratin' again; whoever wanted me, wanted me bad. I left Maxie all ruffled up on the couch and picked up the phone. Normally, I don't answer numbers I don't recognize, but I got a funny feelin' about this one.

"Spinelli," I said.

"It's Robin . . . Scorpio Drake."

"Heya, Doc. What's shakin'? And I sure hope it ain't your hands."

"Uh . . . yeah. Look, I need to talk with you. Something's come up and it's serious . . ."

"It's kinda late, y'know? And I was right in the middle of . . . a delicate operation, if you get my drift."

"Spinelli," Robin said, soundin' real serious-like. "This could cost me my career . . . maybe my family. Everything. I'll pay you anything you want; I'll give you everything I have, but please . . ."

"Whoa . . . hold up there, sawbones. No need for talk like that. I'm sure whatever it is can be fixed . . ."

I looked at Maxie, the front of her sweater-set doin' a little heave-ho, and I was about to tell Robin that whatever it was could also wait until morning. But then Maxie gave me the look—the one that said "Go . . . somebody needs you more than I do right now." On occasion, that look had also said, "I may be here when you get back, or I may be under a table at the Metro Court, collecting a little pocket change. Take your chances." But I counted on the sixteen ounces of steak and the sour cream to keep her home. I kept my eyes on my non-bride as I talked to Robin.

"Coffee shop. Corner of Adirondack and Crescent. Twenty minutes."

"I'll be there," she said, and clicked off.

"Baby . . ."

"Just go," Maxie said, shakin' her pretty blonde hair. "I'm going to curl up with the latest issue of *Crimson* and check out my work. I'm the real brains behind that company, you know."

"I know," I said, smilin'.

"I want to see if the layout of the Maha Chang show came out as good as I think it did. Or I may read some Proust. So . . . just go already."

She grinned at me as I bent down to plant one where it counted. I was halfway to my car when I stopped cold.

"Proust?!"

I found Robin already sittin' in a corner booth, way back, her fingers wrapped around a cup of coffee, black as the mascara streaks runnin' down her face.

"C'mon," I said, slidin' across from her, "can't be bad as all that."

"What'll it be, Jackal?" Candy asked, stridin' up, her waitress uniform just a little too tight.

"The usual, Candy, thanks."

"One cuppa coffee with an orange soda chaser. Comin' right up."

When Candy got a good distance away, I turned to Robin.

"Tell me what's got you lookin' like Alice Cooper."

"Where do you want me to start?" she asked. I could tell she was barely holdin' it together.

"Take it nice and slow and start from the beginning."

She took a deep breath.

"You won't tell anyone else?"

"That's what you're payin' me for."

"Okay. When I was in med school at the Sorbonne . . . in France, I had a professor . . . Mr. Xavier. He was nice enough and I always did really well in his classes. But more than that, I always felt like I could go to him if I had a problem understanding organic chemistry or submolecular biology, and he wouldn't laugh the way some other professors might have done. So, I liked him. When I came back to the States . . . before I started my residency, I got a letter from Professor Xavier saying that I had accidentally skipped one course in France—an important course in ECG interpretation—and the Sorbonne was going to deny my diploma until it was completed. He went on to say that, as luck would have it, he just happened to be coming to the States to teach that very course over the summer in a little college in New Hampshire. He could get me in, the Sorbonne would be satisfied, and no one here would ever know. So I spent the summer in Monadnock. And it was easy, you know? It was pretty basic stuff, so I was acing it. Then one day, my lab partner didn't show up for class because she'd contracted cholera . . . or something, I don't remember . . . and Mr. Xavier stepped in real quick and offered to partner up for the lab portion of class. So, one thing leads to another,

and as I'm sliding the sample ECG across the desk, our fingers touched and . . . and . . . that was it. We sort of . . .
saw . . . each other for the rest of the year. And it was
great . . . he was great. He'd joke with me all the time that
just because I was dynamite in the . . . uh . . . just because I
was a good girlfriend, he was still going to grade me fairly and
all that. So the summer ended and I told him I was leaving to
start my residency. Only . . . only he didn't want to let me go.
He told me that he'd been in love with me ever since I started
at the Sorbonne and he'd arranged the whole summer teaching position just to be close to me. Now he was going back to
France and I was going to come with him and be his TA while
I also took care of our kids. I told him no thanks . . . but in
a nice way . . . and suddenly he turned into this completely
different person. He became a monster; telling me that if I
didn't spend the rest of my life with him he would find a way to
destroy me. And, if I ever had a child with someone else, he
would visit me personally to make me miserable. I got away
from him so fast . . . I just ran. Back to the dorm, threw my
clothes in my car, and got out of town. I tried to disappear.
My dad called in a favor from one of the doctors here at General Hospital and he got my residency changed, but I didn't
tell him why. I didn't tell a soul. And I didn't come home right
away, either . . . I drove to a few towns, just for a few days
apiece. I finally threw Phinneas off the scent."

"Phinneas?"

"He was English . . . and French . . ."

"I wouldn't even have a drink with someone named Phinneas. Just on principle," I said, downin' my orange Nehi.
"So he was a dirty rat, eh? Reminds me of a few book-heads
I squared off with myself. But why the tears? You left him on
the side of the road and your life's great, right?"

"It was . . . it has been, pretty much, up till now. Losing Stone
was tough. And getting AIDS . . . that pretty much changed
everything, some things for the better, some others . . . not

so much. And there have been a few bumps in the road with Patrick, but nothing we couldn't get over. But now . . . now I have Emma. And somehow, some way, Phinneas found out about it. He showed up two weeks ago . . ."

She started gettin' a little wild-eyed and her hands were grabbin' at the edge of the table.

"Hang on, Doc. Hang on. I know what you need," I said. "Candy!? An order of onion rings with a side of ranch, pronto!"

"You got it," Candy called from behind the counter.

"Easy now, okay?" I said. I reached across the table and she clutched at my hand like it was a life preserver. I wasn't used to touchin' anyone but Maxie in that strong-but-silent way, but this dame needed a little human contact.

"I was with Emma in the park," she said. Her jaws were clamped together and she was spittin' out the words like she'd just gone twelve rounds and they were broken teeth. "And he walked out from behind a tree. He's gotten gray. And he's really skinny. I almost didn't recognize him at first. And then I realized who it was. He told me his life became a complete wreck after I left him. He didn't go back to France, couldn't get a teaching job here, was arrested for lewd behavior, spent six months in jail, and ended up working behind the counter at Lottaburger outside of Albuquerque. Then he told me he's never forgotten his promise: Now that I had a baby, he was going to destroy me."

"Why now? What's the baby connection?" I ask.

"He said he felt that, without a child, he could always win me back. But a child ties two people together . . . and if I wasn't tied to him, he was going to ruin me."

"Makes sense. In bizarro-land," I said. "But what can he do? He flips burgers in the Southwest."

"That's just it! I was standing there and I realized this guy shouldn't have any power over me. He was nothing . . . and a skinny nothing at that. So I laughed in his face and walked away. And then . . ."

The onion rings arrived and Candy, God bless her, just set 'em down with another Nehi and scuttled away. A good waitress knows when a table wants to be left alone.

"Slow down. Have a ring."

She ate in silence for a minute. Then she reached into her purse and pulled out a piece of paper.

"A week ago I got this," she said, handin' the paper to me.

It was official lookin', like my draft papers or a warrant. Had a seal and everything. It said that after a review of her med school transcripts, it had been determined that she had actually failed her ECG interpretation class. Therefore, her residency was now null and void, and steps were being taken to revoke her medical license.

"Two more arrived a few days ago," she said, her mascara runnin' down off her chin. "One said that I was no longer board certified and the other said that all my grades are being reviewed, beginning with kindergarten! I have one week and unless I can show proof that I actually got an A in that one stupid class, I won't be able to . . . to . . . be a doctor . . ."

"Wait a minute," I said, startin' to get all tingly. "You mean to tell me that all you need is proof on a piece of paper?"

"It has to be a printed school transcript. And now everything is computerized. Somehow, Phinneas hacked in and changed my grade. What do I do?"

I smiled . . . real big. And I thought this job was gonna be hard.

"Sister, you are talkin' to the master hacker, the wizard of the Web, and the bigshot of binary code. I am the king of cryptology and the ace of apps. In fact, I'm the one who put the 'i' in iMac. I am the scourge of the SEC, the interloper of the IRS, and the Pentagon's perennial pain-in-the-ass. My physical mastery of the martial arts is nothing compared to my cyber kung fu, and I have never met a firewall I didn't love. I'm on it. Gimme a day and a half at most. I'll call you when I have news."

I left her sittin' over a plate of cold onions. And the bill.
But she was smilin'. When I leave 'em, they always are.

I went back to Maxie's and gave her a little tickle. I left her a
few hours later, gigglin' in her dreams, and went to my place.
By morning, I had cracked this wise guy's code . . . or so I
thought.

The first few hours gave me exactly the kind of malarky I'd
expected: generic passwords, common phrases, and such. It
was pretty obvious; this maroon had taken a couple of night
courses in computer programming . . . probably just to make
Doc Scorpio's life hell, and now he thought he was . . .
well . . . me. But it's the amateurs that usually write the un-
crackable code . . . because they make a mistake. Only one,
and they usually don't know they've done it or what it is . . .
and that's the reason it can never be undone. It's the little
finger comin' down on the wrong key . . . or the extra
number . . . or it's a wrong number that they think is the
right one . . . or the cat walkin' across the keyboard when
nobody's in the room. Well, this joker hit something he
shouldn't have and the possible combinations were endless.

I did discover one thing, though. Somehow, Xavier had
hacked into Robin's files on a computer back in Monadnock . . . there were screens I shoulda been seeing that I
wasn't . . . things that told me her files had some serious
network protection. This guy's one stupid mistake was keepin'
the firewall up, and my only chance of breakin' through was
to get onto a computer at the school and hack into the network
at the source.

At six o'clock that night, Robin called.

"I . . . I haven't heard from you," she said. "Is everything
okay?"

"It will be," I said. "I just need to take a little trip, is all."

"What? Why? Where?"

"Monadnock . . .'cause ol' Phinny slipped up somewhere. It's kinda technical, but the only place I can make it right is at the source. I'll be in touch in a . . .'"

"I want to go with you."

"Not necessary, Doc. I'll call you tomorrow."

I got my shavin' kit together and headed toward the car. Now, usually I stand behind the Ford Motor Company all the way . . . it's like cherry pie and baseball . . . like we're raisin' the flag for America on Iwo Jima or somethin'. But lately I'd been havin' trouble with the alternator, and tonight of all nights, the damned car wouldn't start.

"Robin," I said, on the squawker back in the apartment, "I been thinkin'. Maybe it's a good idea you do come with me, y'know? I'll bring the car around in about ten minutes."

"Why don't we take my car?" she said . . . like I was hopin' she would, otherwise I was gonna have to hot-wire somethin' in the neighborhood. "I know the campus and I don't mind the drive at all. I would insist on paying for gas anyway. It would be easier, don't you think?"

"Well . . . okay, if you really wanna," I said, leanin' back in the Barcalounger.

"I do," she chirps . . . like a little bird. "I'll be there in ten."

———

I could barely see Robin behind the wheel of her SUV.

"Nice getaway car," I said, climbin' up the side and into the passenger seat.

"We're just trying it out for a few days," she said. "We needed a bigger car now that we have Emma. That's really why I wanted to drive; I want to see how she does on the open road. Mileage and stuff."

"Let's open her up," I said.

Turns out that an SUV doesn't exactly qualify for LeMans,

and Robin and I had some time ahead of us on the road. After a bit, she came clean about just what it was like livin' with a could-be-fatal disease and the strain that put on damn near everything she did. If I hadn't known it before, I got to realizin' that this was one swell dame. Smart, a looker, and enough courage to lead the Cavalry up San Juan Hill; I hoped Patrick knew just what he had.

We pulled onto the Monadnock Community College campus just after 4:30 the next mornin'.

"Where do we start?" she asked.

"Administration," I said. "That should be the biggest stash of computers, and all the sensitive dope, like grades, should go there. But we're gonna ditch the ride."

She wheeled the SUV back behind the Student Union Dumpsters, and we hoofed it to the Harriet Tubman Administration building. My skeleton key got us in the side door without a hitch. Place was dark as Rickles's sense of humor.

"Do you want some light?"

"Do you wanna flash a big sign for the coppers sayin' 'We're breakin' in . . . bring the Black Mariah!'?"

"Oh, right. Sorry. What should I do?" Robin asked.

"Keep quiet and look pretty."

"All right."

I disabled the security systems and started casin' the cubicles for a decent place to work. Robin and I both saw the green glow at the same time.

"What's that?" she whispers.

"Stay here, Doc."

I made my way toward the center of the room. The cubicles were like a maze, and I started feeling like I was one of those lab rats lookin' for a piece of cheese. I turned a corner and there it was: a computer screen lit up with two words in big, green letters.

WELCOME JACKAL

I started smellin' cheddar.

That's when the lights went out.

When I came to . . .

"Hold it," I said. "Do you mean to tell me that somebody got the drop on you?"

"To use the strictest parlance of the moment and atmosphere, I do, Sassy Solicitor."

"I don't know why, but I find that shocking."

Spinelli grinned a funny, sideways grin and, for just a moment, I understood utterly why Maxie loved him.

When I came to, I was tied to a chair like roadkill on a bumper. Robin was trussed up in a chair next to me, except she had a gag around her cake-hole. Right in front of us, leanin' real casual like against the wall of the cubicle, was a skinny mook with long gray hair. He had something in his hand, but I couldn't make it out.

"Jackal, I presume?" he said. "I am Phinneas Xavier, but then you already know that."

This chump was channelin' Sydney Greenstreet. And I never liked Sydney.

"Such a pleasure to meet you," he went on. "I assumed my little bird would go to you for help. And naturally you would come here to undo all my hard work. Right into my trap. I just didn't expect to see my darling Robin again so soon. I thought I would simply kill you and continue to have the pleasure of seeing her fall from grace into poverty and despair for at least another few weeks."

"Sorry to bust up your plans, Cugat," I said.

Next thing I know, he sticks me real quick with that thing he's holdin' and I gotta 'lectric current runnin' through me that had to measure over two hundred volts if it measured one. I heard Robin screamin' and then it all stopped. I damn near took a tumble to the floor, almost takin' the chair with me. The rat had a cattle prod. He laughed and hit me again. I jerked around like a freshwater trout in a bucket.

"*Au contraire, mon ami,*" he said. "You have sped them up quite nicely. Now I can kill you and plant the entire thing on the fair physician here, accelerating her demise most wonderfully."

"You always talk like you get your words from a florist?" I said. That bought me another two hundred volts.

"'Op ihhh!" Robin tried to scream through the gag.

"Don't worry about me, Doc. I'm okay. It's Cugat you gotta feel sorry for."

Another shock.

"It's Xavier!"

At that moment, I knew Cugat had seen every action flick to come outta Tinsel Town. He'd tied these ropes himself, probably thinkin' he knew what he was doin'. Lucky for me, I'd seen those movies too. And my hands started twistin' the sappy knot behind my back. Just as I suspected, the ropes started to move . . . just a little . . . but it was enough.

"Tell me something, funny man," I said, movin' my hands real slow. "How'd a palooka like you go from slingin' sliders in A-bee-que-que to knowin' how to turn on a computer?"

"I left the Southwest years ago. I have been takin' night classes in computer programming."

"I thought so," I said.

"At MIT."

"Okaaaay," I said. "I gotta admit, I didn't see that comin'."

"I knew the best way to destroy my little scorpion was to go after the thing she loved the most: her damned career! So I have been planning this for some time. Naturally, all anyone talked about at MIT was you and your particular genius for . . . everything. It became so annoying that I developed a singular hatred for you. I discovered I was not alone in this; we formed a club. When I realized that you were acquainted with my darling, it was an easy matter to devise a plan to destroy her and you."

"With a cattle prod?" I said. "The both of us? And then you're gonna pin it on her? So she commits suicide, but first she kills me? And we're both tied up . . . which will leave marks on the skin, case you didn't know. Perhaps you ain't thought this through like you shoulda."

"The cattle prod is simply to disable you until I have time to make my getaway."

"Headin' back to the Blue Parrot?"

"What?"

"Nothin'," I said. The thing I loved most about evil-doin' mooks is that they loved to hear themselves talk. Tellin' you all about their plans, which, o'course, gives you time to figure out how to beat 'em at their own game. "Go on. I'm real interested."

I got my hands free, but kept 'em behind my back.

"Once I'm safely away," he said, pullin' a little box the size of a pack of ciggies out of his Members Only jacket, "I will press this little red button right here. And . . ."

He stepped away from the wall. Right behind him, sittin' pretty as a picture, was an alarm clock with ten sticks of dynamite taped to it.

"You went to MIT and that's the best you could do?"

"I prefer old-fashioned things," he said, then he bent real close to Robin. "That's why I love you so much, my little scorpion. Nice old-fashioned girl with old-fashioned values. Which is why I know now that you'll never leave your husband and your baby. So sorry it had to end this way."

"One bomb isn't going to cover up what you've done."

"No," he said. "But ten will. I have them strategically placed all over the building. This one goes off, which will trigger the rest. The ensuing conflagration will destroy any evidence that I was here. And, if anything happens to me and I am unable to press this button, although that's highly unlikely, this bomb is on a timer. It's foolproof. Now it will simply look like she murdered you when you couldn't help her, and then decided life was no longer worth living. And now, I think one more shock ought to knock you out until the big kaboom."

"That's right, Cugat," I said. "That's all it's gonna take."

He made his move, but I sucker-punched him in the jaw with my right as I grabbed the cattle prod with my left. Xavier fell back, but not out of reach, and I zapped him, but good. Now, all that juice was flowin' right back into laughin' boy. He shook like someone fresh off the Green Mile. Smoke started comin' outta his ears. Finally, when I sensed he was nearly done, I let him go. He fell back like a rotted oak. I finished untyin' myself, then Robin. Then . . . I took a look at the bomb.

"Can I help?" Robin said, a little shake in her voice.

"You can clam up, doll," I said. "And if you do say anything . . . you might wanna make it a prayer."

I took the trigger device off of Xavier. That just left the clock and the detonator.

"You've got less than a minute," Robin whispered.

"No foolin' Doc?" I said. "Really? All that, huh?"

"Sorry."

The whole works was so crude it was almost brilliant; I hadn't seen anything like it since my fourth-grade field trip to that big museum in D.C. . . . lots of antiques there, too, walkin' around and behind glass. This contraption has two wires, one red and one blue. I had to cut one, and fast.

Thirty seconds.

I flipped open my Swiss Army knife and went for the red wire. Then I thought about Cugat . . . what he assumed I would cut if ever given the chance. But maybe he knew that I would know. And if I knew that he knew . . .

Seven seconds . . . six . . . five . . . four . . . three . . . two . . .

I cut the blue wire.

Silence.

Until Robin threw her arms around me and damn near burst my eardrum with a whoop.

Then I made a phone call.

The cops took their own sweet time in gettin' to us, but once they were there, they were pretty interested in what we had to say. Phinny was still out, but by the time the dean of students at Monadnock arrived, he was comin' around. He really woke up when the paramedics tried to pry his melted Timex offa his wrist. He confessed to everything and the dean promised Robin that, come twelve o'clock high the next day, the lady doc would be in the clear: license safe, board certified, and no one would be lookin' into any kindergarten shenanigans.

Starbucks was just openin' up as we hit the road back to Port Charlie. She drove, so I bought.

"How'd you know which wire to cut?" she asked.

"C'mon," I said, sippin' my joe. "That's like askin' Houdini how many minutes he gave the crowd before he stuck his head outta the milk can. Or like askin' Da Vinci how he knew the *Mona Lisa* was done. Or how you and Patrick know when Emma's really gone down for the night and you two can finally get some shut-eye. You just know, y'know?"

She smiled.

"Yeah . . . I know," she said.

"I know you know."

"I know."

(*pause*)

(*pause*)

(*pause*)

"I know."

(Sometimes . . . nobody needs to know that you didn't really know. That, for that one moment, you were fumblin' in the dark just like a regular Pete, and you only walked away because God was on your side. That much, and only that much, you knew . . . y'know?)

10

Damian Spinelli

and the Case of the Dame Who Knew Too Much

Walkin' into the Port Charlie cemetery . . . final lie-down, boneyard, rotter's rest, the six-feet-under club . . . was never a piece of cake. Too many memories.

Actually, if I'm bein' square, I didn't have any relatives stashed in pine boxes in that particular God's Acre. In fact, I didn't know where my folks were; so I just invested the head-stones and grave-markers of the townspeople with a sorta bond, if you get my drift, and made them my own.

"Evenin', Mr. Richard Overton, born 1813, died 1865. Nice night, ain't it? Mrs. Stocking, devoted wife and mother . . . lookin' sharp as usual, doll."

I didn't know them, and they sure as hell didn't know me . . . but they were my folk.

I reached the place we'd agreed on, marker 284F, Col. Marion "Have Mercy!" Barrows, sat down, and waited. I didn't have to wait long . . . this dame had manners.

"Good evening, Jackal," she says, stridin' up real easy.

"Evenin', Miss . . . jeez, considerin' what I know about you, I ain't sure what to call you."

"You have everything, then? It's all taken care of?"

"I may have missed a photo or two, 'cause there were a lot, sister, lemme tell you. But I think I got everything, yeah."

"May I see it?"

I handed her a large manila envelope I'd had tucked under my arm. She opened it with one perfect nail and started combin' through.

"Excellent . . . excellent. Heavens, I could be here all night. Just give me a rundown, will you? Tell me everything you did."

"You were a busy bee from the time you left Princeton to the moment you first set your dainty foot in Port Charles a few years ago. But, thanks to me, we're gonna be the only two who know it. In that envelope are all the records I've destroyed. No one's gonna know that, when you took up modelin' in Japan, you also took up with the Emperor for about three months. Evidence of the two girls you had with him? Gone."

"Miyuki and Saiko," she whispered. "They're young ladies, by now. I miss them so."

"Well, I hope you said your good-byes, mama-san," I said, my voice soundin' a little too cruel. "Because as far as you're concerned, they don't exist. And no one is going to know that you ran that country for six weeks while the prime minister had dysentery."

"Good," she said, wipin' away a tear.

"Japanese ambassador to Hungary? Gone. Hungarian minister of internal affairs? Gone. As well as fine art attaché to the Louvre. No one will know that you 'fixed' the *Mona Lisa* during that hushed-up arson attempt back in '95. Far as everyone's concerned, all the work is still Leo's. Bustin' up that fine art forgery ring from Honduras? Gone. Deposing the South American leader who was about to launch a bio-terror weapon on Nogales? Gone."

"I made that look like a suicide, you know?" she said. "I

caused a scandal from which the *generalissimo* knew he could never recover. He garroted himself."

She was looking around at the headstones, but I knew she was miles away.

"And don't think I wasn't impressed," I said. "But . . . it's gone, doll. So's the fact that you stopped the hijackin' of the *Luriline* off the Côte d'Azur."

"I was working as a double agent," she said with a sad little laugh. "Those pirates thought I was just a pretty plaything, but I showed them. Lured them onboard, gave them the all clear."

"You saved two hundred and thirty-seven lives that day," I said. "But no one's gonna know. People have been paid off, evidence destroyed. That's the way you wanted it, right?"

"Right. Go on."

"There's no record of you startin' the school for rug rats with big brains."

"The Exceptionals," she said, shaking her head. "Gathered from orphanages all over the world. One child came from right here in Port Charles, you know. Her name is . . ."

"Don't say it! Don't speak it out loud. Besides . . . I already know who it is."

"I'm sure you do. Which means you know the history that child was given and what her mission is."

"You got that right," I said.

"But so many other Exceptionals are out there as well! They're already doing exceptional things . . . following their orders! How did you . . . ?"

"The ones in public office have all sworn to keep silent. The ones in the underground wouldn't talk anyway. Plus, if anything ever does leak out, Oprah has agreed to take the credit."

"She's always been so good about that. I have to send her a thank-you note . . . maybe some chocolates."

"Don't do anything, y'hear me!" I said . . . too loudly. "No trail back to you! It's all taken care of. You *didn't* stop

Russia's second nuclear disaster by throwin' yourself on the rods and changin' the heat ratio."

"My hair was curly for three years after that," she said.

"You *don't* have access to Hubble photos showin' space ships circlin' Saturn."

"They're hanging in my bathroom in Manhattan." She giggled now. I sensed she was easin' up just a bit. "People think I'm a science fiction nut. I keep a copy of Asimov short stories by my bed, just to keep up the charade."

"You don't have to keep up anything anymore, sister. You can toss ol' Isaac in the circular file if you want to now; although my personal suggestion would be to read him. He's good. Although you already know more than most about science 'fiction,' am I right?"

"Ah," she said, with a sideways glance. "You mean the time travel."

"No one will ever know that you were pulled off a NASA shuttle mission at the last moment and sent to Switzerland to test the 'Tempest 3 Portal.' But, just 'tween you and me and the colonel here . . . how far into the future did you go?"

"Twenty-five years," she said. Then her smile got real big. "It's funny, you know. People think I have my pulse on the latest trends in fashion. Truth is, I just stole what I saw from the future and brought it back to the present."

"I disagree, Ice Queen. I say you started leadin' the pack now . . . and then you saw the results when you traveled ahead in time."

"You're sweet, Jackal," she said, squeezin' my arm for a second. "Go on."

"That's it for the majors. Let's see . . . you *weren't* the produce manager for Gelson's supermarkets in California. You didn't become a cobbler in Milan. You didn't invent the Cosmopolitan, Coke Zero, or the Frappuccino. You didn't insist that Subway stick with the oil-and-vinegar mix when they wanted to discontinue it."

"Such good sandwiches," she whispered.

"You didn't take over for Mother Teresa when she had scurvy for three days."

"I might want to keep that," she said.

"Then you risk everything else comin' out. This is a tight little fishnet stocking you've woven, doll. One snag and the whole thing unravels."

"Fine . . . lose Calcutta."

"You didn't cap an oil well outside of San Antonio. You didn't score thirty-six goals in the one and only season for the Ottawa Ovaries. You didn't invent the Snuggie. You don't know where Jimmy Hoffa is buried. You didn't translate the complete works of Dostoevsky into Swahili, and you weren't on the rodeo circuit for two years under that name of 'Catastrophe Sal.' "

She sighed. Even her sigh was pure class.

"That's it, then."

"That's it," I said. "The cover story's in place. Photos, articles, scandals, the works. As far as anyone will ever know, you just went to the Big Apple and started workin' to become a fashion tycoon."

I took a long pause.

"But I don't get it," I said. "Why? Why the cover-up?"

It was her turn to get real quiet.

"I want to go back home . . . even if it's just for a little while. I've been lucky so far; none of this has found me. Most of it I did out of necessity. Hell, most of it I did to survive. I covered my trails well, crossed my 't's' and all that. But I want a clean slate. I may come back to Port Charles from time to time, but from now on I just want to live on my own terms . . . no fear."

"But, and I never thought I'd say this to anyone; you've done more than I have. You're out there, fightin' the good fight. Helpin' those who need it the most and puttin' the bad guys outta commission. *And* lookin' like cake while you're at it.

You're . . . you're a real special dame. The world should know . . ."

"Come on, Spinelli," she said, lookin' me square in the *ojos*. "You've saved this country from complete destruction three times already and no one will ever know about *that,* will they?"

"Nope."

"You understand, don't you?"

"Yeah. Yeah, I do," I said, and I was on the level. I did.

"Take care, Spinelli," she said. "Thanks."

"You, too. And . . . I'll just say it. You got my respect." She nodded her head and smiled.

Then I watched Kate Howard walk away into the mist.

11

Damian Spinelli

and the Case of the Contrived Contralto

Maxie and I didn't get to the flickers much. Mostly 'cause I was a little twitchy at leavin' her alone to go get popcorn. Twice I'd come back and found her in the back of the movie house playin' "Who's Got the Goober?" with some joker neither of us knew. If I didn't have such a good grip on my manhood, I mighta taken it real personal.

"You can't say that," I said, flipping off the tape recorder and putting my head down on the formica table.

"Innumerable and heartfelt pardons, Beautiful Barrister, but what has you so exasperated?"

"You cannot say that you have or had a grip on your . . . your . . ."

"Oh! But of course not. Naturally, what you are thinking that I was thinking is not at all what was meant. I only wished to infer that I am dealing with any insecurity issues regarding my masculinity and my non-bride with forthrightness, clear thinking, and a great deal of therapy."

"I can only imagine," I said, flipping the "record" button back on.

However, that night it was a double feature at the Port Chuck Bijou: *The Prisoner of Zenda* with Stewie Granger, and *A Stolen Life* with Miss Bette "Don't You Get Fresh with Me, Jack Warner!" Davis. My blonde baby hadn't known flickers were even around before the early '70s, so this was one set of peep-shows I didn't want to miss.

First, we watched James Mason take his final powder and Maxie loved it. Then, Bette Davis was just confessin' *her* whole mess when suddenly my cell phone started to vibrate. It was a country code I didn't recognize at first.

"Spinelli," I whispered. (I hate rubes who think the movie theater is the perfect place to have a real, real loud conversation. Makes me wish I had a taser.)

"Thank God! It's Alexis. I'm in trouble, Spinelli. It's bad. She kidnapped me. I'm on the island . . . and . . . and she's gone crazy! Really crazy this time! Oh, God . . . I . . . I have to go. Do something. Help me!"

I was almost up and outta my seat when the line clicked off . . . dead; I didn't have a chance to even open my puss.

"Wrong number?" Maxie whispered.

"Nope," I said, real low, slippin' the phone back into my pocket, realizin' the mystery country code was for Greece. "She knew exactly who she was callin'. You stay, baby. Don't miss the end. I gotta get packin'. The dame's in bad shape from the sound of it."

"Dame? What dame?"

"Alexis Davis."

"I can finish the movie another time. I want to help you, if I can. What's wrong?" Maxie asked, followin' me outta the movie house.

"Don't know yet. All's I know is that I'm headin' east. Next stop . . . Cassadine Island."

Suddenly, I had a funny feelin' that there might have been a reason we'd been watchin' those two particular films that night.

———————

There was a twelve-seater at the Port Charles airstrip, and I thought about hot-wiring her for about a minute, until I realized that I didn't know how much fuel was in her tanks and a whole lotta questions might be asked if I needed to gas her up. It was a lousy idea all around. I fished my Greek passport out from my "travelin'" trunk and was at Kennedy within two hours of gettin' Alexis's call.

"Mister . . . Papadopolis?" asked the stew in first class, leanin' over so's I could get a whiff of her Jean Naté After Bath Splash Mist.

"Sweet Jesus, you shouldn't *know* those things, Spinelli!" I said.

"What?"

"You shouldn't know that Jean Naté comes in an 'after bath splash . . . whatever!'"

"Mist."

"STOP IT! Right there! THAT! You're gonna get beat up in an alley if you keep this up. You need to say something like 'a whiff of her perfume. It was expensive, like she probably was.' Something like that."

"But, and with all due respect, Brassy and Somewhat Ballsy Barrister, I do recall you saying that, although these are the stories of my life which involve your clients to a certain degree as well as other peripheral members of Port Charles's 'who's who,' they would only live in note form. Yes, they must be told, but after the telling, you said they would only live on in secret . . . on your computer, I believe."

I sighed.

"Yes . . . yes . . . you have me there. I did say that."

He clapped his hands together.

"Then 'Jean Naté' may stay?"

"Why not?"

"That's me," I answered.

"Would you like something to drink before takeoff?"

"He'll have what I'm having," said a voice behind her.

She turned and I looked up to see Nikolas Cassadine . . . "Cassi" I called him when he wasn't lookin' . . . waitin' for the window seat.

"Two gin and sodas, Miss, thank you," Cassi said.

The stew turned to look at me.

"That'll be fine, doll. Put a twist in mine."

"Jackal," Cassi said, settlin' in.

"Prince," I replied. Outta respect, that's what I called him when he was lookin'.

"Doing a little vacationing in Greece?" he asked.

"Maybe. You? Gonna see some sights? The family maybe?"

"I'm going to do just that," Cassi answered.

"You got a lot of family over there," I said.

"I do."

"You're not taking the Cassadine jet?" I asked.

"It's out of commission," he said, real slow.

"You mean you *can't* take it . . . because it's already in Greece."

"Then you know!" he kinda yelped.

"Shhhh," I said. "What are you doin' here?"

"I got a call from Alexis about an hour and a half ago. Helena kidnapped her and the girls . . ."

"Molly and Kristina are there too?"

"Helena has them all. Alexis couldn't get much out except that my grandmother has gone completely mad and she plans to 'do' something to Alexis and make the girls watch. Just like Helena made Alexis watch when she killed Alexis's mother.

I'm on this plane because I didn't want to charter anything. I didn't want to tip off Helena in any way."

"You gotta fun family," I said.

"You don't know the half of it. Now . . . why are *you* here?"

"Alexis called my cell two hours ago. Told me where she was and that she needed help. That's all I know."

"You mean," Cassi said, "she called you before she called me?"

"Looks that way. Now listen, Prince, I don't mind Alexis hedgin' her bets, and I don't mind you taggin' along. Just one thing we gotta get straight. I work alone, see? You wanna play on the beach and get a tan? Fine. You wanna eat some flamin' cheese and throw a few plates? Fine. Just stay outta my way."

Nikolas turned toward the window as the wide-body lifted off. For a second I thought he might be cryin'. About an hour later, he turned back.

"Listen, Jackal," Cassi said softly. "I know you're the best. I know that's why my aunt called you. But I also know why she called me. I can get us in! Onto the island, I mean."

"Piece of cake," I said, flippin' through my in-flight magazine.

"Look, I know you could *do* it," Cassi said. "But it would cost you a lot of money in bribes. People expect to be paid for their silence or their help. And it would take you time. And . . . dammit . . . that's time Alexis might not have!"

"Easy, sport . . . easy," I said. "You're right."

"I am?"

"You bet," I said, and I meant it, 'cause he was. "We'll play it your way until we get onto the island, okay? Straight down the line. Then, once we're on land, you let me take over. You do what I say when I say it. Jake?"

"Jake," Cassi said. "Thank you."

"Cassi, this is the beginnin' of a beautiful friendship."

"Uh . . . okay. Did you say 'Cassi'?"

We made one stop after gettin' off the plane: a little souvenir shop inside the airport. Forty-five euros and two Greek fishing caps later, we flagged a taxi to take us to the coast. Just two nice Greek chumps visitin' the old sod. No limos, no town cars, no helicopters . . . no cushy ride for the Prince. But for all his rich-kid airs, Cassi was turnin' out to be a regular joe, and a smart one. He didn't say one word to the cabbie, made me do all the gum flappin'.

"Everyone in this country has either been paid off, hunted by, nursed by, slept with, or knows someone who has been killed by the Cassadines. One word out of me and my grandmother would know I'm in the country within five minutes," he told me as the plane was landing. "You should do all the talking until we get to the coast. How's your Greek?"

"Souvlaki smooth," I said.

"I had a feeling it would be."

Five hours and a whole lotta silence later, we reached a fishing village on the coast, the nearest launch point to the island.

"I'll get this," Cassi said when I started to inquire about gettin' a boat. He said something real low to an old man sittin' on a bench, fixin' a net. Without lookin' up, the man went inside a little shack. Cassi and I followed. The man reached down behind a counter and pulled out a single key. Cassi slid two hundred euros across the counter and the man went back to fixin' his net.

We walked around the shack and out onto a short dock. The key unlocked a chain around a tie line; on the other end, the sorriest little motorboat I'd ever seen.

Cassi locked her back up and headed for a bunch of trees about fifty yards away. I kept my yap shut and followed until we were hidden.

"What gives?" I said. "Why ain't we headin' out to the 'forbidden island'?"

"Still too light," the prince said. "We'll be on the water for a while, but we don't want anyone here seein' us take off, not if we can help it. The man who got us the boat was the gardener on the island for years. Every day of every visit I ever had here, he gave me a rose to take into the house for the first woman I saw. I adored him, and he was loyal to the family. Until . . . the 'scissors' incident with his daughter and my uncle. I told him I was here for payback. He won't signal my grandmother . . . but there are others here who would. We have a couple of hours; I'm for getting a little sleep."

I set my watch alarm and we both settled in. Two hours later, "Wind Beneath My Wings" woke us both up real sweet. The skies were darkenin' fast; lights were comin' on in the village. We headed for the dock, unlocked the chain, and started the motor. The moon was full, and Cassi knew the way; all's I had to do was sit back and try not to freeze to death. Thought about those pictures of ancient Greek guys, runnin' around in short dresses . . . in *this* weather? Cripes . . . and I thought *I* was tough.

On the way, I asked Cassi what he thought Alexis mighta meant when she said Helena was gonna do the same thing she'd done to Alexis's mother.

"Gimme the story," I said.

"Helena's husband, Mikos, my grandfather, had an affair with a woman named Kristin Bergman, a Swedish opera singer living in Paris. Out of that union was born Natasha Alexandra Mikkosovna Cassadine . . . also now known as Alexis . . . and her sister, Kristina Cassadine."

"Alexis got saddled with the name baggage, huh? Might explain a few things."

"Anyway, Mikos left Kristin and her girls to fend for themselves in Paris. He sent money, but he'd pretty much abandoned them, so my grandmother let it slide for years.

The story goes that she would only mention Mikos's 'bastard-ettes,' as she liked to call them, when she was either drunk, or Mikos wouldn't buy her something she wanted—a piece of jewelry . . . a plane . . . a country, that sort of thing. Finally, though, one day Helena snapped. She flew to Paris and, making sure that Natasha and Kristina were both home, she invited herself into Kristin's apartment, sat down to tea, made a little small talk, then slit Kristin's throat right in front of both girls. Said something like, 'Let's hear you sing now.' "

"Your grandma's a keeper."

"Natasha was so traumatized by the incident, she was sent to live with relatives, her name was changed, and she basically couldn't remember anything. She also lived on the island for a while before coming to Port Charles."

"She lived on the island with your *grandmother*?" I asked. "With 'Hell-on-Wheels'? The Komodo Dragon-lady?"

"For a while, yes," Cassi answered. "But then she went to law school and started a life for herself in America."

"Wait a second," I said, feelin' all the hairs on the back of my neck stand at attention. "Hell-on-Wheels not only kid-napped Alexis, but she also has Alexis's own girls, Kristina and Molly! And she's gonna do to Alexis what she did to . . . ? In front of . . . ? How fast can this thing go? We gotta make tracks."

"The motor is putting out all the horsepower it's got," Cassi said. "If I overload it, we'll be dead in the water."

"I just hope Alexis isn't dead on the island."

———

An hour later, Cassi spotted the little lighthouse on the northern tip.

"The palace is just above it," he said.

Cassi took the boat around to the eastern shore and ran it

up on a decent stretch of beach. We hoofed it through some heavy undergrowth.

"You okay?" Cassi asked, when we stopped to rest.

"Reminds me of my days in Crimea."

"Come on, Jackal," Cassi said. "You couldn't have been in the Crimean War!"

"Bravo, Prince Cassadine!" I said. "He gotcha!"

Spinelli looked at me like I should have been riding a tricycle.

"I shall say to you the very thing that I said to His Highness . . ."

"I never said I was in the war."

We crawled ahead until we came to a wall. In the moonlight, I could see high buildings that musta stretched up at least two hundred feet, and way at the top I could just make out shiny rooftops.

"Big place. The joint has a metal roof?"

"Gold," Cassi answered, which shut me up for a minute. "This wall is at the back of the palace grounds. That way leads to the pool and the formal French *jardins*. This way leads to the stables, the miniature golf course, the shooting range, and the outdoor torture garden."

"You're pullin' my leg."

"Complete with pillory, wheel, and iron maiden."

"Your grandmother's a freakin' nut!"

"Those were my grandfather's. Grandmother just keeps them around for sentimental reasons. Helena's much more sophisticated. Poisoned lipstick, perfume—small stuff. She idolized Catherine de' Medici."

"She's a fu . . . !"

"She's still my grandmother."

I pointed to a little door in the wall directly ahead of us.

"Where does that lead?"

"To the cellars," Cassi answered.

"Okay, pal, here's where I take over. Any special security I need to know about?"

"Nothing out of the ordinary: lasers, trip wires, cameras . . . the usual."

"Then we're off to see the wizard," I said. My skeleton key didn't fail me, and seconds later we were inside and under the Cassadine palace. The first thing we both heard was someone singin' way off in the distance.

"Hang on a second. Don't make a sound," I said, strainin' my ears.

"What is it?" Cassi asked after a few seconds.

"It ain't a what, it's a who," I said. "Callas. *Tosca.* Act 2. 'Vissi D'Arte, Vissi D'Amore.' La Scala. 1953. De Sabata conductin'. The classic."

"You know about opera?"

"Kate Howard gives Maxie her tickets to the Met. She drags me along. I bought a couple of recordings; been pickin' up a few things."

I disabled the cameras, unsprung the wires, and shut off the lasers. I also took out two guards that Cassi had failed to mention.

"Pay no attention to the men behind the curtain," I said, tyin', gaggin,' and stashin' 'em behind a huge tapestry. We headed, real slow, down a corridor. The place gave me the shivers; it was cold and it smelled like . . . animals . . . and bad wine. Looked like there used to be torches in the walls, but now there were only a couple of fluorescent bulbs on single wires hangin' from the ceiling. And, every once in a while, somethin' dripped on me.

We came to a fork in the corridor just as Tosca was guttin' Scarpia like a scrod fillet. I looked at Cassi, and just as he nodded to the left, we heard a scream to the right. A kid's scream. Molly's scream. And then, from behind a heavy wooden door, we both saw crazy flashes of light. I realized that's where the music was comin' from. Cassi started to run ahead, but I held him back.

"What else is down here, chum?"

"I might have forgotten to mention . . . the laboratory."

"Yeah, Highness, you forgot all right."

"We have to hurry!" Cassi said.

"Hang on . . . hang on," I said. "We can't burst through the door. Helena will finish Alexis off in a trice."

"Trice?" I choked. "Trice? Dost thou, in sooth, wish to say 'trice,' verily?"

"Something else?"

"'New York minute.'"

"Great," Spinelli agreed.

"Hey nonny nonny!"

"Helena will finish Alexis off in a New York minute. Your family is screwy, and how. So, if somebody built a lab, I'll lay you odds they also wanted everyone else to get to watch the hijinks. I'll bet it's gotta viewin' gallery, right?"

"Right," said Cassi. "This way."

He started up a wooden staircase straight out of *Vertigo*. If this thing didn't collapse right out from under us, I told God I would start doin' some charity work . . . or at least be nicer to people.

We came out, real quiet, on a little ledge with a railing that overlooked . . . the lab.

Now . . . I've seen some stuff. Between Saigon, Rangoon, and the Baltic, I've seen some stuff. Stuff that would make an average joe toss his Oreos into the nearest pail. But this was something I'd never seen . . . right out of a Hammer horror flick.

Gizmos, geegaws, and gadgets. Beakers full of liquids boilin', steamin', and foamin'. Electrodes, levers, and pull switches three times the size of my head. Sparks flyin' everywhere, currents of white heat arcin' from one metal object to another. Helena standin' at one end of a giant operating table, some curly-haired guy with a huge name tag that read "Larry Saltmann" standin' right beside her, both of 'em wearin' white lab coats and goggles. Molly and Kristina strugglin' and screamin' at the far end of the room . . . the crazy broad had manacled these kids to the wall. And Alexis . . . strapped like Elsa Lanchester to the table, covered in a white sheet, with only her neck and head exposed. Helena walked over to an old phonograph and delicately lifted the needle off the vinyl, just as Tosca was about to take a flying leap.

"Let's get this over with," Helena said, comin' back to the table. "We've stalled long enough."

"The operation will be very delicate," Larry said. "And I'm not certain of its success."

"Don't toy with me, Saltmann!" Helena said, smackin' him a good one right across his puss. "I have this woman booked into Covent Garden at the end of the month and Budapest, Berlin, and Vienna after that. She has to be perfect!"

"What . . . ?" Cassi whispered beside me.

"I'm just sayin' that she might not be performance ready," Saltmann said, rubbin' his cheek.

"Of course she will be," Helena said. Then she walked over to Alexis and very gently stroked her hair. "My husband said you had the greatest voice he'd ever heard. That's why he fell in love with you. Of course, you were easy and rather cheap, but apparently you could sing like a bird. And I took it all away from you, didn't I? One slice and poof! All gone. I'm so sorry. But look! I'm going to give it back . . . and in front of your little girls, no less. I'm going to make it all right again."

"Helena, you've got it all wrong!" Alexis began. "You've got me confused with my mother. I can't sing!"

"Well, of course you can't. Not now. I silenced you, little bird. I cut you down, didn't I? But now . . . this is my chance! I am going to give you your voice . . . back! Your little girls will be witness to me atoning for my . . . sin. Isn't that right, Kristina? Natasha?"

"*I'm* Natasha!" Alexis said. "It's me, Helena. Not my mother! Me!"

Helena looked startled for a second. I cased the joint in an instant. Two ropes on pulleys attached to the table were ready to pull it up and out of a hole in the roof. Only thing was . . . there weren't any counterweights. Not yet. If we could just jump out far enough . . . I looked at Cassadine; he saw what I was gettin' at and nodded.

"Oh, you're trying to confuse me!" Helena said. "Well, that's just the way, isn't it? Some people don't appreciate when others try to help them."

"Helena, I can help *you!*" Alexis pleaded. "You're . . . you're not well. You think I'm my mother, and I'm not!"

Alexis looked at Larry.

"Help me, please! Don't do this!"

Larry shrugged.

"Sorry. I got a mortgage, an ex-wife, and two kids in braces and private school. They like stuff and stuff costs money."

"But she's snapped! A week ago . . . my God, she was in Port Charles! We all were. I came out of a store and saw her on the street with my girls. I tried to get them away, but she followed us. She heard me call to my oldest, Kristina, and . . . and . . . that's when Helena lost it. She tracked us down, kept calling me by my mother's name. Then she drugged us . . . she drugged my daughters! And now we've ended up here! Helena, you're sick! You need doctors, Helena."

"Not smart to call the crazy lady crazy," I whispered to myself. "Not when you're tied to a table."

"I think that's enough talking now. Time to sing," Helena said. "All right, let's begin."

Larry picked up a scalpel the size of a fish knife.

"You're sure you don't want to give her any anesthetic?" he said.

"Of *couuuurse* not!" Helena yowled. "I want her fully conscious of the gift that she is being given. I want her to feel her voice flowing back into her, just as she felt it flowing out so many years ago."

Molly and Kristina started screamin' like banshees as Larry bent toward Alexis's throat. Alexis's eyes were like pie tins.

"Helena, stop! For the love of God . . . !"

And that's when I jumped. I caught the first rope as Cassi flew by me and caught the second. The operating table lifted off the ground, knocking the fish knife outta Larry's hands and, basically, upper cuttin' him into a nice little coma. We both landed on the floor at the same time. But Helena was like a tiger. She was on the knife in a flash.

"I'll handle the nut-job. Go get the girls," I said to Cassi, tyin' off the ropes. He made a beeline for Kristina and Molly, tellin' 'em to simmer down.

Helena and I started circlin' each other.

"Alexis?" I called up, never takin' my eyes off the crazy lady. "You okay?"

"I'm okay!" she called back down.

"I'll get you down in a second, doll, just sit tight."

"Well, now who do we have here?" Helena said, soft and scary.

"Fly in the ointment, nut-job."

"Really? Someone come to spoil my good deed?" she said, handlin' the knife like she was a ninja.

"I'm a finger in your pie, lady."

"You are?"

"Hand in your cookie jar."

"I don't think I can allow that."

She took a swipe at me that let me know she meant business. I ducked out of the way, but just barely. She lunged again and nicked my upper arm. This dame wasn't gonna fall like a house of cards. I needed some distance. She dove for me again, but I saw it comin' and caught her foot. She went flyin' into a wall, but was up again like she was strollin' in the park. She made a run for me, but I threw one of those electronic who-haws in front of her. It burst into flames and stopped her for a moment, then Hell-on-Wheels just walked right over it like it was a crack in the sidewalk. But it gave me time to put a table full of beakers and Bunsen burners between me and the crazy robot-lady. She cleared the table with one sweep of her arm. I skittered to the other side of the room, behind a second table of boilin' liquids. Then I smelled smoke.

Turns out, Helena hadn't walked over the sparkin' gizmo entirely unaffected.

"I hate it when I have to kill someone," she said, her eyes glazin' over like they were Christmas fruitcakes. "It used to make my day. Now it's all such a bore."

"Hey, nut-job?" I said.

"Are you speaking to me?"

"That's right," I said. "Guess what?"

"What?"

"You're on fire."

She looked down at the cuff of her David Hayes pantsuit. I grabbed the closest beaker and threw it low. The flames caught, and the next minute Helena was playin' Joan of Arc to a full house. She stumbled backward, trippin' over Larry, losin' the knife and landin' on her backside. Crazy but smart, she rolled around on the floor, puttin' the flames out. Then she reached again for the fish knife, only inches away, and my foot came down right on her pretty, aristocratic, crazy-ass hand.

"I don't think I can allow that . . . nut-job," I said. Then I tapped her lightly on the head with a cooled-off Bunsen burner until she went night-night.

Cassi and I lowered Alexis, got her freed up and reunited with her girls. Then we tied Larry and Helena to the table and raised it high. Real high. And we tied off the ropes too far away for either of them to get any clever ideas.

"Call the coppers on the mainland," I said to Cassi.

"Won't do any good," he said. "They're all on the payroll. Our best bet is to take the Cassadine yacht and head for Turkey. We can get a safe passage home from Ephesus."

Cassi and I took the point as we walked out of the lab, keepin' Alexis and the midgets behind us. We were ready for the guards. But they weren't there. On our way up and out of the cellar, we saw a few men stationed here and there, but they just nodded and left us alone. One even tipped his cap.

The kitchen staff helped us load the yacht with supplies, just as the sun was comin' up. No one said diddley. I was last up the gangplank and I turned to one of the housekeepers.

"Your . . . uh . . . employer is in the laboratory. Tied on an operatin' table."

She looked at me for a long time.

"Laboratory, sir? I have never heard of a laboratory on the island. There is much work to be done here today but, perhaps later . . . much later . . . we may go searching for this place you speak of. However, I think you must be mistaken."

I just laughed.

"Whatever you say, sister."

We were underway, with Cassi at the helm, in less than an hour. We put into Ephesus the next evening. Kristina and Molly were kinda upset.

"C'mon, Uncle Spinelli . . . just one more game of Sorry! Please?"

"Girls . . . girls, we been playin' for nearly two days straight. Time to get ready to get off this tug."

"You're good with kids," Alexis said as the girls ran below deck.

"Well, I'm a big one myself."

"How can I ever thank you for saving my life?" she said, watching the dock master wave the yacht into a berth. "And the lives of my girls."

"Promise me one thing," I said.

"Anything. Name it."

"Promise me that you'll talk to Kate Howard; tell her to give her Met tickets to someone else. And never, ever suggest . . . even slightly hint to Maxie that she and I might like to spend another night at the opera."

"Deal."

"Then, counselor . . . we're square."

12

Damian Spinelli
and the Case of the Muscle-Bound Mama

It was a quiet afternoon at the offices of Spinelli & McCall. I was finishin' up the second half of herring salad and potato chips on a cheese bialy, but I was already thinkin' about skirt steak that Maxie'd promised to fry up for me later on.

Then I heard the front door close downstairs.

I knew the orthodontist on the first floor was on vacation, the bookie across the hall was doin' six months in county on behalf of the IRS, and I wasn't expectin' nobody.

I heard steps on the stairs; I pulled out my roscoe and set it real gentle on the desk.

A silhouette grew large outside the office door, remindin' me of the time Carly Jacks paid me a visit wearin' nothing but a mink trench coat, size: mini. But this time, it weren't no dame.

The door opened real slow. I pushed the brim of my hat forward over my eyes and leaned back in my chair. I pushed a little too far and went ass over eyeballs onto the floor. But I was back up like I was shot out of a cannon and sitting pretty as you please in no time. I checked the desk for my heater . . . still there. In fact, the mook in the doorway hadn't moved an inch.

"You gonna stand there in the dark and make me guess who you are?" I said, startin' to lean back in the chair again, then thinkin' better of it. "Or are you gonna come in like a regular joe . . . maybe sit . . . maybe chat? 'Cause I'll give it to you straight . . . sometimes I don't do the guessin'. Sometimes my pal here tries to figure it out."

I patted my gun.

The son-of-a-bandolier didn't move. Then I realized he was shakin' hard. Then he sniffed back a nose-full and ran his hand across his face as he stepped into the light.

"I'm sorry," Lucky Spencer said. "I just wanted to be a little more . . . calm when I came to see you. I tried to clean myself up . . . but I can't seem to stop crying."

He sat in the closest chair and started bawlin' like a kid who'd just found out there was no Santa Claus; that it was his parents all along and, either way, he wasn't gettin' the G.I. Joe with the "Kung-Fu grip."

"Hey, pal . . . and I mean you, Lucky . . . not the gun. What's the story? What's got you snifflin' like Maxie when she runs her fishnets?"

But the poor guy couldn't speak. I was cool at first. Even tried to be a little understandin'. But then, after about five minutes, naturally, I started to get a little steamed. I can handle a dame gettin' weepy; I handle it with a few kind words, a bottle of smell-nice, or half a grapefruit in the kisser if it gets serious. But I couldn't clobber this fella . . . or could I? Could I? I was startin' to consider my options on the subject, when Lucky shook it off. He sat up straight and aimed his peepers right at me.

"I need your help."

"You need somethin' all right. A shot of whiskey, maybe?"

"No," he said. "Not that. I've been drinking for six days

straight. I'd been off the sauce for months, but this . . . this has sent me right off the wagon."

"Well, I'll have one if you don't mind," I said, pourin' a shot into a nearby glass. I watched his eyes dance all over the hooch and I realized there were times I could be a cruel bastard.

"Sorry," I mush-mouthed, puttin' the drink away. "What's up?"

"It's my wife," he said. "I mean my ex-wife. I mean . . . God, I don't even know what to call her anymore. It's Elizabeth."

"I just call her the Maternal One, since she has all those kids by all those different . . . uh . . ."

A real bastard. And I wasn't even tryin'.

"What's happened?"

"A couple of weeks ago," Lucky started in, "I was dropping the kids back off at Elizabeth's. But I was earlier than she expected, and when she opened the door, she was out of breath . . . and sweating."

"Glowin'," I corrected.

"What?" Spencer asked.

"Ladies prefer the term 'glowin'.' Go on," I said. "So she was hankin' yet another fella's pank, eh?"

"Well," he said, "that's what I thought at first. Although I've never heard it put quite like that. So, naturally I called her all sorts of names, shoved the kids inside, and took off."

"Naturally."

"But I couldn't get it out of my mind . . . what she's doing and who she's doing it with. So I borrowed an unmarked car from the PCPD and I spent the next three days staked out across the street from her place."

"Ah, the stakeout," I said. "A time for chili burgers and cold coffee. Crossword puzzle books and B. B. King playin' so low you think Lucille might have broken a string."

"May I continue?" Spencer said.

"What the hell."

"The only thing I saw was a delivery man . . ."

"It's always the delivery man."

"But it wasn't! That's just the trouble. He never went in-side. He just dropped off packages or boxes marked 'AI' and left. And they were heavy. He had trouble getting them to her door, and she really had a hard time. Then, a week ago, it was my turn to take the kids again. Only this time, when I went to pick them up, I noticed that Elizabeth had a nice new tele-vision and a new couch. Fortunately, Cameron was late coming down the stairs, so I just eased myself in. Then I saw her kick a dumbbell under the couch. And there was a fire hose nozzle on the floor behind the table. And then she tried to hide a little white hat between two cushions, but I got a look at it. It was one of those little caps that French maids wear."

"You sure it wasn't her nurse's cap?" I asked.

"I know the difference," Spencer said. "Besides, I know she's a nurse at General Hospital; why would she need to hide it from me?"

"Good point. Then what?"

I noticed other new things around the room. New Persian rug. A crystal vase. And Elizabeth had a manicure. She never gets one of those. Claims she doesn't want to spend any money on herself . . . it all has to go for the kids. And then I saw what looked like a policeman's nightstick in the corner, but she was in such a hurry to get rid of me, I didn't have time to ask. I took the kids, but on my way down the drive, I looked into the ga-rage. Jackal . . . there was a new Mercedes sitting in place of her old Honda . . . the car she said she'd never give up!"

"Okay," I said, gettin' up. "What do we have? Costumes, new stuff, a mystery company, and a sweaty dame. That's pretty stan-dard stuff for an in-home call-girl operation."

"Oh God!"

"Easy now!" I put a hand on Lucky's shoulder. "Don't pop the clutch just yet. The thing that gets me is the dumbbell."

"I'm afraid to ask," Spencer said. "But I swear I didn't see anyone else going into the house, front or back . . . and I was staked out for days."

"I'll bet," I said. "Ah, the stakeout. Doughnuts and sudoku. Fightin' to stay awake. Callin' your gal for a little pettin'-via-phone . . ."

"Spinelli!" Spencer snapped.

"Right here! Baked beans . . . I'm on it!"

"I thought I could get to the bottom of this by myself. But I haven't slept for the last three nights. I'm a detective, for heaven's sake, and I can't bring myself to investigate my own . . ."

"That's why I'm here, friend. I'll find out what's goin' on and I'll break it to you gently. Deal?"

"Deal."

———————

The next night, I had a little stakeout of my own. Spencer was a fine detective, one of the PCPD's best. But he wasn't me. I had a pretty good feeling he'd missed something or someone somewhere along the line.

I had two chili burgers with extra pickles, two cans of orange Nehi, a box of doughnut holes, and a thermos of coffee. The Ford Echo was tucked away in a nice little spot where I could keep an eye on both the front door and the back walkway of Elizabeth's house. The night vision goggles were on, the black Lycra was fittin' nicely, and Anne and Nancy Wilson were callin' me a barracuda on the eight-track, soft and sexy.

The hours ticked away and . . . nothin'.

I stayed well into the next day. Lucky Spencer came to pick up the kids and take 'em to school. With my high-powered binocs, I saw lips moving at the front door and thought I made out something like Lucky sayin', "I'll keep them overnight" and Elizabeth saying, "Fine. Bring them home tomorrow after school." Interesting: Now the kids were gone. Made me wonder how she pulled off whatever it was she was up to with the kids at home. Maybe she was only up to her hijinks when the coast was clear.

Elizabeth got a delivery around 10:00 AM, but this time, whatever it was needed a dolly and two men. She answered the door and I could tell, she looked fine. Nicely put together (and this was a woman who put most other dames to shame . . . at any age). At 11:40, she came out for the mail, only now she looked kinda flushed. She was wearin' a bathrobe over . . . dark slacks and policeman's lace-ups. At 12:10, another delivery truck pulled into her driveway. This one was from M. Henry's Fine Appliances. The two palookas in the cab jumped out and, quick as Vegas takes your money, unloaded a new refrigerator into the home of Elizabeth "No Tricks Here" Spencer.

At 1:00, the garage door opened up, and out she rolled in a fire-engine red Mercedes coupe. Her nurse's cap was on tight, and she headed off for her shift at General Hospital; one of the finest needle-stickers that place has ever seen, now or whenever. She was on until midnight. I knew; I checked.

I popped another doughnut hole and waited until the sky got dark. Fortunately, there was no moon, and I slipped out of the Echo like an oyster out of a shot glass.

Suddenly, Spinelli stopped talking. I was so tired that it took me a second to realize that the buzzing in my ears was now only the sound of the bare fluorescents overhead. I looked up from my notepad and saw Spinelli, white as a sheet, staring at something over my shoulder. Another time I would have turned to look myself, but his eyes, growing larger each second, froze me as I sat. *Something* was approaching.

"Is it bad?" I asked softly.

Spinelli nodded slightly. I saw his gaze go high.

"Big?" I whispered.

He nodded again . . . more of a shudder. All at once, I was aware of someone standing next to the booth. I turned slowly and stared at the faded denim surrounding a thigh the size of Texas. I forced myself to look up . . . and up.

"I've been waiting a long time, lady. You have something of mine."

Big Dave. The biggest of the bikers from the bar Alexis and I had stumbled upon on our "Lucy and Ethel" road trip a few years back. Big Dave (Cates was the last name, I'd come to know) had taken a shine to Alexis and, in a moment of panic, I'd taken his gun. We'd also made off with a couple of hunting jackets belonging to Big Dave and his friend, Gunnar, and those we'd returned, but somehow I had never gotten around to sending back his weapon.

"Hi," I wheezed.

"Yeah, hi. I rode in this morning. I was gonna drop by your office tomorrow. Nice coincidence, huh?"

"You bet."

"You have it?"

I nodded.

"On you?"

I nodded again and reached into my purse. I pulled out the standard barrel .38 Special like it was a spitting cobra. Like I hadn't had it in my purse(s . . . including the occasional clutch) for the last two years, give or take. Like I hadn't been packing. I handed it to Big Dave, who stuck it down the front of his jeans. Then he looked at me like he was expecting me to levitate.

"Oh!" I said after a second. Then I took five bullets (I had used a sixth to shoot out an overhead lamp at the biker bar) out of my makeup bag and put them into his pork-shoulder-sized hand.

"Thanks," said Big Dave. "Later."

He strolled out of the diner. Then I turned to Spinelli, who apparently was saying something to me.

"Huh?"

"The Brusque Lady must breathe sometime soon. Other-wise I fear an aneurysm. Possibly a stroke."

"Oh. Oh, yes . . . of course. Uh. Huh. Yes . . . where were we? Wow. Okay . . . you were just getting out of your car like an oyster. Go on."

My skeleton key got me in the back door. I looked around for an alarm system . . . nothin'. This dame was a trustin' sort; it figured: all anyone needed to do was take one look at the mooks, joes, and shmoes she'd been with to know that she was a trout waitin' for a worm . . . so to speak. Too bad, 'cause she was a looker all right. Just needed some knight in a shinin' tin can to treat her right.

I was on my way to the livin' room, where Lucky said he'd seen a lot of evidence of her shenanigans, when my night-vision specs caught sight of something strange in the back room. More than just something . . . a whole lotta things.

As luck would have it, first room I came to, I hit the mother lode.

There was no need to flip on the light; I didn't want to alert the neighbors anyway. I could see everything in front of me just fine.

Elizabeth Spencer had a room full of exercise equipment that would have put any local gymnasium outta business. Weights and machines that, together, musta set her back at least two hundred Franklins times ten.

Then I saw the copper's nightstick that Lucky had mentioned lyin' over by a closet, next to a fire extinguisher, a fire hose, a little kid's school desk, a fryin' pan, a statue of the Virgin Mary, and a feather duster. That's when I looked in the closet.

There was a full copper's uniform that looked fairly jake, an entire Port Charles Fire Department getup, a Hazmat suit, a teacher's dress (complete with ruler and school name tag), a nun's habit, a mother-type outfit (sweater set and pearls),

and a French maid's costume. Each outfit had a mask to go
with it, and everything had a little logo on a front pocket:
"AI."

I looked closely at the Gorgeous George equipment: There
was a tiny "AI" somewhere on each piece. I'd seen the logo
before . . . but where, dammit! I didn't know what to make
of anything.

I turned around and saw the camera.

And the computer.

I walked across the room and flipped on the Mac. After
that, it didn't take long to put all the pieces of this crazy puzzle
together. Pictures of Elizabeth in a policeman's uniform
doin' crunches. There she was, dressed like a schoolteacher,
curlin' her biceps with free weights; as a fireman on the row-
ing machine; and as a nun . . . doing jumpin' jacks. Sure,
she was masked, but I didn't have to be a private dick to know
it was her.

I hit the link that said "videos." And I watched . . . as long
as I could.

You know the sayin' "You can't un-ring a bell"? Well, I
had a whole damn cathedral goin' off in my head. Elizabeth
Spencer, in a Hazmat suit, expertly demonstratin' the
proper way to work a quad. Elizabeth Spencer, dressed like
a nun, yellin' about rotator cuffs. Elizabeth Spencer, sittin'
on the Bowflex, just as pretty as a new bride, with a fryin' pan
in her hand, screamin', "Move maggots! Ten more reps, you
sorry sons-of-a-British-bulldog!"

Only she didn't say, "British bulldog." I ain't gonna repeat
what she said, because I wanna remember her like she was . . .
before.

Suddenly, messages started to appear in her e-mail: "Mistress! You're home! I am ready for my workout"; "Guess you
didn't have to go to work tonight . . . Can't wait to start
breathing . . . hard"; and "My muscles are on fire and I need
you to put it out! Hint: fireman's suit, please!"

Elizabeth Webber Spencer had a side business, all right, and I smacked myself in the noggin for not realizing it earlier; the clues had been right under my nose.

She was an abdominatrix.

Fully clothed and fully in control, admonishin' her clientele via the streamin' Internet to "feel the burn," "stretch it out," and "step and reach and step and reach!" And all of it was under the banner of a completely legit if somewhat unsavory company: Abdomination Industries. The name was right at the top of her computer screen. I knew I'd seen it before: I'd run across the company when I was tryin' to find my mother . . . but that's another story. It catered to lonely men (and sometimes women) who just couldn't get themselves to a gym and needed a goose from someone they respected: a person of authority. If their "mother" told them, in the privacy of their own home, to get the lead out . . . that was all they needed. Nuns, teachers, coppers, firemen, were pretty obvious. And I guess a Hazmat guy . . . well, if he told you vamoose from someplace, you'd go, right?

But none if it was my cross to bear. All I knew was that Elizabeth had a part-time job, whippin' the rotund, slightly or otherwise, into shape, while wearin' crazy getups, via the Net. She was an online abdominatrix.

And "AI" was her pimp.

I suddenly realized that the last time I'd seen Elizabeth, she'd reminded me of Burt Lancaster in *Trapeze!* She was in the best shape of her life.

I was just about to start browsin' through older files tryin' to get a bead on when she'd first started her trip into crazytown, when I heard the familiar click of a heater . . . a Lady Smith & Wesson if my ears told me right . . . behind me.

"Whoever you are, you have three seconds to turn around . . . keep your hands high."

"I don't need three, doll," I said. "Two will be fine."

Elizabeth flipped on a light.

"Who are you?" she asked.

I went to pull my mask off my face.

"Keep your hands up!"

"Then how can I show you who I am?"

"All right, but go slow."

"Bet you don't say that to all the guys," I said, liftin' off the Lycra.

"Spinelli? What are you doing here?"

"I could ask you the same thing," I said, lookin' around the room. " 'Cept I think I already know."

"So what? So, you've come here to judge me? Who sent you? How did you find out?"

"Whoa . . . slow down, sister," I said. "Why don't you do us both a favor and put down the rod, all right? Wouldn't want it goin' off accidentally, would we? Someone might get hurt."

"WHY ARE YOU HERE?"

"Easy . . ."

"This is none of your business," she said, lowerin' the gun a little. "It's none of anyone's business."

"That's right," I said, taking a step closer. Wrong move. Elizabeth brought the gun back up, but fast.

"I'm not doing anything wrong . . ." she said, her eyes becomin' like a coupla swimmin' pools.

"I know," I said. Then I saw her hand startin' to shake, so I took a chance and edged a little closer.

"Stay where you are! I'm not doing . . . I'm not doing anything . . . wrong!" she yelled, but she was shakin' so badly that I grabbed the roscoe out of her hand just like I took little Chippy Dox's ice cream cone back in the third grade. Elizabeth tried to fight me, but I pinned her hands behind her. Then she collapsed, sobbin', into a heap.

"Whoa there, doll," I said catchin' her and sittin' her down on the Bowflex. I talked real soft and slow. "No one said you was doin' anything wrong. You've just started living the high life, is what, and Lucky was gettin' suspicious. He saw all the bright, shiny objects you've got now and he was nervous, see? Nervous about where you might be gettin' 'em, and from whom."

"Lucky's out of my life," she said, then she really turned on the Niagara. She was like some of those pansies online when Mistress Elizabeth would tell 'em they only had five more reps, when really it was more like twenty. I hadn't seen it for myself . . . but I knew the deal.

"Come on, kid. He may be gone, but he's not gone. You know it and he knows it. He still loves you . . . always will. That's why this little side business of yours is such a big deal."

Her eyes went real wide.

"Does he know what I'm doing?!"

"Nope. He asked me to find out . . . and then tell him."

"Oh God . . . please don't, Spinelli. I'll do anything. It would break his heart . . . and his spirit, to know that I've been exercising behind his back. And to know that I've been dominating others to get them into shape. Lucky couldn't get me to run up the stairs. Exercise was just too much trouble for me. I let myself go a little bit and I think it's one of the things that broke us apart. If he finds out that I'm actually taking care of myself just to make money, it will kill him. I just thought I could give the kids . . . a . . . a better life, you know? Oh, God . . . what was I thinking?!"

"Maybe that's just the point," I said, stashin' the heater in my utility belt. "Maybe you wasn't thinkin'. Not with the fully actualized, conscious part of your noggin, that is. Seems to me, you was lettin' your superego control your ego, which then started takin' orders directly from your id. That's how you got yourself in such a goulash."

"You know the works of Carl Jung?" she asked.

"Sorry to disappoint you, doll," I replied, tryin' not to laugh, "but that was pure Siggy Freud. Of course, if you got a dream or two that needs explainin', I can handle the horse, so to speak. The point is, you have to figure out what's inside of you that makes you think this kinda prancin' about, lookin' like a copper or schoolmarm, is jake, see? It's fine for some, but not for the Maternal One. You got class, see? You're a contender. You're a somebody. You need to get that through your pretty little thinker."

She was silent for a bit. I get antsy when dames get silent.

"I think I need to talk to somebody," Elizabeth said finally, snifflin'.

"Hey, you been talkin' to somebody."

"No, I mean . . . for a long time. This is going to take more than a chat . . . even with you, Spinelli. But you opened the door for me. Now I have to find the strength to push it all the way open. I'm going back to Shadybrook. I'll tell Lucky to keep the kids until I get back. Will you . . . will you check in on them every once in a while?"

" 'Course."

"And I have to let Abdomination Industries know that . . . that I am officially out of business."

"Why don't you let me take care of that," I said. "I've got a coupla things to say to a company that does a vulture tap-dance on the souls of decent folks. I can get you offline in a jiff."

"Thank you," she said, gettin' off the Bowflex. "I think I'd like to go pack now."

"I'll drive you to Shadybrook, m'lady. If you'll let me."

"That would be lovely, sir knight," Elizabeth said.

"And we can take your car."

She was almost out of the room, but she turned, a big grin on her face.

"Would you like to keep the Mercedes until I get back? I've paid the first three months of the lease. It's the least I can do."

"Only because you're twistin' my arm. Hey, lemme ask you somethin'," I said. "I thought you were supposed to be at work until midnight. What made you come back?"

"I was invited to a costume party several weeks ago and I didn't have anything to wear. So I had borrowed a French maid's outfit from one of the other nurses; I left today without putting it in the car. I needed to return it."

"Nothin' to wear? You got a closet full of getups!"

"I didn't want to take a chance on being recognized, Spinelli. You have no idea the people in Port Charles that have availed themselves of my services. People in very high places."

"Do I know some of them?"

"Can't tell you."

I followed her into the living room and watched her walk up the stairs.

"How about a hint?"

"Nope!"

"Just one?"

"NO!" she said . . . but she was laughin'. The dame was gonna be fine.

"Is one of them a burly torpedo with blue eyes? Or a swarthy Italian with dimples? Hey! I know . . . fast Eddie Quartermaine! Elizabeth? Elizabeth . . . ?"

I heard her gigglin' down the hallway. Yeah, this dame was gonna be just fine.

13

Damian Spinelli

and . . . There Are Those Who Enjoy It Uncomfortably Warm

It's never a good thing when a "family" moves into the neighborhood. Especially, if another family or two are already there.

Sonny "Have I Met Your Daughter?" Corinthos and Ant'ny Zacchara were finally on a toleratin' basis, even more so since old man Z had been driven out of Russia and had come back to Port Charlie with his tail between his legs. Ant'ny knew better than to pretend his operation was still in full swing, so he'd been layin' low for a while, slowly puttin' the pieces back together. But he was still a force.

Then . . . seems like it was overnight . . . we all got someone new to contend with.

The Cannalzettis.

Basically, they were small time . . . or so we thought. Thugs and petty thieves. Runnin' some numbers, stolen car parts. Nickel-and-dime stuff. Stone Cold Morgan, Corinthos's torpedo and number-one ace-in-the-hole . . .

"**What did you just call Jason?**" I asked, lifting my head up off the formica. It was heading toward 4:00 A.M. and by God if I wasn't tired.

"An ace-in-the-hole," Spinelli answered. "Why? Is there something amiss?"

"No. Not at all," I said. "I just thought I heard you say . . . something . . . Never mind. Proceed."

. . . thought the Cannalzettis would figure out sooner or later that Sonny Corinthos had the town in his pocket. When they did, they'd pick up and amscray. And Stone Cold ain't usually wrong.

Usually.

Morgan came home to the penthouse one evening, lookin' more like a basset hound than usual.

"**If that's even possible,**" I laughed.

He was down in the mouth about Sam McCall, his best gal . . . when he wasn't keepin' company with Elizabeth Spencer; but that's another story.

"**Ain't that the truth.**"

I told him what he needed was some fresh air and a scotch, neat. Morgan agreed and said we should take a walk down by the harbor; Corinthos had a shipment comin' in and his blues were as good an excuse as any to make sure everything was goin' smooth. Fifteen minutes later, I had sea-salt cakin' my ears, and Morgan was spillin' his guts as we watched the longshoremen unload Sonny's tanker.

Seems Sam hadn't been returnin' Morgan's phone call for a day or two. He'd gone by her place; her car was in the garage, but the lights weren't on and the mail was pilin' up. She'd skipped out, he was certain.

"And it's all my fault."

"How d'ya figure?" I asked.

"Because she wants to get married so badly and I just can't bring myself to ask her. I keep wondering what the rest of my life would be like if I had to be responsible to anyone other than Sonny, you know? What it would be like to wake up and see that beautiful face lying next to me, then realize that I'd have to be careful and cautious in everything I did from the time I got up until I went to bed."

"Well, when you put it like that . . . it don't sound like your kinda life," I said. "But you're forgettin' one thing. Sam is like . . . well, like you . . . only stacked. She's loyal and tough and smart and fearless. She's everything you . . . *you* . . . could want in a dame. And dames like her don't come along that often. And you ain't gettin' any younger."

"Thanks."

"I'm just sayin'," I said.

"I'm still not sure," Morgan said. "But I'd like to know where she is."

I opened my mouth to say that, if it was only a matter of a little legwork, I was already on it . . . when . . .

Kaboom!

We heard the first explosion and hit the deck. It came from a pier two down from the Corinthos ship. A second blast followed. We were only down for a moment, but when we got up, the longshoremen had disappeared. We hightailed it to the burning boat. And what to our wonderin' eyes should appear but two rival gangs, one far and one near.

The ship belonged to Zacchara and his men, some of them high in the organization . . . we knew the faces, had run up the pier from the burnin' hunk of steel. Now they were trapped, caught in a group and surrounded by at least six mooks with tommy-guns. Most of them I'd never laid eyes on, but Morgan knew instantly.

"Cannalzettis," he said.

"You sure?"

"Yep. Look."

Walkin' slowly from the shadows was a man in a camel-colored vicuña coat. And this face I *had* seen: newspapers and wanted posters. But not for a long time. This face was older than I remembered.

Don Enzio Cannalzetti.

The flames were dyin' down just a bit and the wind carried his words to the crates where Morgan and I were hidin'.

"Waste 'em all."

The sound of tommy-guns ain't one you forget, not no way, not no how. When the *rat-a-tat-tat* had finished, all of the Zacchara men lay in a heap and there was blood drippin' into the water. I knew we had to stay put for as long as possible. But Morgan decided that while the Cannalzettis were goin' through the pockets of the dead was the best time to vamoose. Naturally, I wasn't a bit surprised when he accidentally knocked over a crate. All heads turned, and we were fingered like the only man in an all female lineup.

"It's Morgan!" shouted Enzio C. "And the scrawny fella! After 'em!"

I've never run so fast, and Stone Cold was outstrippin' me by a good six, seven feet. It's like we'd been born in Kenya; I thought my Buster Browns were gonna fly off my feet, I was movin' so quick. We ran past the car and hid in a Dumpster about a quarter mile away from the water. We waited a good ten minutes, and I thought we'd lost them when suddenly I heard two of Cannalzetti's men not three feet away, talkin' how even if they didn't find us that night . . . they knew where we lived. The word was gonna spread: Morgan and Spinelli were dead men.

The contract on both of us would be out by midnight.

———————

"Spinelli, this will never work!" Morgan whispered as we walked down the train platform.

"Watch it," I said outta the side of my mouth. "My name's Danielle, remember? We're incognito, got it?"

"We're gonna get made!"

"Nonsense," I said, gigglin' and flippin' my fan at him, then yankin' him over to the side of the train. "Look, Morgan . . . this was the best idea I could come up with and it may just save our asses. I'm the only one in Port Charlie who knows you play the piccolo and I haven't brought out my trombone in years, so folks may have forgotten. It's just lucky I happen to have a friend in a musical booking agency. Now this setup is perfect: Masone's Mello Musicales on their way to Florida for a two-week gig. A band that just happened to need some extra wind, and that's us, see? We lay low until Sonny can take care of this Cannalzetti mess you got us into, and I can lose this girdle. Then we come home."

"You're wearing a girdle?" Morgan asked.

"Jeez, never mind that!" I said. "Just try and act natural."

The whistle blew and we joined a group carryin' instruments at the far end of the platform. Sandra, the band leader, was callin' out names.

"Danielle Spinkler?"

"Here," I chirped.

"Jas . . . ?"

"Here," Morgan said.

"There you are," she said, handin' over our tickets. "Glad you could fill in at the last minute. I just have three rules: no booze, no cards, and . . . say it with me, the rest of you . . ."

". . . be punctual!" they all called out.

"Speaking of which," Sandra said, "where's the other new kid? Sam? Sam McConnolly? McConnolly?"

"Here!" came a breathless voice from way down the platform. We all turned to see Sam McCall . . . McConnolly? . . . carryin' a tiny little bongo drum and walkin' toward us in a

way I thought had gone out with pencil skirts. She was sportin'
a platinum blonde wig and a deep red shade of lipstick, but
there was no mistakin' her. I looked at Morgan, his mouth
dropped open like a clown gettin'-electro-shocked. Then I
looked back at Sam. Neither of us had seen anyone move that
way in real life.

"Are you suddenly hungry?" I asked him, not taking my
eyes off "the new kid."

"Uh-huh."

"For Jell-O?"

"Uh-huh."

"I'm here!" she called again. "Don't leave without me!"

She brushed past both of us, not knowin' who we were.

"Sorry," Sam said to Sandra. "It won't happen again, I
promise."

"Better not," Sandra said. "You might be cute as a front-
man, lady, but bongo-playin' singers are a dime a dozen and
don't you forget it. We coulda left you here and found one tonight in Cape Coral, so you be on your best behavior, got it?"

"Got it," Sam said. Then she looked at Morgan and me
and smiled real big. Not like she'd made us, just like we were
all besty-westy friends.

'Round midnight, the band had a jam session in the club
car as we cruised into Ol' Virginny. Sandra was wavin' her
baton, I was playin' sweet on the slide trombone, and Morgan
was gettin' the rust outta his piccolo. Sam was beatin' the bongo
like she was backin' up a '60s poet in the East Village. Didn't
make any difference that the rest of us was playin' Duke
Ellington . . . Morgan and I just liked watchin' her. Suddenly she shifted a little and a heater the size of a Packard fell
onto the floor. Sandra stopped everything and picked up the
piece, her face turnin' all kinds of red.

"I guess I should have made that *four* rules," she said, loomin'
over the band. "No guns! Now whose is this? Speak up!"

Sam was already on thin ice and everyone knew it. If

Sandra found out that the piece was Sam's, we'd be minus one bongo player and Sam would get to see the Virginia country-side, up close. I went to open my mouth, but Morgan pushed me aside.

"It's mine," he said, takin' the rod away from Sandra. "I'm so sorry. I won't let that happen again. I thought I'd put it in my luggage. I didn't know it was actually still on me. It was my father's. I keep it for sentimental reasons. And . . . because . . . well, I'm very popular back home and it comes in handy. You understand, right?"

And then he winked.

And Sandra bit.

"Of course," she said, a little down at not being able to finger Sam. "Just don't let it happen again."

"I promise."

"All right, everyone . . . from the top."

———————————

It was 2:30 in the AM when Sam poked her head between the curtains of our upper berth. I know because I had just asked Morgan for the time; neither of us could sleep in our getups, but we didn't want to take 'em off. *Número uno*, we didn't want to take a chance on somebody seein' us, and *second-o*, they'd been too tough to get into the first time around.

"Hi!" Sam said.

She was wearing a little baby-doll nightie. I recognized it straight off. I'd helped Morgan pick it out for her birthday the year before. Morgan and I pulled the covers tight around our necks.

"Hi there!" I said, with a little wave.

"Hi to you," Morgan said. "I mean . . . hi!"

"Sounds like you're coming down with a cold," Sam said, laughin'. "Good thing I'm the singer, huh?"

"Oh, you bet," Morgan said.

"It does sound like you're getting sick," I said, lookin' at him. "Maybe Sam could rub something on your back!"

"Maybe someone else could rub you out, Danielle!"

"Oh, I wouldn't mind spreading a little vapo-rub," Sam said. "If you think it would help."

"Don't worry about it," Morgan said. "I'll be just fine once I get a little shut-eye."

"Yes, we do need our beauty sleep," I said.

"You both look terrific," Sam said. "In fact, I don't know how you do it. Your faces look just the same as they did this morning!"

"Spackle!" I said.

"Uh-huh."

"Well, listen," she said, lookin' at Morgan. "I just wanted to come by and say thanks for covering for me like that. I've only been with Sandra a few days and already I've done so many things wrong, I've lost count. If she knew the gun was mine, she would have kicked me out for sure and then . . . I don't know what I would've done."

"My pleasure," Morgan said, carefully fishin' the heater out of his getup. "There you are. Safe and sound."

"Thanks . . . I owe you."

"Nonsense," Morgan said. "Consider the matter dropped."

But he didn't drop it.

"If you don't mind my asking . . . what's an adorable little thing like you doing with such a horrid piece . . . I mean . . . roscoe. I mean . . . gun?"

"I use it in my line of work," she said. "Make that past tense. I used it when I was a private dick-ette. That was back home. But I've given it up."

"Home?" I said.

"Port Charles."

"But being a private dick-ette must be so exciting," I said. "Why'd you quit?"

"Oh, the job was fine," Sam said. Then her face fell like a chocolate soufflé. "Well . . . if you must know . . ."

"Yes?!" I said, a little too excited. Morgan shot me a look.

"Oh, I suppose I can tell you . . . after all, we're practically family now!"

"Practically," I said.

"I was in love . . ."

"A man!" I gasped. "I knew it!"

"Danielle, you're not letting her speak. Go ahead . . . doll."

"He's handsome and tall and smart and sexy. He has the most beautiful blue eyes."

"Oh, those blue-eyed ones," I said, lookin' at Morgan. "They're so dangerous. Don't you think so?"

"Not always."

"His eyes are kinda like yours," Sam said, definitely not starin' at me. "Only not as blue and a little closer together."

"He sounds divine," I said. "So what's the trouble?"

"He doesn't love me. Plain and simple. Not enough, anyway. We're perfect together. We know what the other is thinking. We both love the same kind of life. I understand him and he understands me . . . with one exception. I want to get married, you know . . . make that commitment. He doesn't."

"So he'd rather lose you?" I said. "Sounds like he's not that smart, after all."

"Maybe he's just scared," Morgan said, lookin' away.

"He doesn't scare easily, this guy. Anyway, I just couldn't take it anymore. That's why I had to leave. I read an ad for the Mello Musicales and you know the rest."

"I bet he'll come after you," I said.

"He doesn't know where I am," Sam said.

"If he's half the man . . . if he's any kind of man at all, he won't let that stop him," I said.

"Well," Sam said, "I've bothered you enough for one night. Oh, I am so glad you two are here. I feel so comfortable with you both. It's like I've known you forever. Suppose you think I'm silly, huh?"

"Furthest thing from my mind, honey."

"We'll talk later," Morgan said. "You get a good night's sleep."

"Night!" Sam said. Next thing we knew, she was headin' back down the passageway. Morgan stuck his head out to watch her go.

"She's wearing the high heels with the little fur on top. Those drive me nuts. What?"

I was just grinnin' at him.

"What?"

"You are the shmendrick of the century if you let her go, you know that, right?"

"Shut up, Danielle," he said, turnin' away.

"And I'm not even talkin' *this* century!" I said. I was gettin' excited, so I had to drop to a whisper. "Any century. Past, present, and future. You hear me . . . ?"

"Keep it up, and I'm gonna save the Cannalzettis some trouble and kill you myself."

———————

The Cape Coral Ritz was one of those gingerbread joints; looked like someone dumped a giant two-hundred-room wedding cake on the beach. Lot's of "froofy."

On our way up the front steps, we passed a line of geezers, not one of 'em under eighty, rockin' on the veranda and checkin' out the new arrivals. Apparently, this was where millionaires came to die or find new wives. Or both. Morgan got his heel caught on the top step, and I bent over to help him get it loose. Someone wolf-whistled in my direction. I looked up and coulda sworn I saw a real familiar face about ten chairs down, givin' me the once-over. Morgan stood up and looked where I was lookin'.

"Hey," he whispered. "Is that Edward . . . ?"

"Keep it moving," I said.

"What's the holdup?" Sandra called from the front drive. "We have a show in less than two hours, You've got your room keys, now *ándale!*"

"Jeez, it's like we're a couple of lobsters in a tank," Morgan said as we walked past the front desk, turning heads as we climbed the stairwell. "You'd think no one had ever seen a couple of . . ."

"They still haven't," I said.

"Yow-ZA!" came a voice from below. It was a voice I knew well.

"Move!" I said.

Our first show in the grand ballroom was finishin' up nicely. Sam was at the microphone, croonin' the last song, a sweet, up-beat number:

> *Your kisses do things to me;*
> *They make me weak, I can hardly see.*
> *Your kisses do things to me;*
> *You know-o-oh . . . vo-di-o-doh!*

Morgan and I were layin' back to let her voice shine.

"Did you know she could sing?" I asked, sideways.

"Not like that," he answered. "She doesn't even sound that good in the shower."

"Hidden talents, my friend," I said. "Let her get away and I'll take a run at her myself."

"Yeah, well don't look now, but someone's doing a little sprint toward you."

I looked out into the audience and, sure as Maxie's got a bottle of bourbon on her nightstand and thinks fidelity's for suckers, there was Fast Eddie Quartermaine slippin' the maître d' a twenty for a table up front and never takin' his eyes off me. He was holdin' a bunch of roses in his mitt.

"Cripes, what's he doin' here?" I muttered. "He could blow the whole thing!"

"Only if he finds out you're you."

"I ain't gonna let him get that close," I said.

Sam finished her number, Sandra gave a cheerful good-night, and we started packin' up our instruments. I was almost off the bandstand when a hand caught my arm.

"Watch it, buster . . ." I said in a less than feminine voice. "I mean . . . unhand me, sir, or I shall have to call the management!"

"I beg your pardon, miss, but my name is Edward Quartermaine and I just wanted to tell you how much I admire the way you handle that trombone. You have a nice slide."

"Thank you . . . Edward, did you say? Well thanks, Ed. And now, if you'll excuse . . ."

"Might I have the pleasure of your company for a late-night supper aboard my yacht?"

"Your *yacht*?" I said, forgettin' myself. "Your yacht went down in a storm a while back off Farrin's Point!"

"Yes," he said, lookin' all kinds of confused. "But how did you know about that?"

"Uh . . . uh . . . well, it's just that news of that nature gets around. Oh my, yes, it was all over the society . . . yachting columns. Terribly sad. Let's see, what was the name of your ship? That's right, the *Smilin' Lila* . . . I believe."

"Well this is the new yacht: *Lila Smiles Again*."

"Oh, I'll just bet she does," I said.

"Shall we say eleven-thirty? I'll pick you up dockside in the speedboat."

"I'm sorry, but I can't make it tonight. Thanks anyway."

"Tomorrow, then?" Eddie asked.

"You can try!"

I got back to the room I shared with Morgan and found a note.

Walking on the beach with Sam

I chuckled to myself. Morgan might blow it . . . our cover and the opportunity. Then again, maybe not. All night I'd been watchin' him watchin' her. Something was happenin', all right, and I knew he was lookin' at Sam with a . . . fresh eye. When he got back, he was quiet for a bit. Then he started talkin'. If I was hearin' right, their conversation went somethin' like this:

Sam: Oh, I just love being down here . . . the sand, the ocean, the palm trees!

Jas: They've got beaches where you come from, don't they?

Sam: It's not the same. They're cold and kinda rocky, and nobody wants to walk with me.

Jas: Well, you'll pardon my saying so, but you don't seem like the kind of a girl that would be interested in moonlight walks and all that romance stuff.

Sam: I know. That's the trouble when you're a private dick-ette and have to carry a gun. Dressing like hookers and drug addicts. Being held hostage and nearly blown up. And when you have a past like mine . . . real rough, you know what I mean?

Jas: Mmmmm.

Sam: No one thinks you have a feminine side.

Jas: Like your guy back home?

Sam: Yeah. But that's one of the things I thought he loved most about me. The rough and tumble. I was able to hang

with him, not drag him down on various jobs we had. I
was his equal in many ways.

Jas: But maybe he didn't want that. Well, not all the time
anyway. Maybe he wanted a little perfume and lace every
once in a while.

Sam: If he did, I never knew about it.

Jas: Well your guy may not have realized it until now . . .
with you being MIA and all.

Sam: He's not my guy. I sure wish he was. But I'm thinking
now that I have to let him go. Not just physically, not just
by running away, but here (she pointed to her heart), you
know?

Jas: It . . . it would be a shame if you did that.

Sam: I have to . . . for me. I have to . . . learn . . . not to
love him.

Jas: Well . . . some guys don't come around as fast as
others, but if you slip away, he'll regret it. He's probably
up in . . . where is it, again?

Sam: Port Charles.

Jas: Right. Well he's probably up in Port Charles, realizing
you're the best thing that ever happened to him. As they
say, you don't know what you've got till it's gone, right?

Sam: I suppose. But I'm afraid it's too late for me. Thanks
anyway. You sure are smart.

Jas: Oh, I wouldn't say that . . . not by a long shot. In fact,
sometimes I can be pretty dense.

Sam: You know what? I don't know anything about you!

Jas: Nothing much to tell. Just me and my piccolo. Sche-nectady Conservatory for a few years. Some time in Europe. Boring, boring.

Sam: Doesn't sound boring at all. Sounds exciting! Hey, you know what else sounds exciting? A skinny-dip! C'mon!

(*Here, she lost her dress and . . . everything . . . and headed into the water*)

Jas: Oh! My, my . . . look at you in your . . .

Sam: The water's great!

Jas: Heh heh . . . no, I don't think it's for me. I just washed my . . . hair. But you paddle around all you want. I'll just sit here and watch . . . and drool.

Sam: What?

Jas: I said . . . I'm cool! I mean I'm fine. The night air and that cold water . . . I might catch a chill! Take your time, I'll be right here.

———

"From what you're tellin' me, Morgan, you left Sam at her door an hour ago and you just got back here now. What were you doin' in between?"

"I was too worked up to sleep," he said, pullin' off his getup. "Sam came out of the water and I knew I was gonna be up all night. I've never seen her like that before, y'know, Spi-nelli? And I'm not talking about the outside . . . I mean on the inside. She was vulnerable and sweet and kinda shy. It got me. I walked around for a bit, then I asked the desk clerk if he would mind opening the gift shop so I could buy some bicar-bonate and some Sleep-eze."

"Sounds like love has found Andy Hardy."

"Shut up," Morgan said, floppin' down on his bed. "God, Spinelli . . . what if you're right?"

"Yeah," I said. "Yeah, it would be horrible. Terrible. Jeez . . . you might even be happy."

The next coupla days went real smooth. I mean smooth for two "musicales" that needed a shave before each show and kept belchin' in public. Swimmin', volleyball, and gettin' tanned. Morgan and Sam were becomin' thick as thieves; Sam was gettin' a little more depressed about "the guy back home" every day (although Morgan said she was tryin' like hell to hide it). Eddie Q kept followin' me around like a spaniel. I wondered why he hadn't recognized Sam, then I realized her blonde wig and big . . . voice were too much for even Fast Eddie to see through. Guy was gettin' old.

A day later, Eddie had cornered me in the hotel cafe while I was eatin' a bologna and Muenster with coleslaw and honey-mustard dressing on matzoh. He told me the reason he was down in Florida was to find a new wife and start another family, 'cuz he was gonna disown the "miserable spawn I have now." I decided this story was too good to pass on and I said yes to Eddie's invite for a late supper that night on the *Lila Smiles Again*.

"Terrific," he grinned, loosenin' his dentures. "I'll pick you up right after the show!"

Later I met Morgan in the lobby and we started up the stairs to change into our show outfits, when who should be comin' down from the second floor but Berto and Lorenzo Cannalzetti, Enzio's sons and top men.

"Let's take the elevator," I suggested.

"Good idea."

We turned around just as the Don himself strolled through the lobby with two torpedoes by his side. Morgan and I just stood stock-still and looked up at the floor counter. Me, I said a little prayer.

They huddled together, waitin' for the lift. Morgan and I were trapped. One of the sons had news, I could tell, but the others motioned for him to keep mum. The elevator doors opened and the seven of us crammed inside, makin' eight, with the operator.

"Whaddya got?" said Enzio.

"They're here, all right," said Berto. "Room four-sixteen. We just came from there, but they're out."

"Are you certain?" the Don said. "I don't want to have made this trip for nothing."

"Papa, we have the proof," Lorenzo said. "Morgan bought some bicarbonate and sleeping pills at the gift shop two days ago. And he used his credit card. We traced it here . . . and the desk clerk says their room has been occupied since then."

Outta the corner of my eye, I saw Morgan's eyes go wide, then close in what I figured was complete embarrassment; but that didn't keep me from givin' him an elbow in the ribs.

"Oooof!" he gasped.

Stupid of him, more stupid of me . . . now we was noticed. And boy, did they look. Gotta give 'em credit, at least they took off their hats.

"Pardon me, miss," said Berto to me. "But haven't I seen you someplace before?"

"Who, me?" I said, pretendin' to dab at my lipstick. "Oh no, I don't think so."

"Yeah, don't we know you two from someplace?" asked Lorenzo.

"I'm sure you've acquainted yourself with any number of personages, my good man . . . but they were not we . . . us . . . we two," I replied.

"They look familiar to me too, boss," said one of the torpedoes.

"What's your name, toots?" asked Enzio.

"Our names are none of your beeswax," said Morgan.

"I was only askin' because I thought you might like to have a little supper . . . ?"

Just then, the elevator slammed to a stop, then shook three times like a cocktail shaker . . . Morgan and I were the hooch, and the Cannalzettis were the ice.

"Sorry about that, folks," said the operator. "This old girl's been acting up lately. They're supposed to fix her sometime tonight. Just give it a sec . . . she usually starts right up."

And, presto-change-o, the elevator started movin' again with all of us inside tryin' to adjust our hats and whatnot. I was tryin' to straighten my seams. Morgan didn't realize that he'd dropped the room key.

"Fourth floor," said the operator.

"This is us," I said, inchin' past Berto. "Excuse me. Pardon me."

"Goodnight," Morgan said, startin' down the hall with me.

"Hold up a moment," said the Don. "I think you dropped this."

Morgan froze. We turned, and Enzio was holdin' the room key. Morgan gave a little smile and walked back to get it.

"Thanks," he said. But as Enzio was handin' over the key, he glanced down at the number.

"Four-sixteen!" he yelled.

"I knew we'd seen 'em before!" shouted Lorenzo.

"It's Morgan and the scrawny one!" yelled a torpedo.

"Get 'em!" said the Don, as everybody drew their guns.

Morgan slammed shut the elevator doors fast, and we high-tailed it down to our room. But even as we bolted the door, we could hear the whole gang runnin' back down the main stairs.

"Out the window!" I kinda whispered . . . and kinda screamed.

"Where's my piccolo?" Morgan said, rummagin' through the room.

"Forget the . . . !"

"My mother gave me that piccolo, and I'm not leaving without it!"

Enzio's torpedoes were now throwin' themselves against the door. Finally, Morgan found the piccolo, and ten seconds later, we were shimmyin' down the drainpipe to the third floor. We found an open window just as the torpedoes stuck their heads outta our room.

"Third floor! They're on the third floor!"

We ran down the stairs, crashin' into other guests, until we hit the lobby. I could hear Sandra's voice comin' from the ballroom; she was just welcoming the audience and probably wonderin' where we were. For the next two hours we covered the entire hotel and most of the grounds. We managed to lose 'em for a good hour while we sat on the roof weighin' our options, but Lorenzo spotted us from the pool and gave a shout. Lucky for us . . . they coulda snuck up on us from behind and sent us flyin'. We scuttled over the old Spanish tiles, down another drainpipe, then back into the lobby. Suddenly, Morgan took a detour into the ballroom. I followed and found him standin' like a statue . . . just listenin' to Sam. She was singin' somethin' new . . . at least it was new to us. A slow number . . . people shoulda been dancin', but the few couples out on the floor were so stunned by what was comin' outta this gal that they just stood there, arms and hands kinda loose on each other. Sam was tearin' up the joint with a song that started somewhere deep in her gut and was comin' out all molasses, fire, whiskey, and he-ain't-comin'-back-no-more:

> *I'll hide my heart;*
> *I'll keep it locked away.*
> *And I'll find a part;*
> *That's easier to play . . .*
> *For I love you only, darling . . .*
> *And yet you don't love me . . .*

Sam stopped singin', but her voice hovered in the air like a cloud. She hung her head and just sat for a moment. That's when Morgan walked up to her . . . right in front of everyone . . . and kissed her hard.

"Don't cry, Sam," he said, liftin' her face and lookin' into her eyes. "No guy is worth it."

"Huh?" Sam said, in complete shock.

Then we heard Enzio's men right behind us and we took off like bats outta hell.

"Oh!" I heard Sam shout as we headed toward the ballroom doors. I kinda figured she'd figured it out.

We started to run through the lobby for the fourth or fifth time that night, when the Don and Berto walked out right in front of us. Then Lorenzo and the torpedoes came runnin' from the ballroom. They joined each other, makin' a nice little club of mobsters with their heaters trained on us. What they didn't see was that they were all standin' in front of the elevator and a big sign that said:

ELEVATOR CLOSED FOR REPAIRS.
PLEASE TAKE THE STAIRS.

"Well, ain't this nice?" the Don said. "You two just showing up. You know, if you'd made it a little easier on me, I might have made it easier on you."

"Don't be a fool, Cannalzetti," I said. "You shoot us here and you'll have more witnesses than you'll ever be able to silence. Just look around."

The desk clerk dropped behind the counter. Two maids ran up the stairs and the four guests just hangin' around ran out the front door.

"You were sayin'?" the Don said with a smile.

"Thanks!" I called out. "Thanks a lot . . . everybody."

"People here are real cooperative and nice," Enzio said.

"Yeah, pop," said Berto, leanin' real casual against the wall.

"Once we take over Port Charles, let's bring the operation down here!"

Only Berto didn't realize he'd hit the elevator "call" button with his ass. And that's the moment when the doors opened . . . onto a big, dark nothing. And that's the same moment when Sam McCall came runnin' out of the ballroom and into the lobby.

"Jason!" she yelled.

Every head turned to look at the bombshell and, on pure impulse, I ran forward with my arms out. Morgan was right with me . . . 'cuz we think alike when it counts. We shoved the three Cannalzettis and the two torpedoes into the elevator shaft and closed the door.

"Hey, fraidy-cat behind the desk," I said, as Morgan grabbed Sam and we went tearin' out of the lobby. "How many parkin' levels underground?"

"Uh, three . . . and a basement," said the clerk, stickin' his head up.

"Sweet!" I said as I hit the open air.

We didn't stop runnin' till we were at the end of the pier. Fast Eddie was just pullin' up the speedboat.

"I hope you don't mind," I said, climbing in. "I brought a few friends along. I figure if this works out, you might as well meet some of our wedding guests now."

"Oh, I like the way you think," said Eddie, as he gunned the boat toward a sixty-foot yacht half a mile away.

"Sam, I have been such an . . . idiot," Morgan was sayin' in the back.

"I know."

"I love you, you know that."

"I know."

"I'm thinking we should . . . we should . . . give it a try. That is . . . unless you've already learned not to love me."

"Nope," she grinned, then pointed to her heart. "It's still there."

"But I'm still me . . . I can be difficult," Morgan said.

"I know."

"I'll have to stay out late. And be in danger a lot. And . . ."

"That's right," Sam said. "Pour it on . . . talk me out of it."

Next thing I knew they were lip-locked.

"I called my kids back home," Edward said to me, a big grin on his face. "They weren't too happy. In fact, Tracy . . . my daughter . . . said she was going to find my first wife's wedding dress and shred it, just so you couldn't wear it."

"Listen, Edward," I said. "I couldn't wear your wife's dress anyway. We're . . . we're not the same size."

"That's all right."

"Look, Edward . . . I might as well tell you . . . we can't get married."

"Why not?"

"Well, in the first place . . . I'm wearing falsies. This isn't really my figure."

"I'll buy you a boob job."

"I . . . carry a gun. I'm packin'!"

"Sounds exciting," Edward said.

"I have a partner . . . it's another man. And I'm with him all the time."

"It's a big house. He can have his own room."

"Edward . . . I can never have children!"

"We can adopt . . . from Russia!"

"Oh . . . for heaven's sake, Eddie!" I said, whipping off my wig. "I'm a guy!"

"Well, nobody's . . ."

14

Damian Spinelli

and the Case of Dante Falconeri, DOA

As a rule, I don't like walkin' into my private office and findin' someone sittin' in my chair . . . unless it's a dame with a plate of food, a peek-a-boo nightie, or both. Anything else and I have to pull my heater.

I had been workin' late, finishin' up some paperwork on the Elizabeth Spencer case, and I needed a sandwich, so I headed to Rossi's Round-the-Clock for a gefilte fish with provolone on pumpernickel. I'd been outta the office fifteen minutes, tops. So when I found the outer door open and my desk lamp glowin' through the doorway, I reached, nice and easy, for my gun: There were a coupla mystery butt-cheeks on my private patent leather.

Bein' dark outside, I couldn't see who it was clearly; I could only make out a mop of brownish hair that kinda reminded me of both "Joanie" and "Chachi." Suddenly, whoever it was spun the chair around so that it faced the window.

"You're in my office, friend," I said. "You're even in my chair . . . and now you wanna go and turn your back on me? Not polite. Not polite at all."

There was a long pause.

"You ever notice how beautiful this city is, especially at night?"

It only took me a second to recognize the voice; I knew I wasn't gonna be enjoyin' a plate of meatballs or baby-doll pj's anytime soon.

"I don't see much of the city from this window, Dante. Alls I can see is the launderette, the Easy Vegan cafe, and Branco's Butcher Shoppe across the street. Sometimes, Mr. Fairman on the second floor over there decides to give himself a sponge bath, so I get a little treat, but I ain't sure what you're talkin' about, sport," I said, keepin' my finger on the trigger. "What's with makin' like a mole and hidin' in the shadows?"

"There are parts of this city that are gorgeous. And this state . . . hell, the whole country is a paradise, if you choose to see it that way."

"I suppose," I said, realizing that something somewhere was way off. "Why don't you tell me what you're doin' here?"

"We take it all for granted, you know what I mean?" he went on. "I never bothered to appreciate anywhere I've been. Bensonhurst, Manhattan . . . and now here. Such wonders, right in front of me, and I just looked the other way."

I felt the urge to belt him. Only this was one mook who would belt back, and hard. One smack from Detective Falconeri and I'd end up across the street in a plate of vegan slaw.

"You gonna start singin'?" I asked.

"Maybe," he said with a little laugh.

"Well, I have some nickels to throw, so turn around and let's hear it."

He spun away from the window and brought my desk lamp up to his face.

I nearly dropped my gun. Like I've said before, I've seen some things; some I wanna remember, some I'll never forget. Like this. Only thing was, this wasn't the first time.

Dante Falconeri . . . was blue.

"Still want me to sing?" he asked. "Some Billie Holiday . . . or Ma Rainey? A little Bessie Smith, perhaps?"

I sat down across from him.

"Start talkin'," I said. "And I'm guessin' you'd better be quick."

"I just came from General Hospital. They didn't want to let me go, but all the tests said the same thing. My vital signs are slowing down and there's nothing they can do, so I didn't want to spend my last moments staring at monitors and ceiling tiles. They told me I have only . . . only . . ."

"Twenty-four hours to live," I said.

"Yeah," Dante said, after a bit. "How'd you know?"

"You only get twenty-four hours with *Dendrobates azureus*."

I flashed back to my days helping the Colombian government in a few hush-hush raids on their local drug thugs.

"Come ON!" I said. "Look, it's . . . God, it's four thirty-five in the morning, Spinelli, and I can't tell if I have heard one word of truth out of you this entire evening. Now you want me to believe you were working to bust up drug cartels?"

"It would be hard to imagine another circumstance where and when I might have encountered the Blue Poison Dart Frog, Steel-tongued Solicitor. It is native only in certain parts of South America. So, yes, I have sojourned to points south and . . ."

"I'm sorry, Mr. Jackal-hopper. I just don't buy it."

"Then where, pray tell, would I have gotten this?"

Spinelli lifted up his T-shirt just above his "utility belt," and there on his left side was a small, blue patch of skin surrounding a one-inch scar.

"What's that?"

"The drug lords enlisted the help of several native Indians. Their arrows usually don't miss."

"Go on," I said . . . once again caught in his web and too
tired to fight.

The *federales* hoped to score a large amount of uncut fairy-
dust, but the drug lords had made a deal with a local native tribe
and they were waitin' with arrows tipped with poison from the
frogs. Most of my team turned into blueberries right in front
of me. I got hit as I made my escape. I crawled to a local village,
where a kindly native girl sucked all the poison outta me with
a 1978 Hoover, set on reverse, as her grandmother banged on
the generator for electricity. It was only thanks to Miranda
and Abuela Vicky that I was still kickin'. I never saw any of my
men again. But I'd heard they'd all . . .

"Only twenty-four hours," I repeated to Dante. "And then
your heart's gonna stop. When did you get hit?"

"That's just it," Dante said. "I never got hit with anything.
I have no idea how this happened. That's why I came to you,
Spinelli."

"Fine. Here's the sixty-four-thousand-dollar question," I
said. "When did you go blue?"

"About three hours ago. Around eleven, I guess."

"What were you doin' before that?"

"I don't kiss and tell," Dante said. "Let's just say I was with
a lady. Lulu Spencer."

"Uh-huh."

"But Lulu left my place around ten forty-five. That's when
the cab arrived . . ."

"You sent your girlfriend home in a cab?" I asked him.
"You didn't drive her home your own self?"

"I was tired."

"Classy. And before that?"

"Well, before that . . . we . . . we . . ."

"Yeah, I meant before *that*."

"We left the restaurant around nine, I guess. And before
that . . ."

"Hold up," I said. "Which restaurant?"

"O'Connor's."

"The sushi joint on Lexington?"

"Yeah . . . it's Lulu's favorite. We even have two seats reserved just for us at the sushi bar."

"They knew you two were comin' in?"

"Every Wednesday night, seven-thirty. Regular as a Swiss watch."

"And you didn't do nothin' out of the ordinary after that, huh? You didn't bump into anyone? Go into a shop? Buy the lady some Juicy Fruit?"

"Nothing."

"Then it doesn't make any sense. From what I know and what I've seen of this poison, it takes effect fast . . . like that clean-you-out stuff they give you to drink before they stick a scope up your keister."

"I know I'm a goner, Jackal," Dante said. "I've made my peace with that. But I have to know who did this to me and why. Lulu will want those answers too. I have one day to find them."

"Hang on . . . you probably ate around eight o'clock . . . turned blue at eleven. Two AM now . . . so actually you got about eighteen hours."

"Okay, thanks for that update."

I walked over to the office closet and pulled out my spare fedora and a pair of winter gloves.

"Put these on and flip up the collar of your coat. Try to act natural. O'Connor's is closed now, but they're probably still cleanin' up. Let's take a drive."

"Spinelli, if you don't answer that phone, I will. Now let me have it!" I said to him when I saw that now-familiar twitch for the fourth or fifth time.

"Whoever possesses this number is no longer calling, per se; I have received a text," he said, looking down.

"Well, what does it say?"

Even I was curious as to who it was, exactly, that could plague Spinelli to such a degree.

"It only says 'S, need your help. B.' There is nothing further."

"Well, who's 'B'? Not Sonny, not Jason," I mused.

"I am still of the mind that it is a prank and I shall treat it as such. The morning fast approaches and I have little time to finish."

"Lay on, MacJackal-hopper!"

Now I was just getting silly.

The back door of O'Connor's was wide open. We brushed past an old man sweepin' fish parts into a bucket and headed for the manager's office. Dante stayed behind me as best he could. A few sushi chefs were still there and the conversation was pretty wild from what I could tell as I got closer. I turned on the Japanese translator in my noggin and halted outside the office door to listen. Turned out that an unknown chef had worked the bar that night from the hours of 7:15 to 9:30. No one knew his name or where he came from. Everyone was too busy mindin' their own beeswax, slicin' and dicin' pretty for the people. And it just so happened the new guy worked right in front of the seats holding Dante and Lulu's derrieres. The problem with the guy wasn't that he was no good . . . he was *too* good, and the other chefs were runnin' scared. Mystery man could do the work of three people all at once . . . and he brought his own fish in a small industrial cooler . . . the kind they reserve for totin' hearts and kidneys. The manager told the chefs not to worry, that the guy had just been hired for the evening at the request of an investor, and that's the last anyone would ever see of him. Then I heard a sigh of relief from someone and the unmistakable sound of a sake bottle being unscrewed.

I backed Dante into the parkin' lot and got him into the Mercedes . . . the one Elizabeth Spencer had let me borrow. The one I had no intention of givin' back. I had to think.

"What did you find . . . ?"

"Quiet, hear me? I gotta work this out. The chef you had was a substitute. He was only there for one night: tonight. So he had to be the muscle. But you say you never got hit with anything . . . you never felt it. But what if you . . . ?"

I turned to Dante.

"What did you eat tonight?"

"The usual," he answered. "A crab hand roll, two orders of smelt eggs, and cucumber salad."

"That's it?"

"Well, Lulu had me try some sushi that the chef had given her. We didn't even order it. He said it was made special, just for Lulu. But she was feeling kinda flirty so she fed me one of the two pieces. But . . . oh, jeez, now I remember . . . she didn't eat the rest of it 'cause I said it tasted strange. But she didn't want to offend the guy, so she wrapped the second piece in a napkin and I stuck it in my coat pocket."

"The coat you're wearin' . . . now? As you sit your ass in my car? This coat?"

"Yeah!"

I belted him one right in the puss. I couldn't help myself. And I musta looked pretty heated 'cause Dante didn't so much as raise an eyebrow.

"Gimme!"

He fished the napkin out and unwrapped it carefully as I turned on the overhead light. It was a piece of yellowtail sittin' on top of some crumbled rice. Real ordinary.

Unless you counted the blue streak runnin' down the middle.

"You didn't think a piece of blue fish was somethin' strange, huh?" I yelled at him. "Something not to be eaten, maybe? And it comes to you from a guy you've never seen before? Huh?"

"But it didn't come to me, Spinelli."

"You got enemies in this town, pal," I went on. "Just 'cause of who your pop is. That makes you a target anywhe . . . what did you say?"

"The chef didn't give it to me. He gave it to Lulu. It was for her. Oh, God . . . this poison was for her! But why!?"

"Your pop on the outs with Lulu's?"

"No, Luke and Sonny are fine. They're great."

I sat back. Who would want to off Lulu Spencer?

I was quiet a long time; Dante finally spoke up.

"Aren't we gonna at least go back and talk to someone in there?"

"Don't need to, pal," I said. "I learned a lot. And if we start yappin' and that boss gets a peep at you, someone's gonna blab that the hit went wrong and now we're sniffin' around. I wanna keep this on the QT, see?"

"But what did you hear in there? All I heard was Japanese!"

"What I heard was that we have to get to O'Connor's investors list. I happen to know that the owners use the First Port Charles Bank and Trust. Maxie and I used to go to O'Connor's before she wound up in a Hot Night Roll with Yashiro, the rice-maker who was also the accountant before he found himself at the bottom of the harbor—but that's another story. He told her a lot. Probably shouldn't have, but it works in our favor. Let's go."

The skeleton key worked its usual voodoo on the back door of the bank and I took out the security system before Dante was even out of the Benz. He followed me into an office with a huge row of filing cabinets. I grabbed the flashlight off my utility belt and started lookin' for the "O's."

"Why don't you just hack into their computer system?" Dante asked.

"Because this bank works the old-fashioned way . . . they keep hard copies of all their files right here. I could try to hack in, but finding a password might take some time, and this way is a lot . . . well, lookee here," I said, pullin' a file out of a cabinet. "'O'Connor's Sushi and Pie.' Let's take a peep."

I rifled through the scraps of paper until I came up with the original documents for the start of the restaurant. And there, right at the top, was exactly what I needed to see.

"What does that say?" I asked Dante, pointing.

"The Corinthos-Morgan Coffee Company owns forty-one percent of the restaurant. But . . . that makes no sense. I already told you; Sonny and Luke are at peace. There's no reason for my father to put a hit on Lulu."

"No reason that you know of," I said. "Let's go have a chat with your old man."

The light was comin' up in the east as we headed toward Sonny "Mister Sir" Corinthos's compound. There was no an-swer at the gate. I could tell that Dante was startin' to slow down; he only had about twelve hours left. I pretty much or-dered him to wait in the Benz, promisin' him I'd bring his father out. Then I disabled the alarm system and scaled the wall. I came around the back way and got in through the liv-ing room door. I found . . .

"Oh GOD!" I yelled, waking up the waitress as she leaned against the counter. "You mean this was *that* time? That was *this* time? When you found Max and me in Sonny's living room . . . *this* is what you were doing?"

"I can see why Mister Sir keeps you in his employ, Brusque and Bellowing One. Nothing gets by you!"

"Well, now I have to know how this turns out."

Sonny's mouthpiece . . .

"Watch it."

"A thousand pardons. May I continue?"

"Tread carefully."

Sonny's legal eagle and her boy-toy, Max, asleep on the couch. I tried not to wake 'em, but Lady Law had one eye open.

"I thought you might have been Sonny . . . then I realized there was no way you could be. That's why Max and I had indulged ourselves on the softest couch in the world! Never mind. Go on. I won't say another word."

She gave a shout, which woke up the big guy, and ran into another room. Max woulda pounded me, but good, until he finally realized who I was. I explained why I was there, but alls I could get outta him was that his boss was outta town. He wouldn't tell me where, at first, but then he slipped up and said Caracas. I asked him to put me down and then I backed outta the house the same way I came.

Back at the car, I told Dante that Sonny had taken a powder with a side of rice and beans. Dante just looked at me, and outta nowhere, a single tear ran outta his blue eye and down his blue cheek.

"I spoke to my father yesterday morning," he said. "We talked for a good half hour. He asked me how things were going with Lulu, if it was really serious. When I told him it was, he got quiet for a long time. Then he asked what I was doing last night and when I told him we were gonna have sushi, same as every Wednesday, all he said was, 'Enjoy yourself, son.' He never mentioned a word about going out of town."

"For some reason, it looks like your pop wanted Lulu Spencer dead. But I can't figure why."

"That's it, then," he said. "Dead end."

"A lot you know, pal," I shot back, pullin' the Benz out onto the road. "You may be dyin', but we ain't licked yet!"

"Where are you going?"

"We're gonna go see the man."

"The man?"

"Shaddup!"

The only person who knew more 'bout Corinthos's business than he or Stone Cold Morgan or Lady Law Miller was his accountant, Bernie. And we woulda been at Bernie's in short order, but the Mercedes had a flat at Third and Craft streets. We were downtown but it was still too far to walk to Bernie's office, and Dante was gettin' worse by the minute. While we waited for the auto club, I told Dante I'd stand him to a tongue sandwich with lettuce and grape jelly on sourdough at Stacy's Sandwiches right around the corner. He puked a little, but Falconeri was usually as tough as they came . . . tougher actually . . . so I chalked it up to the poison and led the way. We got back to the car around II:OO AM, just as the parkin' cop was puttin' a boot on the back tire . . . the one the auto club had just replaced.

"What gives?" I said to the copper.

She didn't say squat; she just turned on her double-wide patootie and walked away. Now I was mad. I was gonna get Dante to Bernie's, come hell or high water.

I was havin' trouble gettin' a taxi; they'd pull up, take one look at Dante, and peel off. I got us to the bus stop and told Dante to turn his back. I shoved him into a seat and paid the fare before the bus driver knew what hit him. Now, anyone tells you that the Port Charles transit system is a good one, you pop 'em in the mouth. Two hours and five transfers later, we end up in front of Bernie's building. I figure Dante has about six hours left, give or take. Then the elevator breaks down and that eats another two hours while we wait for the fire department and my tongue on sourdough starts comin' back on me. Finally, we get outta the elevator, but we're on the wrong floor. We take the stairs, then we get locked in the stairwell. After an hour of poundin' on the exit door, some dame lookin' for the ladies' room opens it up. We get into Bernie's office and his gal Friday tells us that Bernie won't be back until 5:30 . . . 'cause his tee-off time got pushed. I tell the dame that she's gonna get pushed outta window if she don't get Bernie back here, pronto.

She gets Bernie on the squawk-box and he says he'll be on his way as soon as he gets his balls out of the rough. At 6:30, still no Bernie, 6:45 and Dante is dozin' on a couch in Bernie's private office. Finally, Bernie walks in with some song and dance about takin' the Reverend Guzagnelli for all he's got on the last three holes when he sees Dante, who's now pretty much unconscious. Bernie stops fast, but doesn't say anything for a good twenty seconds . . . like he's considerin' his options. Then he tries to amscray out the door, only we're standin' there . . . me and my pal.

"Easy, easy," I said. "Why you rushin' off, Numbers Man? You just got here. You don't wanna blow when we came such a long way to see you, right? Besides, this place smells like a brewery, real hoppy . . . and I like it. Now, tell the broad with the nail file to clock out and sit down. We're gonna have a chat, see?"

"I don't know anything," Bernie said.

"That's okay," I said, reachin' in my pocket. "You be silent. We'll both be silent."

I started puttin' a silencer on the end of the roscoe.

"Okay . . . I'll talk."

"Let me wake up Blue Boy," I said. "He needs to hear whatever you have to say."

Dante was groggy and weak, but I propped him up against my shoulder and motioned to Bernie with the gun that he should start singin'.

"There's been a big mistake," Bernie said, looking at Dante. "This wasn't supposed to happen . . . not this way."

"Yeah?" I said. "And exactly what way was it supposed to happen? Whatever it is?"

"I have to make a call," Bernie said, headin' for the desk. "Sonny has to know . . ."

"Keep your mitts off that phone!" I said, standin' up. Unfortunately, Dante crashed back down on the couch.

"Ow."

"Sorry, pal," I said, proppin' him back up against my leg. "Bernie, start talkin'. The guy doesn't have much time."

"Well . . . it's very simple, really. Mr. Corinthos is in the middle of negotiations with a . . . business associate in Venezuela. Talks that could enlarge Mr. Corinthos's holdings and territory roughly ten times over. Only he and his associate felt that the deal should be set in stone, if you will. The associate has a daughter, slightly younger than you, Mr. Falconeri. Beautiful, from what I am told. And your father and hers decided that a union of the two families would cement the alliance. But yesterday morning, after talking with you and realizing that your love for Ms. Spencer is as strong as ever, Mr. Corinthos knew he needed to take a drastic measure if you were to be free to marry. So I hired a certain Mr. Yakazuki and arranged to have him placed in your favorite sushi restaurant for the evening. It was to be an . . . accident. A poisoning at a local restaurant by a rogue chef, never to be seen or heard from again. You would grieve for a few months, at the end of which your father would suggest a trip. From which you would return . . . with a wife."

Dante was makin' noises in his throat, like he was a chained dog. He tried to get up and take a swipe at Bernie, but he fell down like the wheat stalks I used to cut when I worked on the farm in Nebraska.

"It wasn't supposed to be you, don't you understand?!" Bernie said.

"Yeah, I don't think that takes the sting out, Numbers," I said.

"Ki . . . kill . . . you," Dante coughed out.

"I'm so sorry," Bernie kept sayin'. "The two pieces of fish

contained just enough poison to kill Ms. Spencer quickly. Dante's extra weight is what's causing his prolonged suffering."

That struck me like a fryin' pan in the face . . . and if you've ever had that happen, you'll know it can be surprising.

"Dante didn't eat both pieces," I said. "He only ate one."

"Only . . . one?" Bernie said as if I wasn't speakin' English. "Then . . . then . . . I think you may be in the clear, my boy."

Dante tensed up beside me.

"Come again?" I said.

"The instructions were exact," Bernie went on, excited now, like a kid rattin' out his sister for smokin' reefer. "One ounce of venom from the Blue Poison Dart Frog placed in a spicy food to hide the taste. It was all based on Ms. Spencer's weight. Señor Vaca was very specific when he told Sonny, and Sonny repeated it to me verbatim."

"Vaca!" I said, takin' a step forward, which pitched Dante onto the floor. Only I didn't notice. I was right there, as heated as Bernie, as if I was spillin' somethin' on my own sis. "You mean Vicente 'the Vengeful' Vaca? That's who Sonny's doin' business with?"

"I am not at liberty to say, but . . . yes."

"That means drugs, Numbers! You know that, right?"

"Not anymore," Bernie said. "They're out of drugs, which is the only reason Mr. Corinthos considered an alliance. They're into stolen fuel cells and oil/water separators, the kind they use for oil spills." He looked at Dante, lyin' on the floor. "You'll be marrying into a very nice, respectable family now, Mr. Falconeri."

"I will . . . kill you," he wheezed. "And my . . . father."

"What's gonna happen to him, Numbers?"

"Señor Vaca was not specific regarding Dante on that issue; none of us thought that Dante would ingest the poison. But he did make reference to a few hits he knew of where the victim had taken too little. They became blue . . . that part you already know . . . and their vital signs slowed. But instead of dying, they went into a coma for about a month and came out again right as rain. Some were still the color of a robin's egg, but not always. Naturally, they had to be hit again."

"Of course," I said.

Bernie looked at Dante.

"You won't have to worry about that, Detective. And I can make arrangements for a day and night nurse if you'd prefer to spend your coma at home."

I didn't want to admit Dante back into General Hospital. There would be a lot of questions that I didn't want to answer. And word would spread.

"Do that," I said, hoistin' Dante to his feet. "And call us a cab, pronto. And do yourself a favor, Numbers. Don't do nothin' to Lulu Spencer. Her father finds out about this, and he will . . . and he'll come after the things Sonny values most. The kids will be fine, 'cause Luke Spencer doesn't off children. Which leaves Sonny's dough. That's where your neck gets stretched. I'd take a vacation for a while, *capice*?"

"Good idea."

I gave Dante's address to Bernie and got Dante back into the repaired elevator.

"Hang in there, pal," I said. "Gonna get you home and you're gonna stay there for a month. When you come outta this, outta the blue . . . no pun intended . . . you're gonna be jake, see? You might look like a cornflower, but you'll be fine where it counts."

On our way down I did some fast thinkin': I'd make up a story for Lulu that would keep her away from Dante's loft for a few days, but that was the best I could hope for. Someone was gonna have to tell her sooner or later. And tellin' Lulu would be the same as tellin' Luke. Once Luke found out that Sonny Corinthos had tried to have his daughter killed so that Dante could marry into the fuel-cell mafia, Luke would be on the next plane to Caracas.

I had to get there before he did.

15

Damian Spinelli

. . . MIA

I opened my eyes and, for a split second, had no idea where on earth I was. The diner waitress was poking me in the shoulder.

"Listen . . . miss . . . the Jackal paid the bill and told me to let you sleep, but it's getting on breakfast time, and if you're not going to order anything else . . . we need the table."

I raised my head off the formica, realizing that my hair had been soaking in the cold grease from my steak and hash browns. I checked my watch: 6:17 AM. I was in the Night Owl, where, presumably, I'd been for the last five or six hours listening to that crazed computer geek and his wild tales. I'd missed my evening with Max: a full body massage and a sexual thrill-ride with the most elastic man in the contiguous United States. I remembered at some point in the evening being almost won over into thinking that Damian Spinelli had actually *done* everything he'd claimed. Now, in the bright light of day, I couldn't believe how gullible I'd been. Trapeze artist. Brain surgeon. Freudian analyst. Trombone player!

The boy must be running around Port Charles at that very moment, crowing about how he'd put one over on Diane

Miller . . . Esq.! I started to see red. I started to see a court date and litigation for wasting my precious time in the future of one little Grasshopper.

Then I saw the tape recorder on the table with the B side recorded to the end. He must have hit "stop" after I'd gone to sleep. And there was my notepad lying beside it, full of scribbles.

"So what's it gonna be?" asked the waitress.

"Uh . . . yeah, I mean yes, I'll be going. Just give me a minute to get my things together. You can have the table in a moment."

"My excitement knows no bounds," she said, walking away with a hip thrust that screamed "I was supposed to be a dancer!"

I started gathering my belongings, stowing my pen and the recorder in my bag. Then I went for the notepad and, underneath the top page, I saw the corner of a folded white piece of paper poking out. I opened it up and there in black and white was a travel itinerary from Port Charles to Caracas, Venezuela, on a plane that had left at 6:05 that morning and a handwritten note:

> *Brusque Lady . . .*
> *I humbly thank you for your indulgence of last evening. You are now in possession of the full details of many of the most important events of my life for the past two years . . . or so. I ask that you guard them well and, in the event of my demise, I would only ask that you put them down on paper and give them to my non-bride, Maxie. Tell her that I loved her and will miss her, as Dorothy said to the Scarecrow, "most of all." I know that you still have your doubts as to the veracity of my ramblings. I have left my travel itinerary as proof. I have no need of it as I have committed it to memory. You may call the airline if you wish and verify that I am on the flight. There is one case whose tale is yet to be told and it is the one on which I find myself now. I shall attempt to send you updates as I am able. Keep a weather eye out for*

*them, if you will. Perhaps we shall meet again . . . if not, it
has been an undiluted pleasure . . .*
   Regards,
   The Jackal

So he was on his way. Of course, it would be a piece of cake for
a technological whiz like this kid to create a phony itinerary . . .
and even have a stooge on the other end of a phone line if I was
foolish enough to check up on him. A piece of damn cake.

And yet . . .

And yet, for reasons I couldn't pinpoint, I suddenly had a
strong feeling that, crazy or not, he was indeed soaring overhead on a puddle-jumper to JFK, and from there he'd be on
an overnight to South America. In fact, I was certain of it. Just
as I became instantly certain that Damian Spinelli, while he
might or might not be channeling Sam Spade, had *done* all
of those things he'd told me, not simply that he believed he'd
done them. But, even *if* it had all played out only in his rather
fevered mind, in many ways it didn't matter anymore. I knew
then and there that the Jackal-hopper was one astonishingly
special individual. And, it was my great gift to know him . . .
no matter how stark raving mad he drove me . . . and everyone else.

As I left the Night Owl, I looked skyward and said a prayer
for the skinny kid in the cargo pants and the fedora, that God
would keep him safe and bring him back home . . . where we
all loved him a hell of a lot more than we realized.

16

Their Man in Caracas . . .

and Los Teques . . . and Esmeralda . . . and Damned Near Every Place in Between

(**Miller note: The following was personally transcribed by me from three microcassettes that arrived within the course of one week after my meeting with Spinelli.**)

The flight to Caracas was a pain in the keister. After clearing customs, which took a few pesos more than I remembered from my days smugglin' rare plants back to the States for medical research, I was in a taxi headin' south through Los Teques, then out into the countryside, north, east, and west of nowhere. I'd learned that Luke Spencer had also headed out of Port Charles just about the same time. Different airline, different stops, but if his information was anything close to mine, he'd soon be in a taxi on the same road. I only hoped he wasn't ahead of me. My final destination: just outside the city of Esmeralda on a southern arm of the Rio Orinoco . . . 'bout six or seven hours away. Or twelve, if the taxi you was ridin' in had bad shocks, like mine. It had taken

almost two hours of cyber-hackin' kung fu to access the
location of Vaca's secret hideout. Before gettin' on the plane,
I had put together the pieces of the Corinthos-Vaca puzzle as
best I could. Seems Sonny had been dealin' with Vicente Vaca
for about three years and no one had gotten wise until Sonny
had put out a contract on Lulu Spencer so's Dante could
marry a Vaca daughter and cement the partnership. Vaca had
a big house in the capital city of Caracas and he spent enough
time there to put on a grand show, as if he was actually a
stand-up guy, an upright citizen and all that. But his main
compound was far south, halfway between Brazil to the east
and Colombia to the west. It was supposed to be a secret
hideout . . . but I never met a secret I could keep; all it took
was several clicks of my wireless mouse to activate the heat
sensors and high-definition camera in the NASA satellite I'd
already tapped into. I needed to get to Sonny before Luke
Spencer did; needed to warn him that serious trouble was
on the way. Although it was beyond me why I gave a rat's ass.
Mister Sir Corinthos has always made it clear that he would
just as soon wipe me off his shoe as look at me. But he was
good to Morgan . . . and that was enough to get me on a plane
to try to convince Corinthos to either take it on the lam for a
year or so, or try to make nice with Luke Spencer.

The taxi driver took me through every little backwater village, most of 'em not on any map anywhere. Beautiful but
dirt poor . . . and I mean dirt. No electricity, no pavement—
hell, no roads. Just ramshackle buildings, lean-tos, an occasional *mercado* and always a cantina. All the towns began to
look alike, including the people. Real pretty, but sad around
the eyes. They all seemed to have these sad, dark eyes . . .
especially the kids. The little kids. Damn, but there were a lot
of little kids.

And then it hit me.

All these kids looked *exactly* like Sonny Corinthos. Well,
sure . . . damn, o'course! Sonny Corinthos had been travelin'

this same road for the last three years and he musta got out of the taxi or limo or llama or whatever at various points to get a drink or a *pan dulce* or an *empanada*. And that was all it took. Just like back home in Port Charles, Sonny would only need to look at a dame and *bang!*, nine months later, there'd be a new rug rat somewhere. Then I started seein' the signs; I'd been seein' 'em all along, I just hadn't realized that "Sonny" wasn't a comment on the weather, but was actually a name. Women of every age, and every stage of bein' preggers, holdin' signs that read "Señor Sonny . . . *te necesito!*" "*Sonny, mi amor . . . este es su niño!*" "*Sonny, mi corazón!*"

Jeez . . . the guy was single-handedly populatin' Venezuela. And from the looks of it, he was gonna be just as hands-on an old man to these kids as he was to his legits back home. Actually, maybe *these* kids would have it a little better . . . maybe he'd leave 'em alone so's they wouldn't be likely to get shot in the head or land in the slammer . . . etc.

I understood the draw: His dimples alone made most dames fall over sideways. And I'd seen him be generous and, yeah, charming. But this! I was just amazed at his stamina; there musta been at least fifty kids, and ten more on the way.

Just before sunset, the taxi driver suddenly stopped short, sendin' me into the passenger side headrest.

"Six hundred eighty-five American dollars, *por favor*. You get out here."

"You ain't gonna take me all the way in?" I asked, knowin' full well what the answer was gonna be.

"You get out here. Señor Vaca knows my taxi; he has seen me before in Caracas. I took a big chance in bringing you here in the first place. Out now."

"Okay . . . okay, pal . . . I'm goin'," I said. "Here's seven hundred fifty U.S. presidents. Now, I don't know how long this will take . . . whatever it is I gotta do, but if you're around in a day or so, when I need to get back . . . there's plenty more *verde* where that came from."

"Maybe yes, maybe no. Out."

He left me standin' at the head of a dirt road (big surprise) that led straight into some dark hills. I started walkin' into the overgrowth, kickin' pebbles and stuffin' my hands in my pockets. I was just an ordinary Yank out for a stroll in God-forsaken territory. It wasn't ten minutes before I had a sense there were at least three long-range pea-shooters pointed directly at my own *corazón*. Fifty yards farther along the road and I knew I was also bein' followed on foot. I saw some twin-kly lights ahead and decided to just keep walkin', even though the "bird" calls and the "wolf" calls all around me were sig-nalin' my every move.

Twenty minutes later, with darkness fallin' fast, I hit the main *hacienda* and a double line of muscle with semiauto-matics. Obviously, someone had given the word that I was to be left alone. I walked up the steps, across the veranda, and into the house without so much as a peep from any of the hired guns.

Two of Señor Vaca's enforcers met me at the door.

"Raise your arms, if you please."

It was polite . . . but it didn't leave any room for doubt; I didn't do what the nice man said, and I was dead in my tracks. They patted me down, took the roscoe and the mini-roscoe hidden on my lower leg. Suddenly I felt naked . . . like Maxie must feel when she got out of the shower . . . or bed . . . or while she makes breakfast . . . or sits at the computer . . . etc.

I was escorted into a long, low room lit entirely by candles . . . the drippy kind. Little hardened piles all over the floor. Some of it drippin' onto the boots of the sentries posted at every window. Señor Vaca was standing at the far end, and next to him, Sonny Corinthos. They each had a tumbler in their hand and Señor Vaca, with a nod of his head, indi-cated that one be poured for me. Tequila's not my favorite, but when an underworld kingpin says you should drink, you drink.

"You are very brave . . ." Señor Vaca began, then he turned to Corinthos. "What is his name again?"

"Spinelli."

"Ah, yes, Spinelli," Vaca said, lookin' back at me. "Most *hombres*, they know not to venture too far down my road, but you . . . you like to take chances, eh?"

"When I need to," I said.

"Why do you need to, Spinelli?" Corinthos said.

"The best-laid plans, Mister Sir."

"What the hell does that mean?" Corinthos asked.

"Simple. Your hit on Lulu Spencer didn't go off as planned, and now her father is on his way here to . . ."

"What?!" Corinthos said, stunned. "What are you talking about? I never put a hit out on Lulu Spencer!"

"Now's not the time to clam up, Corinthos," I said. "Dante knows that you tried to poison his gal so that he would be free to marry Vaca's daughter. Only trouble is, Lulu didn't take the bait . . . Dante did. He's in a coma right now . . . and he looks like a blueberry . . . but he's gonna be fine."

"Dante . . . ? My son is in a coma? And you think I had something to do with it?"

"Dante let me know that you were pokin' into his private life only a few days ago. Now, c'mon, Corinthos . . . shoot straight!"

"I only asked Dante about Lulu because I wanted to be certain when I came down here that I could call the wedding off!"

"What?"

I suddenly noticed that it got very quiet outside . . . no night noises. Nothin'.

"It is true, Señor Spinelli," said Vaca. "We have been discussing the best way to tell my wife, Anita, that our daughter will not be marrying the young Corinthos-Falconeri."

"Then why did you order Lulu to be poisoned?" I asked.

"Been meanin' to ask you the same thing, my friend."

I turned and saw Luke Spencer standing in the doorway, a rod in each hand, one pointed at Vaca, the other at Corinthos.

Instantly, the guards in the room had the business ends of their own guns pointed at his head.

"You must be Vicente Vaca," Spencer said, with a half-smile. "Tell your men to put down the metal and walk out of the room. If they fire, I'll be able to get off at least two shots and that just might leave your daughter and little Dante without papas . . . and I don't mean potatoes. Get it?"

The room was as tense as Kate Howard . . . on a good day. For a moment, I thought Vaca was gonna give his goons the go-ahead to fire. Then he gave the signal and his boys lowered their weapons and exited single file. And not one of 'em so much as glanced at Spencer on their way out. These men were finely tuned.

Now it was just the four of us.

"I have done as you asked, señor," Vaca said. "Now you will put your guns down, yes?"

"No. I want Corinthos here to tell me why I shouldn't blow a hole the size of Texas in his rotten hide."

"Spencer, I had nothing to do with an attempt on Lulu's life. As your friend . . . as one professional to another . . . I swear on my own kids' lives. Now, c'mon . . . put down the guns."

Luke didn't move.

"Spinelli," Corinthos said. "He'll listen to you. Tell him. Tell him I am just as shocked as he is."

"Luke," I said, real quiet. "Luke, I believe him. When I arrived he had already broken the bad news to Vaca. Dante is in love with Lulu and that's it."

"And I had just told my good friend Sonny," Vaca piped up, "that all is 'jake' as you say in America. My daughter has run off with someone else. Someone whom she truly loves."

"The milkman," Spencer sneered. "The village blacksmith, maybe?"

"No. The village midwife."

There was dead silence in the room. Then . . .

"Oh."

"Oh!"

"*Oh!!!*"

"But that doesn't change the fact that somebody tried to kill my peanut," Spencer said, lowerin' his arms. "And if not you, Corinthos, then who?"

That's when the heavy curtain over the far window was pulled aside and a fifth person stepped into the room.

Bernie, the numbers man who'd been hidin' in the corner for God knew how long, a nine-millimeter semiautomatic pistol in his big, fat paw.

"Excellent question, Mr. Spencer . . . don't!" Bernie yapped when he saw Luke about to level his guns. "Don't move a muscle or, believe me, sir, I will not hesitate to . . . what's the phrase you thugs use? Spinelli?"

"Blow us away?" I said.

"Exactly! Thank you, Jackal . . . although I should be putting a bullet into *you*, seeing as how you spoiled my plans."

"Sorry to hear it," I said.

"That's all right; it's one hitch in an otherwise brilliant scheme."

"You know this man?" Vaca said to Corinthos.

"He's my accountant. Been with me for years. Thought he was loyal," Corinthos said. "I don't believe this."

"Of course you don't," Bernie said, steppin' into the room. "Spencer, Spinelli . . . join us over here please. Vaca, Corinthos, center of the room, if you will. That's it. Of course you don't believe it, Sonny-boy. After all, I'm just the accountant, right? Happy in my office, calculating all of your ill-gotten gains while I got next to nothing."

"I paid you well."

"A fraction! A damn fraction! And who was the one who really made all the moves in the organization? Who was the one who kept you two, three steps ahead of your competitors? How difficult do you think it really was to plan the assassination attempt? To get the poison shipped from Venezuela? To bribe an out-of-work sushi chef? To make it look like you were behind the whole thing? Who has the brains, Sonny-boy . . . really? You? Don't make me laugh!"

"You can't take all of us, Numbers," I said.

"My thoughts exactly," Spencer said.

"Wanna bet?" Bernie said. "I'll even tell you how I'll do it, because you'll never be able to stop me and I, the lowly bookkeeper, will finally run the Corinthos empire. You see, it's like chess . . . you have to know how your opponent thinks and *will* think five, eight . . . ten moves ahead. Which is why I am fully prepared for this little snafu. What was supposed to happen is that Spencer was going to arrive here tonight just as he did, take out all the guards who were in his way, just as he did, then enter the hacienda and blow Sonny's head off without even a courtesy hello. And that's what you would have done, right, Spencer?"

"Sounds good," Luke said.

"At that point, Señor Vaca would have brought out his gun from under his desk and killed Spencer. Then, while his back was turned from me, I would have stepped out from behind the curtain and shot Vaca."

"In the back?" I said.

"Oh, for heaven's sake. You want to talk honor? In front of these men? Ridiculous."

"Yeah, silly me."

"But because you were here, Spinelli, and Spencer heard you talking, he decided to actually find out the facts before he came in, guns blazing. Because he respects you. And here we are. But I'm a chess man. You all . . . checkers on the front porch. So here we go. First, I'm going to shoot Spencer, since he's armed. Then I'll shoot Spinelli, because he's annoying and shouldn't be here in the first place. Then I'll take out Vaca, before he can get to his desk gun, and then . . . my dear, unarmed Corinthos. The man who has made my life hell for the last . . . how many years is it, Sonny-boy?"

"Wanna wait while I count?" Corinthos said.

"I don't think so," said Bernie, and he took aim at Luke Spencer.

"Knight to Bishop 4," I whispered to myself, then, "Wouldya look at that?!"

I pointed to the fireplace. Bernie turned his head, and I shot him right between his kidneys and his liver. Clean through . . . very little blood. Corinthos was on him in one second and I was pullin' Corinthos off the next.

"Don't kill him!" I said. "The authorities are gonna want to have a few words with bookkeeping Bernie here, and they can't do that if the guy has no teeth!"

I threw Sonny into a chair.

"Vaca, keep him there, will ya!"

"Sí, señor. But I must ask . . . where did you get the gun? My men searched you, no?"

"No one ever checks the hat, Vaca."

"Ahhhh. The hat."

I looked down at Bernie, sobbin' into the rug.

"Guess I got your queen, huh, Numbers?"

"The oldest trick in the book," he moaned.

"For the greenest tough guy in the world," Spencer said, comin' over.

"How did you know I would fall for it?" Bernie asked.

"I was in Russia for a while. Made a few friends. You might know one of them . . . name's Kasparov. He kept a summer house in St. Pete's. I learned a few things . . . beat him a couple of times."

"You beat Garry Kasparov at chess?"

"Candy from a baby, Numbers. Vaca, call the local witch doctor and tell him he's got a patch job. Then tell the local office of UPS that you gotta crate goin' back to the States. Get your men in here and get this wanna-be punk outta my face!"

As they were draggin' Bernie outta the room, I saw Spencer and Corinthos shakin' hands. Then they both thanked

me for savin' their lives, their friendship, and their businesses. Vaca's daughter walked in, arm in arm, with Florencia,
the midwife, and Florencia's two-year-old boy, who looked
exactly like Corinthos. Then Vaca's wife came in and an-
nounced that dinner was ready. We all had a good laugh.

As we were walkin' into the dinin' room, however, we
heard a shout from the direction they'd taken Bernie, and
somethin' caught the corner of my eye. I saw the flash of gun-
powder before I heard the shot. Bernie musta gotten loose.

As I fell, I heard Vaca's wife scream. I smelled the chiles
rellenos on the table.

And then . . . it all went away. . . .

(Miller note: At this point, Spinelli's voice on the third and
final tape faded out, and there were almost thirty seconds of
silence. Then another voice began, a deeper accented voice,
male, stating that "Mr. Spinelli had been taken to a hospital
in Esmeralda and treated for a gunshot wound. His brief stay
was relatively uneventful except that a nurse had once heard
him talking in his sleep, repeating the word 'Istanbul.' Shortly
thereafter, Spinelli disappeared from the hospital one night,
unnoticed by any member of the staff, and now could not be
located." As previously stated, what immediately preceded was
an accounting of Spinelli's travels through Venezuela as recorded on three microcassettes and sent via the United Fruit
Company to my apartment, "special order," in several crates
of bananas (if nothing else, the cooperation of such a mega-
conglomerate has all but solidified my belief in the truth of
Spinelli's stories). Aside from a tarantula bite and a spike in
my potassium levels, they arrived without incident. The same
could not be said of Damian Spinelli. I didn't know where he
was or in what condition. I had alerted Maxie that I had "something" for her and would deliver it if Spinelli didn't show
up within the month. That month came and went; Maxie
demanded to see what I had in my possession . . .

. . . but I held back. For some inexplicable reason, I had
refused to count the Jackal out. I had faith that he would return soon, spouting yet another whopper.

I was not to be disappointed . . . in a way: I got my story, all
right. However, it arrived in a similarly bizarre fashion as the
Venezuelan tale. Several days after I'd told Maxie that I wanted
to wait just a little longer, that turning over Spinelli's tales to
her would mean that I had surrendered to the idea that Spinelli was dead and, even though it was roughly six weeks after
my all-nighter with the Jackal, I wasn't ready to do that, a package was delivered to my home with no return address. Inside, a
packet of instant hot chocolate from Angelina's and a wedge of
the finest brie from a little cheese shop on Paris's Left Bank . . .
a place I knew well and talked about often. Not knowing who
sent it to me . . . and not particularly caring, I sliced into the
wedge and found . . .

. . . another cassette.

Unfortunately, Spinelli . . . it had to be . . . had neglected
to encase the tape in plastic, and I had to freeze it for a few
hours to harden the cheese enough so I could chip it all off,
but finally, I was able to push "play" . . .

Damian Spinelli

and the Case of the Lady on the Train

It's real simple.

I hate to disappoint a dame.

Normally, I'd bend over backward for a dame, and Maxie had a few polaroids to prove it.

But when I was flappin' my gums to Miller-for-the-Defense that night back in Port Charlie, I was so eager to get it all out, all my stories; to sing like a canary and have her record it all for posterity . . . and Maxie, that I'd ignored some phone calls and a text. I didn't recognize the number. I thought it was an unknown wiseacre, havin' a little fun with the Master Hacker.

But I shoulda known better than to pass on a phone call. If it's a dame, she'll keep callin', and this one did. And a skirt don't keep callin' unless she needs somethin', real bad.

A few days after my conversation with Lady Law Miller, I was laid up in a hospital in Venezuela, cute little town just north of the Equator named Esmeralda. I'd just squared a rift between Spencer and Corinthos and forced a double-dippin' rat named Bernie right outta his rat hole. Then, somehow,

Bernie got the upper hand and put a piece of hot lead into yours truly. They got me to the hospital, where I went in and out of consciousness for a bit. Then one night, while I was awake, but just barely, I heard a "plop" next to my bed. I leaned over and saw that my pants had fallen off a chair onto the floor; they were shakin' a little. I reached down and fished out my phone, still vibratin'. I checked the number . . . same crazy number, same wise guy. Then I checked the log. This mook had called roughly thirty-five times since that first call in Port Charlie. Finally, it hit me through the morphine that maybe I should answer the damn phone.

"Spinelli."

"Oh, thank God!"

The voice on the other end was scared all right, but definitely dame-ish and definitely flirty. Didn't take long for me to start imaginin' the face that went with it. Wow.

"I have been trying to reach you for days. Jason gave me your number. Jason? Jason Morgan?"

"I know my partner's name, lady."

"I called him for help, but he's behind bars at the moment. He said you were the man for this anyway. Look, I've been on the run for eight days. I made it out of the United Arab Emirates and I just got to Istanbul. I'm leaving on the Orient Express for Venice tonight. From there I have to get to Paris. I thought I had got away clean, but for the last four or five days, I know I've been followed. I need your help to reach Paris alive. You've got to meet the train, Spinelli . . . somewhere . . . anywhere. If you don't, I won't have much time. And this is a matter of . . . oh, no . . . I have to go! I see one of the sheik's men."

Her voice dropped to a whisper.

"I'm counting on you!"

"Who is this!?" I said.

"My name is . . . Brenda."

And then the phone went dead.

The night nurse came in to change my morphine drip; apparently I was goin' through the stuff faster than most. I dropped off with only one thought: Stone Cold Morgan had placed this gal's life in my mitts and I wasn't gonna let him down. Where did she say she was again? Oh, yeah, Istanbul . . .

Istanbul . . .

Istanbul . . .

The closest major airport was in Colombia, a few days away walkin'. If I kept a sharp eye on my stitched-up side, I knew I'd be okay. Three days later, I had the control tower in my sights.

There's only one thing worse than pickin' thorny Venezuelan and Colombian undergrowth and the fangs of a large green viper outta your derriere, and that's sittin' on said derriere on a trans-Atlantic flight from Bogotá to Budapest. At first I was a little worried about the snake bite, then I got wise and realized that my days in the Colombian coffee fields had provided my system with plenty of *Bothriopsis bilineata* anti-venom. I was fine.

Somewhere over Nova Scotia, when I figured the flyboys pretty much had a handle on the flight, I pulled out my phone. I needed to do two things and I couldn't let any pansy-ass airline navigation equipment regulation blah blah get in my way. First, I needed a ticket on the Orient Express outta Budapest. The reservation link said the train was full up.

Not for me.

I chose a name at random.

"Good-bye, Mr. Frons . . . and wife," I said, hittin' the "cancel reservation" button. "And thanks very much for your suite on the Express. Hope you enjoy Hungary, 'cause you're gonna be there a little longer than you thought."

Then it was time to do some research on Brenda.

My in-flight readin' began to turn up some interestin' facts about one Brenda Barrett, the woman who had been the talk . . . *the* talk of Port Charles. She had proved to be just too much woman for both Jax and Sonny . . . which had made me choke a little on my coach-class salisbury steak: too much for Dimples Corinthos? How was that even possible? She was in love with them both at various times, but the timing never seemed right with either guy for anything to stick. She had been married to Jax for a few years early on, then she bounced to Sonny, but he'd left her at the altar.

That's when the story got really strange. Apparently her mom, Veronica, had some sort of nasty disease, Huntington's chorea, and odds were pretty good that Brenda and her sister, Julia, would have it too. Then there was the car accident which sent Brenda and her mom off a cliff and into the big drink, where Brenda was fished out by Luis Alcazar. He kinda held her hostage on his yacht and then . . . wait for it . . . fell in love with her. Luis took Brenda to Switzerland for tests and promised to stick by her if she was really sick. But he tricked her into thinking she actually had HC, when in fact she was just fine. Brenda then discovered Luis had evil business dealings involving Sonny that could put him in danger; she knew she had to warn Sonny, and that's when everyone back in Port Charlie realized Brenda was still alive. She got her heiny back to the States, but it turned out both Sonny and Jax were now married to other gals. So what did Brenda do? She married Jason Morgan, of course. Why? Because she knew he wouldn't have any trouble at all stickin' her in an institution when the chorea started takin' away her mind.

Then, somehow, Brenda found out that she wasn't sick after all. She divorced Morgan and set her sights back on Sonny . . . who just happened to now be married to Carly, so he was a no-go. Change of plans and Brenda decided to marry Jax . . . again. But she made the mistake of kissing Sonny good-bye, which was witnessed by Carly who couldn't wait to tell Jax. Jax left Brenda at the altar.

Being jilted in a white dress twice in one lifetime is too much for any gal, and she decided to get lost. Good ol' Morgan was the only one who'd drive her to the airport so she could amscray outta Port Charles. That was the last anyone had seen of Brenda Barrett.

And that was only the first page of notes.

Strange enough, there was no snapshot of her mug to go with any of the dirt I was pullin' up. Someone, somewhere was keepin' Miss Barrett's face a secret.

I leaned back in my seat.

So *this* was the dame that Morgan never liked to talk about . . . hell, never even liked. I popped a few pretzel sticks as I realized that this was the woman who truly got under his skin . . . and not in that smooth, bubbly Elizabeth way . . . and not in that scratch-that-itch-'cuz-it-feels-so-good Sam way. This was the "pain in the ass" that drove him nuts.

I didn't know what the minx had been up to in the last few years, but I had a feelin' she'd tell me once I found her on the train.

I had calculated the travel time of the Express from Istanbul to Budapest and, with my days of hoofin' it from the hospital to the airport, and with flight time factored in, I was gonna be on the platform just as the grand gal pulled into the station.

And damn if I wasn't.

I had bought some new duds, done a quick re-block on the fedora, and got myself a little steamer trunk. I looked like a regular swell climbin' aboard.

As I passed the ticket agent, I heard a man shoutin' at the top of his lungs, "What do you mean my reservation has been *canceled*?! We have been booked on this trip for months! I want to speak to your supervisor!" I tipped my feddy down low and thanked Mr. Frons again . . . real silent like.

I stowed my baggage in the compartment—felt like I had walked into a room for a king . . . Mr. Frons knew how to travel. But I didn't have time to look around at the bric-a-brac. I knew I needed to find Brenda, and fast; I hadn't heard a peep from her since that phone call in the hospital.

I also knew I couldn't just go bangin' on every door in the consist. Only one place to go, only one fella who was gonna know everybody on the train (and probably more about 'em than he ever wanted to). I felt myself a little parched, so I went in search of the club car . . . and the bartender.

Three cars down, I hit it. Walked back in time about a hundred years . . . which was just fine by me. I bellied up to the bar and asked for a Tom Collins with an orange soda chaser. That's when I knew this train was pure class: I didn't even get a smirk from the guy in the white coat and bow tie.

"Right away, sir."

"Maybe you could help me," I said, as he set the drinks on cocktail napkins.

"What would you like, sir?"

"Little information."

"If I am able to help . . ."

"I'm lookin' for a dame . . . travelin' alone, see? Probably keeps to herself a lot. She's a looker, this one. The kind that makes you think twice if you gotta ring on your finger. Stats say she's got dark hair, a hundred pounds drippin' wet . . ."

"Say no more, sir," the booze-master said. Then he pointed to the end of the club car. "We have several ladies with us who're traveling alone this trip. But one and only one comes close to your description. I believe you'll find her at the back-gammon table."

Then he leaned in, real palsy-walsy.

"Myself, I am not particularly fond of the fairer sex, yet even I was breathless when she came aboard."

"Riiiight. Okay," I said, leanin' back. "Thanks for that. Keep the soda iced for me, will ya, friend?"

I slapped a Jackson on the bar for his trouble and picked up the Tom Collins. The club car was crowded with new passengers claimin' seats like they were dogs stakin' out hydrants. Folks were trippin' over themselves tryin' to find space, and my Collins splashed about as I fought my way through. Finally, a space cleared, and I saw the back of a head of long, dark chocolate-brown hair. There was no one sitting across from her and I swung around her seat and faced her like I was just another tourist on his way to Venice. Just another schnook. One look at her and I realized how right I was: That image that I'd started to build when I'd first heard her voice on the other end of my phone? Not even close.

Brenda Barrett was Ava Gardner, Liz Taylor, Lana Turner, and Vivien Leigh all rolled into one. Then the good Lord coated her with a little Venus just for kicks and good measure. My stomach fell flat on the floor. I knew I had a gal back home: "Maddie"? "Maggie"? I tried hard to picture her . . . but . . . but . . . and her name began with an "M" . . . I coulda sworn it was an "M."

Then I remembered what Dickie Burton had done the first time he'd seen Liz. He was so startled . . . so completely speechless . . . that he just laughed.

This was that moment. I started to chuckle, which made Brenda Barrett scowl.

Beautiful.

Then, I followed with Burton's famous lame-o first line:

"Has anyone ever told you you're a very pretty girl?"

Brenda stared at me as the Express went into a tunnel. She was still starin' when we came out the other side.

"The answer to your question is . . . yes," she said.

"Miss Barrett?" I whispered.

Her eyes went wide; they looked like two Oreos floatin' in bowls of milk.

"Spinelli?"

"At your service," I said, sittin' down, keepin' my voice low. "What are you doin' out in the open like this? You say you're bein' followed and you're givin' 'em a clear shot at you."

"It's because I'm out in the open that no one will risk making a move," she said.

I thought a moment.

"Smart gal," I said, lookin' around. "You're sure they're here? I don't see anyone suspicious."

"The fellow chatting up the lady with the Pekingese? One. Then there's a man reading the *London Sunday Times* . . . upside down. The third man is eating cashews and talking Kafka to a deaf woman by the bar."

She had them all pegged.

"Fine," I said. "Cashews, Pekingese, *Sunday Times*. Got it. Then we're not goin' anywhere for a while. You're a friend of Morgan's, so that makes you . . ."

"He's no friend of mine," she said, real simple . . . but a little too fast. "He's just the only man I trust. And he trusts you, so that's good enough for me."

"Tell me how your potato landed in this stew."

"I left Port Charles almost eight years ago. I bounced around for a while, odd jobs, modeling . . . nothing serious. Then I was recruited by Interpol and went to work in international counterespionage. Oh, and I did some charity work on the side. Interpol got a tip that a minor sheik in the United Arab Emirates had the code for a new kind of weapons technology and a taste for leggy brunettes. I was sent on a 'modeling' job for a phony magazine and one day, the sheik's men kidnapped me . . . just as we thought they would. For the last three months, I have been in a harem of over three hundred women. I started out as 'number eighty-five concubine' . . ."

I *had* to wonder what numbers eighty-four and up looked like.

". . . and I worked my way up to number three. Which meant that I was invited into the sheik's private rooms and that I had the opportunity to steal the code, once I found it."

"Did you?" I asked.

"You bet I did," she said. She reached into her blouse which, of course, made me knock over my Tom Collins.

I bent to pick up the glass and when I straightened, Brenda was holding a ruby the size of a tomato. Not a beefsteak . . . but not a cherry either. Maybe a Roma.

The man eating cashews started choking a little.

"The code has been etched onto this. And this is also the triggering device for the weapon, once it's built."

"Double trouble," I said. "Where did the sheik hide it?"

"His navel."

"Which means you had to get real close."

"I did what I had to do," Brenda said, tuckin' the ruby away. "For my country. For humanity. It wasn't easy."

"I bet not."

"He was an 'outty.' "

"Huh," I said, tryin' to get *that* image outta my head. "So what's your plan, beautiful? Be . . . Uh. Be good, for goodness sake . . . uh . . . Brenda. What's your plan, Brenda?"

"I don't have one. I just know that I have to get the ruby to Paris. My connection from Interpol is waiting. This train only goes as far as Venice, which I thought might have thrown the sheik off the scent. But his men are here. I have to either lose them or kill them. Then I have to get back home to Rome. I have a modeling job waiting."

"Right," I said. "What is it this time? Stolen documents? Chemical weapons formulas?"

"Italian *Vogue*."

"Oh, it's an actual . . . modeling . . . job. Gotcha."

The strength of Crawford, the smarts of Stanwyck, and maybe the insecurities of Monroe.

"Okay, well we ain't gonna lose these mooks," I said. "So we'll do it the hard way."

"I've never killed anyone before. That's why I called Jason."

"And that's why he told you to call me. Here's the plan . . ."

———

Eight hours later and the sun was starting to dip. We were cutting through Austria on our way to Italy, the Express slitherin' like a serpent past castles and along rivers . . . or were we in Slovenia?

Earlier that morning, as we'd left the club car, I made a loud show of tellin' Brenda I'd see her for dinner that night . . . I'd pick her up 'round seven at her suite.

"Which one is it, again?" I asked in my loudest "American" voice. I figured the sheik's men already knew where Brenda was storin' her bags, I just wanted to make sure.

"Three cars down, right in the *middle* of the train," she answered back.

"Got it."

She slipped into her suite and, making certain we'd been tailed, I slipped into mine . . . right next door. Sweet. Thanks, Frons.

Two minutes later I opened my window and, using the suction hand-grips from my utility belt, I crawled onto the side of the train. I reached Brenda's window just as I saw a headlight in the distance. Eastbound engine on the next track and she was movin' fast. Brenda was supposed to have opened her window for me, but I caught her sittin' at the vanity, dabbin' a little perfume behind her ears. I banged on the glass and she looked up, startled, then raced to the window. I fell into her suite just in time . . . five seconds later and some part of me would have been heading back into Hungary.

"Sorry! I'm sorry," she said. "I just got caught up in this new perfume . . . it's the one I'm advertising in *Vogue*. It's called 'Naughty Flowers.' Do you like it?"

"It's real special, doll. Now how's about helpin' me get my ankle out from behind my ear."

I straightened up and poured myself a whiskey from the minibar.

"All right," I said. "The sheik's men think you're all alone in here. Odds are they'll try something soon. What they don't know is that I'll be waitin'. So right now, that's all either of us has to do."

I looked at her and caught the scent of "Naughty Flowers" as it settled on her skin.

"Unless, of course . . . you had something else in mind?"

"Nope," Brenda said. "I'm good."

She'd pulled out a stack of fashion mags, I found the pretzels, and that's the way we'd played it since. I was beginning to think I'd read the sheik's men all wrong, that they were gonna try some other attack, but then around six o'clock, when they assumed she'd be primpin', I heard a noise in the passageway. We both saw the outer door handle turn slowly. It was locked, but I knew what they'd try. Brenda ducked into the lavatory while I slipped behind the door, just as one of the men fired a roscoe with a silencer into the lock. The knob popped off and rolled across the floor. The first man in didn't notice me and made straight for the lavatory door. He opened it and got a face-full of "Naughty Flowers" and then a bean on the noggin with the big glass perfume bottle. The second man saw the first man fall and started to shout. That's when I clobbered him from behind with the non-business end of my heater.

Two palookas on the floor of the suite: Pekingese and Cashews. Obviously, these two were the dirty-work guys, but *London Sunday Times* wouldn't be far behind. The first two were probably sent to get Miss Barrett nice and quiet, then *Sunday Times* was gonna come in and get her to turn over the ruby . . . by whatever means necessary.

In a flash, we lowered the upper berth, stowed Pekingese and Cashews, then hid the berth again, locking it from the outside. I opened the window and told Brenda to get back against the wall. Then I closed the compartment door and leaned against it. Sure as my gal back home is named Mallory, the third man was at the door in less than a minute. There was no knob, so he pushed . . . and pushed. I threw my voice across the room.

"Help! She got the drop on us!" I said in muffled Arabic.

Sunday Times pushed harder and then, when I knew he was really gonna try and build a little speed in the two-foot passageway, I opened the door. *Times* went flyin' across the suite and landed halfway out the window. He was pushin' himself back in when I lifted his legs, ready to give him the heave-ho. But the guy was holding on to the casements. Suddenly, I saw a spark of light from somewhere west flash off the metal window. Another eastbound consist. We only had seconds.

"Brenda! Help me! Get his hands loose!"

She ran over and tried to pry his fingers off the casement. He went to strangle her, but that only made it easier for me to shove him farther outta the train. He struggled, but the delightful Miss Barrett and I were too fast. I heard the whistle from the approaching train, and just at the right moment I yelled for Brenda to let go and look away.

The next instant, *London Sunday Times* had a new front page story . . . make that front *train* story. We dumped what was left of him off the Express just over the Italian border and repaired to my suite for a private supper . . . where she told me all about Jason, Jax . . . and Sonny.

The next morning, Venice appeared out my window. Brenda had taken the bed, I'd taken the upper. She'd woken up first and I felt a poundin' in the small of my back as she tried to get me to open my eyes. I looked over the side of the upper . . . no makeup, hair mussed, and this gal still looked like Snow White.

"Wake up! The bells of the Campanile di San Marco are tolling and it's a beautiful day!"

She kinda lost the Snow White spunk when I told her that public transportation was out once we got off the train. Too risky, I said; we'd be thumbin' it to Gay Pairee. In chicken trucks, if I could manage it.

You have no idea how many poultry and produce trucks are willing to stop and pick you up if you're travelin' with Brenda Barrett.

Did I mention that she had the legs of Claudette Colbert?

We made it to Paris in three days, she turned over the ruby to Interpol, and we treated ourselves to a little coq au vin. We said good-bye on the rue de Rivoli, right in front of Angelina's, the place where they serve hot chocolate for 'round ten smackers a cup. I knew odds were I'd never see this dame again and I thought long and hard about plantin' one on her . . . then runnin' like hell.

But she was a lady and a fine one at that, so I shook her hand like a gent and strolled away.

(Aside to you, Brusque Lady: I'm sending a packet of cocoa to you . . . it's pricey stuff, don't spill it. And I spent two days lost between the 6th and 7th arrondissements before I found the cheese shop you've canaried about. Enjoy the brie. I should be home within a week, give or take. Hope you ignored my request and haven't given the rest of these stories to Maxie . . . MAXIE! THAT'S her name!)

(Miller note: The tape ended there. But I found out what I needed to know: Spinelli was alive and trying to get home, bless his crazy heart.

I continued to wait and fend off Maxie. Finally, coming home or not, I realized I was losing the battle against Spinelli's non-bride and her insistence to know what was going on. She deserved at least to be apprised of the facts. I had transcribed everything into my computer and was getting ready to make a printout of my scribblings.

Then, three days ago, four months to the day of my wild, sleepless night jotting down notes, Damian Spinelli showed up on my doorstep with several weeks' growth of beard, a yellow Nehru jacket, and a chimpanzee. I ushered him in and he began to speak . . .

. . . but that is another story.)